Bake It 'Til You Make It

Kassie Jones

First edition: April 2026

Cover design by Caravelle Creates
ISBN: 979-8-9932639-1-5

Printed in the United States of America
Author website: **www.kassiejones.com**

*For the dreamers and optimists who were told they couldn't have
it all...*

Fuck that.
Have the cake.
Eat it too.

You deserve the whole damn thing.

A Note from the Author

Content Warnings

Before you dive into *Bake It 'Til You Make It*, I want to take a moment to let you know that this story is intended for adult readers (18+).

My goal is always to create a reading experience that feels safe, enjoyable, and full of heart. To help with that, I want to share a few things you'll find within these pages so there are no surprises along the way.

Content Notice:
✓ Strong language
✓ Explicit sexual content (open-door scenes)
✓ Mature themes and adult situations

This book is, at its core, a romance.

Which is to say that it's full of tension, connection, a little bit of chaos, and hopefully a lot of moments that make you smile, laugh, and maybe even blush a little. If any of these elements aren't your thing, this may not be the right story for you, and that's okay.

If you're still here, I'm so glad. I hope you fall a little in love with these characters, get swept up in their story, and enjoy every bit of the ride.

Thank you for choosing to spend your time with my words—it means more than I can say.

With love,
Kassie

Chapter 1

Subject: Congratulations! You've been selected for America's Next Great Baker!

The words glare back at me from my laptop screen, bold and impossible. For a full three seconds, I forget how to breathe.

Then my coffee mug slips from my hand, splashing lukewarm hazelnut roast across the stack of unpaid bills spread over my tiny kitchen table. Brown swirls bleed into the red *PAST DUE* stamp on my power bill, turning it into a watercolor of my questionable life choices. My heart is racing too fast, my hands too shaky.

My mind too blown.

I should reach for the roll of paper towels on the counter and try to save the electric bill from its soggy fate. I should, at the very least, stop staring at the email like it might sprout wings and fly out the window if I look away from it for too long.

But I don't.

Because—*no way, this can't be real!*

I blink once. Then twice. Then lean closer until my nose almost touches the screen, but the words don't vanish; they stay exactly where they are. Crisp, proud, glorious black text on a stark white background breathing hope into my life.

Congratulations, TAYLOR ROSE MADDEN. You've been selected to compete on the PREMIER season of *America's Next Great Baker!* Filming begins in Los Angeles on May 3rd. Please confirm your availability at your earliest convenience.

Holy. Freaking. Cupcakes!

I clamp a hand over my mouth to stifle the sound that bursts out of me. Something between a gasp, a laugh, and a full-on scream. It doesn't work. A shrieking giggle escapes around my fingers anyway, echoing off the chipped tile backsplash and bouncing around my tiny, first-floor apartment like a runaway balloon.

"I did it," I whisper. Then louder, "Oh my god, I *did it!*"

The smile stretching across my face is unstoppable, wide enough to hurt. I press both palms to my cheeks, feeling them warm under my fingers. I can already smell the cinnamon rolls, the sugar and butter, the vanilla that never seems to leave my hair when I go on a baking binge, no matter how many showers I take.

In my mind, I see the bakery I've always dreamed of come to life.

The tiny bell that sings a sweet, silvery melody when customers walk in. Bright pink awnings propped on the outside of the building that make the whole street look happier just by existing. Glass cases lined with pastel macarons, glittering cupcakes, and flaky croissants stacked like towering pieces of art.

Taylor's Treats.

A place where people smile and remember that life can still be sweet, no matter how ugly the world around us gets. A bright oasis in a life full of gray.

I close my eyes, just for a second, and I can almost hear my grandma humming along to Dolly Parton as she kneads dough beside me, telling me that "baking is just another way to say I love you." She used to say flour was magic and that if you used it exactly right, it could turn the hardest of hearts into marshmallow.

A lump forms in my throat. I miss Gran so much, but I smile thinking of her, knowing she pulled some strings as my guardian angel to get me this chance. Proof that magic and love don't abide by time and space.

They're endless.

Then, faster than I ever thought possible, reality crashes through the sugar haze like a wrecking ball.

Rent. Bills. Work coverage.

Coffee destroying everything on my kitchen table.

"Oh, crap!"

The words burst out of me as I grab a dish towel to dab at the mess, but I'm too late. The coffee's curling the edges of my overdue notices like burnt pie crust. Figures. The first thing I've managed to soak thoroughly in this kitchen isn't a tres leches cake.

I flop back onto the wobbly chair, rubbing my temples as the excitement begins to war with the dread gathering in my gut.

How am I supposed to disappear for *weeks* to film a TV show when I can barely afford to take one unpaid day off? When my checking account balance is already sailing somewhere south of pathetic?

I glance around my apartment—the cramped galley kitchen that doubles as a dining room, the couch that's seen better centuries, the stack of empty shipping boxes I keep telling myself I'll turn into artsy storage bins someday. It's small, messy, and perpetually smells like sugar and coffee, but it's mine.

A dreamer's headquarters, even if the rent check bounces more often than I'd ever admit aloud.

I rest my chin in my hand, staring at the screen again. If I lose my job, I lose my health insurance, my car, maybe my apartment. Dreams don't keep the lights on. Trust me, I've tried. What kind of lunatic risks everything on a long shot?

Apparently, *this* kind.

The kind who grew up baking birthday cakes out of boxed mix and decorating them with her mom and grandma because store-bought was too expensive. The kind who wrapped up tins of cookies as Christmas presents because that's what love looked like when money was tight. The kind who dreamed hard when it made no sense, believing that a bakery could be more than just a business.

That it could be a cornerstone of the community.

I scroll down the email again, rereading every word as if one of them might suddenly say, "*Just kidding*". But none of them do; this is real.

It's signed.

It even has an attachment at the bottom titled, "Contestant Welcome Packet."

My stomach flips on the word *contestant*.

That's me… I'm a contestant.

I shove my phone closer and snap a photo of the email, heart still hammering. The image is a little blurry and has those weird horizontal lines through it. For a second, I hover over my contacts—my mom, my brother, my best friend Kara—but my thumb stops before hitting send.

They're going to freak out. They'll start crying, which in turn will make *me* cry, and I can't afford to cry right now.

I need to think.

I stand, pacing the length of my kitchen, which takes approximately four and a half steps before I hit the opposite counter. My brain feels like it's spinning in the bowl of an overworked mixer.

Joy, fear, disbelief, and excitement, all blending together.

I catch my reflection in the microwave door: curly blond hair in a messy bun, an oversized T-shirt, and bright hazel eyes that look a little too hopeful for someone who can't afford to fix their car starter that sporadically started failing last week.

"Okay," I say aloud, pointing at my reflection. "You can do this. You'll figure it out. People on TV *always* figure it out."

The microwave version of me doesn't look convinced.

Not at all.

I grab a bright orange dry-erase marker and start jotting down a stream of consciousness to-do list for myself on the fridge in my loopy handwriting, because that's what I do when things feel too big. Break them down into bite-sized pieces.

Contact the show to confirm I'm not hallucinating. Tell my boss; maybe beg her to hold my job. Budget for flights. Figure out what to pack. Buy a better whisk since mine literally snapped in half last week.

Don't panic.

DON'T PANIC!

My phone buzzes on the counter as I'm putting the cap on the marker. I drop it into the wire basket attached to the refrigerator and scoop up my phone with its sunshine-themed case.

KARE-BEAR:
u survive audit hell or did
the trunch make u cry?

I stare at it, thumb hovering over the keyboard, then grin wider. Kara and I started calling our supervisor *The Trunch* last year after she yelled at someone for taking an extra three minutes on their bathroom break.

All that was missing was the chokey.

The nickname stuck, and now, every time she stomps past our desks, Kara hums *Send Me on My Way* under her breath, and I have to bite the inside of my cheek not to lose it.

And to answer her question, The Trunch sure did try to make me cry today, but I held it together, because my call logs this term have been flawless.

ME:
guess who's about to
be famous?? ··

Three dots appear immediately. Then vanish. Then appear again.

KARE-BEAR:
???
WAIT
WHAT
DID YOU GET IN?!?!

My grin transforms into full-blown laughter, ricocheting through the little kitchen as I spin once in the middle of the floor, arms out like some kind of flour-dusted Disney princess. I clutch my phone to my chest and bounce in place, unable to control the excitement buzzing through my body. Before I can reply, the little bubble pops up again.

KARE-BEAR:
girl u better not quit bc i refuse
to suffer at this place alone 😭

I glance at the clock on the microwave. Ten fifty-seven p.m., which means in about nine hours, I'll be back in my cubicle at *Elite Connections Customer Solutions*, headset glued to my ear, pretending not to hear Kara snort-laugh whenever someone asks to speak to a manager because our manager is objectively terrible.

"Thank you for calling *Elite Connections*. This is Taylor. How can I make your day brighter?" I mutter under my breath in my cheerful, customer service voice, mocking the greeting I say on the phone at least sixty times a day. My brain is already tired just thinking about the rest of the week.

It's not a bad job, exactly... but it is a *soul-crushing* one. Eight hours of angry customers, hold music that is severely outdated, and the smell of burnt popcorn clinging to the break room microwave.

Why is that smell so hard to get rid of?

But Kara and I make the best of it by passing notes during team meetings, doing a baked goods swap on Fridays, and making eyes at each other over our shared cubicle wall when we have a particularly hostile client on the line.

But still.

It's not what I'm meant for.

Every time I say that chipper greeting, a little part of me imagines what it would feel like to say a different greeting instead.

"Welcome to Taylor's Treats. How can we make your day sweeter?"

A smile tugs at my lips. The same one that got me through dozens of shifts, and the customer who once yelled at me because his router's blinking light was, and I quote, *too aggressive.*

Kara always says I was born to make people happy, not handle complaints from people who don't know the difference between the internet and cable.

My best friend is the realist to my dreamer, but she also never rolls her eyes when I talk about pink awnings and always taste-tests everything I bake.

She's actually the one who made me apply to *America's Next Great Baker* in the first place.

"You're wasting your frosting magic on cranky customers," she'd told me over tacos one night. "Go be famous already."

I'd laughed it off, explaining to her that people like me don't get chosen for TV. But, after a few margaritas, she filled out the application for me, uploading a photo of me holding a whisk like a microphone as my headshot.

Now here I am, staring at the proof that she was right.

Again.

My phone vibrates in my hand, shaking me from the memory.

KARE-BEAR:
r u gonna do it??

ME:
i think i have to 🐹
this might actually be my
chance

KARE-BEAR:
u bring cookies.
i'll bring champagne.
and if the trunch tries to fire
u for it, i'll fight her 👊

I laugh, blinking against the happy sting in my eyes. Leave it to Kara to make my whole chest ache with gratitude and panic at the same time.

Because she's right, if I take this chance, there's no safety net. No extended paid time off, no backup plan. Just me, myself, and a dream I've been kneading into shape for years.

I set the phone down, my smile wobbling a little as I glance back at my laptop.

This isn't just a hobby anymore. It's a crossroads.

"I GOT IN!" I shout at nobody, then realize the window's open and Mrs. Delgado from next door is outside watering her plants even though it's the middle of the night.

My eyes go wide when our gazes meet.

She peers through the screen. "You okay, sweetheart?"

"Living the dream, Mrs. Delgado!" I call back, leaning against the counter to bring my face closer to the window.

"Good for you, honey. But it looks like you left your oven on again." Her watery pale eyes soften, and she smiles, inclining her head my way.

I whip around. "Oh my gosh!"

Sure enough, the faint aroma of almost-burnt sugar hits my nose. I dash to the oven and pull out the tray of lemon cookies I'd been working on before falling down my email rabbit hole.

Half of them are golden perfection. The other half... not so much. Is charcoal chic a thing?

Sighing, I shake my head at myself, then laugh again. "Better now than in May."

I grab one of the good ones, biting into it, and letting the crumbles melt in my mouth. Crunchy edges, soft center, a hint of lemon zest, and sweet hope dance across my tongue. It's not perfect, but it's getting there.

My eyes flick back to the laptop screen. The email that is offering everything I've ever dreamed of is still there. Still glowing. Still daring me to say yes.

I swallow the last bite, then whisper to myself, "This is it. My life's about to change forever."

And without giving it another thought, I type out a quick acceptance email and hit send. I can't give myself the chance to rationalize my way out of this.

This is my one shot, and I'm going to take it.

I close my laptop, press my hands to my cheeks, and let myself imagine the smell of all kinds of sugary goodness rolling through a tiny little bakery that's all mine. Maybe this is crazy.

Maybe it'll never happen. But hope blooms in my chest, and for the first time in a long time, I can almost taste it—and nothing has ever tasted so sweet.

Alex

Chapter 2

The kitchen of my family's Michelin-starred flagship in Vancouver is chaos. Steam rises in thick waves, utensils flash, pans clang—but none of it touches me. I'm standing at the center of it all, a statue of control: apron crisp, sleeves rolled up to my elbows, eyes sharper than any knife you've ever seen.

I move along the pass like the calm center of a storm, scanning the dishes with surgical precision. Every plate is a judgment. Every garnish, a potential failure. I bend forward, eyeing the set of dishes before me, not missing the subpar presentation.

It's close.

But close isn't good enough at *Prism*.

"Potato puree," I snap, voice low but cutting. "Ridges are uneven. Again." A sous chef to my left freezes mid-garnish, brow furrowed, hands trembling.

"Chef," he stammers, fumbling the garnish again.

I close my eyes and take a deep, steadying breath. The air is a robust mix of seared meat and reduction sauces—butter browning to a nutty edge, garlic just shy of burning. Every aroma layers into the next, culminating in a perfect, ideal balance.

Even the smoke smells intentional.

Letting everything that's going well temper my irritation, I exhale slowly and keep my voice low, controlled. "I refuse to let this service fail because of sloppy, amateur work. Do. It. Again."

He mutters something under his breath.

A single, careless word reaches me: *Bastard.*

My jaw tightens at those two syllables.

Unbelievable.

I don't have to raise my voice to command the room. "Out," I say without raising my eyes from the botched presentation in front of me. "Pack your knives. Leave. Now."

The entire line freezes on the spot. Fear? Yes. But respect, too. They know this is the standard, or it's the door. There will never be an exception.

My ex-sous chef gives a curt nod of understanding. He had to have known this could be the outcome, and he risked his position here anyway. He doesn't put up a fight, just rapidly gathers his knives and retreats to the back of the kitchen, out of my line of sight.

I grab my father's set of knives from under the pass and move to the now vacant station. All thoughts hone in on my new mission while I wipe down the station with speed and precision as a reset. Clean. Correct. Perfect.

Julian, my cousin, meets my gaze. "Expo," I bark. "Now."

He steps in, breath steady, and takes inventory of the ticket line-up. *Good.* At least someone else here understands that this is serious.

Taking over the first plate, I inspect and adjust for perfection. Every sauce flick, every microgreen: *flawless*. If it's not immaculate, I fix it myself.

I feel no satisfaction in firing the sous chef.

I feel... *nothing*.

Passion was trained out of me a long time ago, replaced by precision, by legacy, and by expectation. Everything here is to be executed without error. Anything to the contrary is unacceptable.

Falling into the rhythm of a station is second nature. Muscle memory overtakes any thought I might have, and I'm lost in the ebb and flow of service.

Eyes always scanning; hands always moving.

"Hot line!" Julian's order cracks the commotion. "Four short rib, three chicken, two octo, three lobster, and four pork!"

"HEARD!" Every voice, including mine, resounds in unison. Synchronized movement erupts across the kitchen as each line cook springs into their designated actions.

My heart rattles hard in my chest, but my face is the picture of careful stoicism. The pace is quick, but I'm quicker.

"Hot line, six out!" Terri yells from the back of the kitchen. She is the best damn grill cook I've ever seen, and it takes every ounce of willpower I have to not watch her precise, methodical movements.

"HEARD!" Another battle cry rings out.

Julian swipes his forehead with the back of his arm and passes off an order to one of the waiting servers, who disappears out of view in a hurry. The pass sits ready for action.

Knowing I only have minutes, I move down the line to Gordon on sauces. I taste the glaze for the chicken. Too sweet. I fix it with a touch of vinegar without hesitation. "Watch your heat on the sauté," I warn, sliding in beside him and tilting the pan myself. "We're not burning a single clove of garlic tonight."

"Yes, Chef!" His response is immediate. Quick, but not bitter. I clasp him on the shoulder, squeezing firmly. The most praise anyone on my team gets from me. Gordon's exhaled breath fills the space between us with the faint scent of spearmint. He's new to his position, but his willingness to take correction without backlash is going to take him far in this industry.

"Hot line! Start plating!"

"HEARD!"

Every free hand rushes the pass for the final push to get beautiful, delicious creations in front of our guests. I feel the soft brush of a shoulder against my side as Terri slides in and passes off her work. It's always impeccable, but I check out of habit anyway.

She's gone as fast as she came.

The service continues, plates moving past me in choreographed chaos. Every flaw noted, every misstep corrected, every dish leaving the kitchen as close to perfection as humanly possible.

Julian calls the last ticket. "Final fire—two rib, one veg."

Then the kitchen noise dips, tension twisting tighter rather than fading. Final plates matter most; every critic in town loves a late seating.

My team doesn't miss a beat. These are some of the most exquisite executions I've ever seen from them, which makes my job easy. When the mains clear the pass, I check my watch.

"Savory's done. Pastry, bring it home!"

With our part of the service finished, the scent of caramel and sugar replaces garlic and char throughout the kitchen.

For the next hour, I watch our pastry team put out intricate tarts adorned with meticulously placed edible flowers, perfectly torched crème brulés, and stacks of multi-colored macarons.

The lump that rises in my throat is sudden, but I turn away and start helping the rest of the cooks with clean-up. No time to dwell on what could have been.

Only once the chrome gleams spotless and everything is reset for tomorrow's service do I venture to the front of the house, where Julian and one of our servers are lounging on the tall stools near the bar. My eyes, stinging from the smoke and seasonings in the air, have a hard time focusing in the dim light.

"There he is," Julian says, slowly clapping. "The man, the myth, the legend! Not a single dish was returned all night. That's a new record!"

"It really shouldn't be," I grumble, sliding my hands into the pockets of my slacks. Praise for doing the bare minimum? Pathetic. My job tonight was to produce perfection. And that's exactly what I did.

Not fucking it up shouldn't be impressive.

"I don't know, Alex." Charlene props her chin on her hand, turning my way. She bats her eyelashes as she takes a sip of wine that I assume Julian gifted her on the house. "The way you move back there is something else."

Her tone is flirtatious and laced with suggestion. I recognize her intentions immediately for what they are.

I've never had a problem garnering female attention. I'm tall with a full head of thick brown hair and blue eyes that are often described as captivating. I spent the better part of six years with an expander and braces. I also come from a good family with a strong reputation.

I'm not naïve. I know the effect I have on women.

Too bad I don't care in the slightest.

I lean my forearms against the bar, the cool, polished wood chilling my skin on contact. It feels so damn good. I've been on fire all night.

For a brief moment, I take her in. She's pretty enough, I guess. Long dark hair, big doe eyes. Pouty lips. But she's like every other pretty girl I've already met in this city. Nothing special.

Julian grins my way, inclining his head subtly in her direction like he's encouraging me to lean into her attraction. I don't take the bait.

"The bar is in Hell." My tone is clipped as I take a seat, leaving an empty stool between us. Her eyes cast down at it, then back to my expression. Understanding has her face falling, but she's dejected for only a moment before turning her attention to Julian.

Even though we're cousins, we look like we could be brothers. The only difference between us is his dark eyes in contrast to my blues. If she's attracted to me, she's definitely also attracted to him. Which is perfect, because she's exactly his type.

He notices her attention on him and immediately runs his hand through his hair, preening. Unbothered by being the second choice. Without missing a beat, he downs his glass of whiskey and says, "We were just finishing up here. Want to walk out together?"

"No, you guys go ahead. I'm going to hang out for a while, maybe rest my eyes a bit."

"Okay, man, we'll see you tomorrow." He stands, draping an arm around Charlene's shoulder as she beams a bright smile up at him. Weird how women can turn it on and off on a whim. Dating in this city has shown me enough to know that you can't trust any of them. They're all the same.

"Good night," Charlene says sweetly, tracing fingers along my still-exposed forearm as she passes. Julian looks back over his shoulder as they're walking out and mouths, "Thank you", in my direction.

I wave a hand in dismissal.

My head feels like a ton of bricks. I cross my arms on the bar top and drop my head against them, yawning. I don't know how long I stay that way, but I must doze off at some point, because the sound of the kitchen door snapping shut startles me awake.

My head whips up, neck cracking in the process, and I wince at the sharp popping sensation. My heart races, breaths shallow, as I squint my eyes and try to make sense of the figure moving toward me. Between the dim lighting and my still-unfocused gaze, it's hard to make out who it is.

"Alexander," the deep timbre of my father's voice slices through the darkness. I'm equally relieved and put off by his presence. "How did the night go?"

I rub my eyes and groan. "Went off without a hitch, if you don't count my firing Lawrence as a hitch."

No reaction from Chet Harrington, per usual. He's even more cavalier than I am.

"You'll find a replacement, I'm sure. We have a queue of applicants a mile long." He's not wrong, but his nonchalance grates against my nerves.

"It was good being back on the line again. Maybe I'll take the open position." I say it jokingly, but once the words leave my lips, it doesn't feel humorous at all. Being in the middle of it all silenced my mind in a way I haven't felt in a long time.

I was the eye of the storm, and it felt... *Fuck, it felt good.*

"Absolutely not," my father quips, unbuttoning his suit jacket and sitting on one of the plush stools. He reaches across the bar and grabs the crystal decanter of Crown Royal XR. He pours a measure into one of the heavy tumblers, the amber liquid catching the overhead light as he swirls the glass in one hand.

Honey and spice drift toward me.

My mouth waters, but I don't partake. Father doesn't make casual visits to his restaurants, which means he came here specifically for me. I don't want to think about how he knew I was still here when the rest of the staff is long gone.

Asshole probably has a tracker on me.

"I'm going to cut right to the chase because neither of us has ever appreciated small talk." He takes a sip from his glass, then sucks his teeth as he sets the tumbler down.

Dread sinks in my gut, tight and heavy. Nothing good has ever come from a sentence like that. I roll my shoulders and crack my neck before leveling my gaze on his. "Go on."

"We have decided—"

"Who is we?" I immediately interrupt.

His steely eyes flare at the intrusion.

"The board." My father's voice is laced with warning. "We are sending you to the States as an ambassador for The Harrington Group on an upcoming project. It's not our usual scene, but we all agree that we need to extend our reach beyond Canada. We've made our mark here; it's time to expand."

Expand into the States? I haven't heard anything of the sort until this moment. To be fair, I haven't attended any of the "mandatory" meetings this quarter either, but there's no way I *completely* missed that discussion.

When I don't say anything, he continues. "This is a chance to showcase Harrington excellence to the U.S. market. Culinary prestige, media reach, potential partnerships. It's the logical next step for the business."

I press my lips together and force a smile that feels suspiciously like a grimace. "That's still pretty vague."

"FluxTV has a new series it's cooked up that they're pitching as the American reality TV version of *The Great British Bake Off*."

The words land like a sucker punch. I choke on the air trying to enter my lungs. "You aren't serious…"

"I never joke about opportunity, son."

"Because nothing screams prestigious opportunity like a trashy reality series." I don't even try to keep my disdain at bay. There is *no way* I'm doing this.

"Alexander," my father almost sounds reasonable. "We need a way into American households. As I've said, they are a massively untapped market for The Harrington Group. You leave for LA the first week of May."

I can't believe he wants me to do this. Reality TV is degrading. It's embarrassing. It's a waste of all my training and expertise.

"Right, so it's already decided then? They have no idea who we are, and I have no choice but to spend all of my free time performing for people who don't care if I'm there or not?"

Father's expression doesn't change. "Performing, yes. But also representing Harrington standards. Innovation, precision, refinement. Alexander, you've been training for this your entire life. Now it's time to apply it beyond the kitchen. *Make* them care that you're there."

"The contract is already signed, isn't it?"

"Yes." Father's eyes sharpen. "And we've coordinated with the production team. Dates, logistics, wardrobe suggestions, camera coaching. You'll be working with the best in the industry."

"And what if I simply refuse to go?"

There's a tick in my father's jaw as he considers me.

"If you refuse to go," he says, clearing his throat. "You can forget about any investment from the Harrington Group for you and Julian's pet project."

My gaze snaps to his, resentment and panic surging through my veins. "You wouldn't pull funding from Northern Flame."

My father cocks his eyebrow. "Care to try me?"

I press my fingertips together, measuring the room's silence. Measuring myself against how much of me they actually want. I'm not loud or flamboyant or prone to tears at the smallest critique of my work.

People like me don't make for good TV.

My father finishes his drink, knowing he has me backed into a corner, and stands, straightening his jacket. "You'll do fine, Alexander. You always do."

I wait until he's gone before I reach for the decanter. I pour myself a measure of the whisky, letting the burn trail down my throat.

If I'm going to be paraded for the world's entertainment, then I'll make damn sure they remember my name.

I set the glass down, eyes on my reflection in the polished bar top.

"Fine," I mutter. "Let's give them a show."

Chapter 3

POP! —A burst of red and gold confetti explodes over my head the second I shut my car door. I blink through the glitter raining down on me to see Kara beaming from the sidewalk, the empty cannon still smoking in her hand.

"There she is!" She calls, throwing her hands in the air for emphasis. "America's next great baker, live and in color!"

My best friend crushes me in a bear hug, bouncing up and down as she squeezes me in excitement. I'm sure we look ridiculous to those driving past as we laugh to the point of gasping for air. I barely register the Tupperware full of lemon cookies smashing into my ribcage before Kara leans back and uses both hands to smooth my reckless mane away from my face.

"You're going to do this, Taylor. I know I'm not always the warm and fuzzy kind of friend, but for this? This competition has your name written all over it."

Warmth floods my face. Searching her eyes, I find nothing but sincerity swimming in her rich umber stare. My cheeks ache in the best possible way, and I bite the inside of my cheek, trying to get myself back under control. It's hard to stay level-headed when Kara is radiating this amount of excitement.

She links an arm through mine and swipes the Tupperware from my grasp in one fell swoop. "Are these the citrus butter bombs you've been working on?"

"Your name for them, not mine." I toss my head back in another laugh. "I was thinking something a little cuter. Maybe Sunny Melts, or Lemon-Butter Drops?"

Kara unlinks our arms, pops open the container, and pushes an entire cookie into her mouth, chewing slowly. She closes her eyes before she audibly moans and reaches for another. I can't help laughing because that's precisely the reaction I was hoping for.

I nudge her with my shoulder while she double-fists cookies beside me. The confetti sparkles fade behind us as we push into the building, the fresh air instantly replaced by the chemical bite of old carpet cleaner and the unmistakable scent of stale coffee grounds.

The lobby looks the same as it always has: water-stained ceiling tiles that sag at the corners, flickering fluorescent lights that buzz overhead like a fly caught in a bug zapper, and a patch of industrial carpet that's so worn it's almost completely smooth. I didn't even know that was possible, but the faded navy textile under our feet is living proof that it is.

Our footsteps hush as we cross the cubicle maze, each fabric wall covered with faded memos and ancient motivational posters. There's a comically passive-aggressive reminder on every third row to keep the break room clean. Somewhere in the distance, the printer complains over another jammed tray, followed by someone muttering curses under their breath.

My steps slow, a tingle of nerves blooming in my belly as I picture myself actually asking our boss for the time off. Kara notices and whispers, "No backing out now, Sunshine."

I swallow hard against the lump forming in my throat. We slide into our cubicles and sit on our worn-down swivel chairs, the earlier enthusiasm colliding with the monotonous hum of the office.

"But first," Kara says, popping the cork on the miniature bottle of champagne she brought. "A little bubbly before you go face your fears."

I watch the tiny, fizzing bubbles rise to the surface, trying not to spiral over the task looming ahead of me. My stomach performs another somersault at the thought.

Our supreme overlord doesn't like anybody on our team, but she harbors special disdain for me. The Trunch doesn't try to hide her feelings, nor does she sugar-coat anything. Every conversation is peppered with disgruntled sighs and countless eye-rolls.

If I weren't so well-adjusted, it'd be a real bummer.

"I don't know if I can do this," I admit, raking my lower lip between my teeth. I instantly regret it when my lip gloss smears across them in the least glamorous way possible.

Kara smacks my arm playfully. "You *can*. You've been dreaming about this for so long, you've earned it. Now strut in there like the baking rockstar you are, and get that time off!"

"Alright." I pass the champagne into her waiting hands, and crunch the last bite of my cookie before standing and making the world's least confident shuffle down the hall to our boss's office.

I take a deep breath and square my shoulders, trying to appear more self-assured than I feel. I knock three times and step back to wait.

"Come in!"

The cheap wood door feels heavier than it should as I push it open. The musty aroma of The Trunch's office hits me before the door swings all the way back on its hinges. It smells like old paper, burnt coffee, and a cloying floral air freshener that somehow makes everything worse.

Stacks of manila folders teeter on the edge of the desk, forming lopsided towers that look one breath away from disaster. A dusty fake fern slumps in the corner, and the prehistoric desktop computer emits a low grinding noise, the tower rattling against the peeling laminate like it knows it should've retired a couple decades ago.

My boss sits behind her desk, arms crossed. Her expression is laced with that special brand of annoyance she seems to reserve exclusively for me. "The shift just started, Taylor. What could you possibly need?"

I swallow hard. *It's go time.*

"Good morning, Karen!" I plaster on my brightest smile and make my voice as cheerful as humanly possible. "I have something I need to speak with you about, but if it's not a good time, I can—"

"Taylor!" Her voice crashes through the otherwise quiet room like a clap of thunder. I wince. "Spit it out. The faster you say what you have to say, the faster you leave my office and go do what we pay you to do."

Bracing both hands on the back of a plastic chair in front of her desk, I try to steady myself and my racing thoughts before speaking.

"As you have probably gathered, baking is my entire life. My passion, really. And I've always wanted the chance to do that professionally, rather than just as a hobby or small—"

"TAYLOR!"

"Right, sorry. Straight to it, then. I've been accepted as a contestant on the first season of *America's Next Great Baker*."

An exasperated sigh escapes as The Trunch props her head on her hand. "Great, congrats. What's that got to do with me?"

I roll my shoulders in an ill-fated attempt at releasing the tension that's built up in the middle of my spine. "Well, filming starts next month, which means I need to take some time off."

"You can't be serious..."

"Oh, I'm very serious. It's technically only on the weekends, but they provide a house for the entire time because it's also a reality show, and I'd really like to be there for the entire experience..." I trail off, figuring she probably couldn't care less. "I only need one week off from work to start."

She snorts. "One week? What's the point of going at all if you don't think you're good enough to make it past the first week?"

"I'm going against the best of the best, Karen. You never know what'll happen. But, you're right. I might need longer than that, and I only have one week's worth of PTO. Are there any other options? Please, Karen. I need this more than I've ever needed anything."

I'm not above groveling if it gets me to LA.

"We'll see if you get further than that." She taps a pen against her desk, tired eyes flicking back and forth between her computer screen and my face. "Fine. One week of PTO. After that? Unpaid. If you last longer, that is. Don't make me regret this."

"Thank you, I won't," I stammer, doing my best to hold back a smile as I back toward the door. "You won't. I mean—I won't make you regret this!"

An audible groan of frustration chases me as I make a quick exit before she can change her mind.

I sink against the closed door, hands coming up to cover my face. Forgetting the makeup I put on this morning, I press my fingers into my eyes until I see stars.

She really said yes. I'm actually going to LA.

I'm going to be on *America's Next Great Baker*.

Walking back to my cubicle feels more like floating on a cloud than trudging through an office. The entire customer service team is already on its feet, waiting in a hush to hear the verdict. Apparently, Kara's been busy broadcasting my news to anyone who will listen.

My eyes bounce over each waiting stare before a megawatt smile breaks across my face, and I nod my head enthusiastically. Claps and hoots ring out from every direction, and I feel tears prickle my eyes, warm and unexpected, as everyone cheers.

"Good luck!", "You've got this!", and other congratulations fill the room.

Kara sneaks an elbow into my side. "See? They get it, we all know what you can do. Now go show the rest of the country why you really are America's next great baker!"

The next few weeks are a curious mix of lightning-fast and slow-motion moments, packed with long days at the office and evenings full of practice that feel far too short. But every moment is worth it because today is the day I've been waiting for.

I dash out of work a couple hours early, eager to finish packing. Last night's email from our producers came with the address for our LA house and a not-so-subtle demand: *be there by 7:00 PM*.

By the time I catapult through my front door, the adrenaline high has simmered into a softer, sweeter kind of excitement. My vision sparkles at the edges, and my hands tremble ever so slightly as I unlock the door.

The apartment looks the same as always: tiny, sunlit, a little cluttered, but completely mine. My suitcase sits open on the couch, half full of folded clothes I'm already second-guessing.

As soon as I drop my keys, a familiar knock rattles the door. I crack it open and Mom's standing there, beaming. She breezes in, a grocery bag hooked around her wrist.

"Hi, sweet pea. I figured you might forget to eat in all the excitement." Her bright, singsong voice bounces around the room.

"I ate!" I protest without thinking, then pause. Did I actually eat anything of substance today? I narrow my eyes as I mull that over.

Mom raises an eyebrow in question, but her warm brown eyes sparkle with amusement as she watches me try to sort it out.

"Okay, okay." I relent, hands raised. "I drank coffee, nibbled on a leftover practice cookie from last week, and called it lunch."

"That sounds about right." She kisses my cheek, then continues straight to the kitchen in that purposeful, unquestionable way only moms possess. "You look like you're vibrating. Is that caffeine, nerves, or happiness?"

"All three. Definitely all three!" I fold my arms and lean against the counter, watching her pull out fruit, a box of granola bars, and what looks suspiciously like a premade sandwich, cut into fours.

"Mom...you didn't have to—"

"Hush. Yes, I did." She straightens, eyes turning glassy. "It's not every day your baby girl sets off on a once-in-a-lifetime adventure like this."

Warmth spreads through me so fast it makes me dizzy. Tears prick my eyes, but I blink them away before she notices. Knowing Mom, if she sees me get emotional, she'll get even more emotional, and we'll both end up a puddle on the tile floor.

She spins around, eyes sweeping the apartment like a general surveying a battlefield. "Okay, suitcase first. Let's see what we've got to work with."

I gesture toward the couch. Mom marches over, plants her hands on her hips, and lets out a slow breath as she picks up whatever's on top of the pile next to my suitcase.

"Honey, these are pajamas."

"Not just any pajamas, Mom." I defend with a half-smile. "They're *cute* pajamas."

"They have a cartoon avocado riding a skateboard, Taylor. You can't wear that on TV!"

"Why not? They're playful and show everyone that I don't take myself too seriously. They make me *approachable.*"

"You're not going to a sleepover at Kara's," she says lovingly, balling them up and tossing them onto the armchair.

I flop down on the far end of the couch, grabbing a pillow to hug to my chest. "Part of it is kind of a sleepover, if you think about it. All of us strangers will be living in a house together."

Mom hums a noise from the back of her throat, nodding her head in partial agreement.

"I honestly don't know what I'm supposed to wear. I know I need the judges to take me seriously, but I just want to be me."

Mom's eyes soften in understanding, then she grabs a flowery sundress from the closet—one with flowy, tulle sleeves that I wore exactly one time when I was a bridesmaid in my cousin's wedding almost a decade ago. "What about this?"

"I'd rather wear my avocado pajamas for every shoot."

She shrugs, totally unbothered. "I'm simply pulling options, hon. I don't know why you insist on keeping clothes you don't actually want to wear."

We fall into an easy rhythm with her holding things up, me making horrified faces, and both of us laughing more than packing until suddenly she goes quiet, her hand lingering on the hem of my worn jean jacket.

Her voice gentles. "I'm so proud of you, Taylor."

"Mom," I swallow hard against the emotion I can't hold down anymore.

"No, really." She turns to me, eyes twinkling with pride in a way that makes my chest ache. "You've been dreaming about this for so long. And you worked hard for it. You chose this even when it scared you. That matters, hon. You're so brave."

The swell behind my eyes returns with full force, blurring the room around me. I reach over and squeeze Mom's hand, letting her steady support anchor me.

"Mom, I don't even know how I'm going to pay rent next month," I confess with a small laugh, burying my face in the pillow I've been clutching like a lifeline. "I only have one week of PTO, and after that, it's unpaid. What if I last longer? But worse, what if I don't? What if—"

I press my face into the pillow and groan before lifting it and smiling despite the nerves. "No matter what happens, at least I'm chasing my dream. I'll figure it out. I always do, right?"

She sits beside me, taking my hands in hers. Long, deft fingers trace circles along the backs of my hands in a steady, comforting pattern.

"Sweetheart. Listen to me. I can cover your bills for a bit."

My eyes snap to hers. "Mom, no—"

"Yes." Her tone is light but firm. "This kind of chance doesn't come around every day. You have to take it and give it your all. Let me help you the way I wish I'd had help when I was your age. I'm sure I can pick up a few extra shifts in the coming weeks. We'll figure it out together."

The tears spill over before I can stop them. Slow, hot, vulnerable. She wipes one away with her thumb.

"I don't want to put that on you," I choke out. "I don't know how long it will be for, or when I'd be able to pay you back."

"You'll owe me nothing," she says as if it were that simple. "You being bold enough to do this is payment enough."

"You're going to make me cry into my packing cubes."

"They could use a little moisture. I've heard it makes them more flexible." She teases.

I nudge her shoulder with mine, sniffling. "You're something else, you know that?"

"And you, my girl, are going to shine," she says, leaning her forehead against mine. "Now. Show me what you've been working on all week as your first bake."

I stand, wiping my tear-stained cheeks, and head into the kitchen to retrieve a small container from the fridge. It's the last test batch of my first challenge for the show. I've been tweaking it obsessively over the past couple of weeks, adjusting the zest, butter, and bake time.

Since I've been on a lemon kick, I figured, why not run with it for week one? I didn't want to do a pie or a cake in case that would be considered too safe or predictable. Instead, I opted for lemon-blueberry crème puffs. A lot can go wrong, but if it all goes right, it's going to knock the judges' socks off.

"They were a little vague, honestly. Something about capturing my *flavor identity*." I air-quote the last words with a laugh. "No idea what that looks like yet, but I'm excited to figure it out!"

"I think you're overthinking it." Mom takes a bite and closes her eyes. Her shoulders relax as she chews. "Oh, Taylor… this tastes like sunshine."

"Do you think it's good enough to keep me there?"

"It's perfect." She squeezes my hand. "This is going to get you noticed. The pop of blueberry is a beautiful touch."

"Okay." I nod more to myself than Mom, letting out a nervous breath. "Okay. Let's finish packing before I have another emotional breakdown."

"But the packing cubes need the hydration!"

I pick up a pillow from the couch and toss it at her, laughing. Together we get back to work, folding clothes, choosing outfits, and filling tiny toiletry bottles. The apartment always feels different when Mom is here, brighter somehow. Full of optimism, possibility, and love.

So much love, I swear it could lift the whole building a few inches off the ground.

Mom squeezes me one last time at the doorway before she heads home for the night.

"You're ready," she murmurs into my hair, hugging me a little tighter. "Go make your mark."

After she's gone, silence settles around me. My suitcase waits by the door. My apartment feels a little emptier now that Mom is gone and all my essentials are packed. A little lonelier.

A little like it knows I'm leaving.

I rest my hand on the knob and give the room a soft smile.

"Goodbye, little apartment," I whisper aloud. "Try not to miss me too much, I'm off to make our dreams come true."

I lock the door behind me, straighten my shoulders, and step forward into whatever comes next.

Alex

Chapter 4

The soft chime of the seatbelt indicator pings on, and the flight attendant's voice cuts through the cabin.

"Ladies and gentlemen, we'll be landing at Los Angeles International in about twenty minutes. Due to congestion in the airspace, we'll need to circle until a landing slot becomes available. Please return your seats to the upright position and fasten your belts."

Incredible.

Regular traffic isn't enough; LA has to bring its overcrowding problem to the sky, too. I shift in my seat, feeling the plane dip through a smear of haze that hangs stubbornly over the city. From my window, the sprawling chaos below spreads out like an invasive species. Freeways twist and overlap, crisscrossing the beige and gray monotony. Even the water looks muted, like someone drained it of its color.

I lean back with a low groan and snap my laptop closed. Already regretting leaving Vancouver. Back home, the city isn't perfect, but it has breath. *Life.* Shimmering sapphire waters curl around inlets, emerald forests climb the hills, and mountains loom majestic, their peaks lost in pillowy clouds.

The spring drizzle has its own appeal, a charm the sun here could never quite achieve. LA doesn't illuminate. It assaults you, pressing against your skin and clogging your senses.

God, I cannot stand this city.

The second I step out of the airport in search of the car the producers arranged for me, my hatred for the city is confirmed. The air hits like a ton of bricks—too warm, too bright, too everything. Vancouver smells of cedar and rain. LA smells of car exhaust and desperation simmering in a smoggy haze.

Anxiety tightens my chest as the driver opens the trunk for my bags. I shove them inside without waiting for help. Sliding across the leather seat, I glare in the direction of the honking, crawling traffic beyond.

Stop-and-go brake lights stretch like a river of red lava, punctuated by oversized billboards and construction zones that feel permanent. A convertible zips past my window and cuts in front of the SUV with inches to spare.

Five miles takes half an hour.

According to GPS, this was *supposed* to be the faster way.

Hours of life are wasted, stranded out here on this damned freeway. Everyone acts like this is normal. I don't understand it—and I don't want to.

Finally, we reach the Hollywood Hills area. The air feels a little cleaner, though that might just be the elevation. Streets narrow, houses climb the hillside, each screaming wealth and architectural one-upmanship. Palm trees sway, and the SUV pulls into a gated driveway.

The house is enormous, its glass walls reflecting the city sprawled below. Immaculate landscaping surrounds an infinity pool that seems to spill seamlessly into the valley. Inside, sunlight floods the open-concept living room through towering floor-to-ceiling windows.

I step out onto the patio, taking in the sweeping view below. Everything about this is designed to impress.

"Gorgeous at this hour, right?"

I flinch, arm flying up across my chest. "Fuck, when did you get there?"

At the far end of the patio sits a sweet, grandmotherly type with a steaming mug of tea in front of her. She has a neat, pin-straight bob, tortoise-shell glasses perched on her nose, and despite the heat, she's wrapped in a cream knit cardigan embroidered with tiny apples.

She gestures to the empty chair.

"Been right here the whole time." Her Boston accent comes through thick. Vowels flattened, r's almost nonexistent. "Well, would you look at you! What's your name, kid?"

I sit with a quiet huff. "Alex."

"Alex, that's a good name. Strong name." Sharp brown eyes bore into mine. I stare back, unsure what she's after.

"This is where you ask me for my name," she says, tapping the table lightly with one finger. "That's generally how introductions work. The name's Diane."

I raise an eyebrow, a smirk tugging at the corner of my mouth. "Nice to meet you, Diane."

She sits up straighter as her smile widens and her eyes flare. Spitfire. I feel sorry for anyone who underestimates her.

Not a mistake I'm about to make.

Cackling voices and booming laughs erupt from inside the house. Diane's gaze flicks to the chaos, then back to me. We cringe at the same time.

"Did you meet any of the others yet?" I ask.

She shakes her head once, rising to her feet.

"No." She smooths her cardigan down and lifts her mug of tea. "We better get to it, though. Before they scream the whole house down."

She's right, but I don't want to. Raucous, chatty types are the worst—too loud, too much, like an ice pick to the skull.

Begrudgingly, I follow Diane inside, cracking my knuckles in rapid succession. She halts for a moment, eyeing me.

"Awful habit, Alex." She tsks. I smirk at her like I used to when my grandma would chastise me for the same reason.

Two of the most camera-ready people I've ever seen descend the stairs from the second floor. The young woman is petite, all energy, and probably not a day older than twenty-one. Her long, wavy, platinum-blond hair sways behind her as she pans her phone around the room, yapping in a high-pitched, energetic voice.

"That's it for now, lovelies! Lila out!"

The man next to her is tall—at least a couple of inches taller than me—and muscular, with a presence that demands attention. Deep brown skin, cropped hair, and a smile that he probably paid a lot of money for.

"Bro, finally another dude! I was starting to think I might be the only one. Not that I'd *really* complain, if you know what I mean." His eyes slide to Lila. "I'm Ace."

"Alex," I say, giving his hand a firm squeeze. To my surprise, he yanks me into a hug, patting my back enthusiastically. Awkwardly, I tap his back with one hand a few times before pulling away.

"Did you see how they have the rooms set up?" I ask as the two of them sprawl on opposite couches. "More specifically, are the rooms assigned?"

"Yeah, bro. They have our names on the doors and everything." Ace stretches an arm across the back of the couch, spreading his long legs out in front of him and nestling into the seat. Lila doesn't say anything; she just gives me a dead stare that's in stark contrast to the bubbly persona she used while recording.

I nod once, heading up the stairs.

It doesn't take long to find the door with my name attached. In crisp gold letters on heavy white cardstock to the left of the door is my name. Right below it, *Brandon*.

I rap my knuckles on the door, but don't wait for a response before entering. Maybe I'll get lucky and he won't be here yet. I need a minute to collect my thoughts.

But of course, luck isn't on my side.

Brandon's pristine chef coat, embroidered with his full name, hangs on a hook by the door. My new roommate is kicked back on one of the beds with his legs crossed at the ankles and arms propped behind his head.

Brandon pops up to stand when he hears me approach. He's tall, with honey-brown eyes, and sandy-blond hair that's somehow overly styled yet still messy. Obviously intentional.

When I introduce myself, he shakes my hand for a little too long as a smirk spreads wide across his face.

"Yeah, I know."

Fuck.

My reaction almost betrays me.

He laughs, claps a hand on my shoulder, then drops back onto his bed. "Don't worry. Your secret's safe with me. I'm not exactly a home baker either, but nobody else here needs to know that."

I don't trust him.

"Right." My response is short. I'm not here to make friends or allies. I have no use for either, especially in this competition.

"Did you meet the ditz twins out there? They're all noise and no talent. Probably just here to stir up drama."

"We'll see."

One thing I've learned throughout my career is that you can't count anybody out. People surprise you every day. I hope he underestimates Diane. That would be gold.

Somehow, my bags have already been deposited next to my bed. Small favors. Snagging my toiletry bag, I head into our ensuite to brush my teeth.

I spit, rinse, and glare at my reflection in the mirror. The minty taste barely cuts through the ghost of coffee on my breath, so I go again.

My father's voice echoes in my head, sharp and biting. The same blade he used to slice through every misstep I ever made in the kitchen. "Precision, Alexander. You're a Harrington. Always aim higher. Perfection isn't optional."

I used to genuinely love baking. I'd spend hours in the kitchen, making gruesome but mouth-watering concoctions that my grandparents raved over. Baking used to be fun. Before my father decided that passion was a weakness.

Before he drilled the whimsy and spectacle out of baking and replaced it with timing charts, perfect plating, and relentless pressure. Every dessert became a performance. Every critique, a test I couldn't pass.

And now here I am, shoved into a house with a bunch of strangers, cameras, and reality TV personalities, expected to smile and charm my way through this asinine show. Lila and Ace are prancing around like this is some social media playground, while I'm here wondering how much patience I can muster before cracking.

I scrub my molars harder, wishing I had a little bit of that old spark still inside me. But it's gone. Snuffed out by Daddy Dearest. Hot rage spikes in my chest that the man who killed my love of pastry is the same bastard forcing me into this confectionery contest now.

With one last swish, I shove those thoughts back down into the deepest part of me. Then spit and exit the bathroom. Brandon is already gone, probably on the main floor with the rest of the group.

And even though I'd rather be doing anything else, I pop a piece of gum in my mouth and head downstairs anyway.

For the next forty-five minutes, the front door is a constant stream of new faces and names I'm not going to remember. Still, I make an effort to match them—because, supposedly, remembering is crucial to my image.

Chloe walks in like she owns the place. Sleek bun, gold hoops, and a no-nonsense look in her eyes. She gives me a tiny nod, polite but unreadable. She's cool and detached, and I appreciate that about her.

Jasper's a stocky guy with a baseball cap and bad jokes for days. It's like he can't wait to fill the silence with a punchline that makes anyone within earshot groan. Right down to his off-white New Balances, he looks like he walked straight out of a suburban dad magazine.

RaeAnn scampers in behind him. She's all freckles, messy bun, and oversized glasses, looking like she sprinted here straight from a PTA meeting. She has frantic eyes and keeps apologizing for making everyone repeat their names.

I'm getting secondhand anxiety just being near her.

Khalil is tall and lanky, with headphones resting against his collarbone. He's wearing relaxed thrift-store layers with an iced coffee in hand, and has sharp, assessing eyes. He glances at the rest of us, sizing us up.

Doing a quick count, I notice there are only nine of us when there are supposed to be ten. I glance at the watch on my wrist; it's a couple minutes past seven.

"Attention, everybody!"

I snap my gaze to the guy in the foyer holding a clipboard—probably a producer. "We're going to start tonight by filming personal introductions. There's an interview room upstairs where you'll each get five minutes to give us your best elevator pitch for why you deserve to be on the sh—"

The front door swings open and cracks him right in the back. Clipboard Guy shoots forward with a yelp, papers exploding everywhere as he hits the ground.

A bright-eyed blonde barrels through the doorway, smile fading fast as she realizes she's committed a door-induced, full-body tackle.

"Oh my gosh, I'm so sorry!" She drops her bags and falls to her knees, scrambling to help collect the papers. "I didn't know if I should knock or just come in, and I definitely didn't expect anyone to be standing right behind the door."

She squeezes her eyes shut and takes a breath. "I'm really sorry. I'm Taylor. I'm here for the baking competition... Are you okay?"

She's stammering, tripping over her own words, face bright red, spiraling. Her curls bounce as she moves, her hair clip barely hanging on.

Looks like contestant ten finally showed up—and she's a fucking disaster.

Chapter 5

No—no, no, no, no... This cannot be happening.

This cannot be the first impression I give to a room full of brilliant home bakers I'm supposed to bond with for the next however many weeks.

Not only was I absolutely, definitively *not* here before seven o'clock, I've already managed to body-check one of the production assistants and catapult him across the foyer like a human cannonball, clipboard and all.

Reaching forward, trembling hands clutching the papers I've managed to gather, I steady our fallen friend and offer a tentative smile while stealing a quick glance at his lanyard badge.

Joe.

He smiles weakly in return, clearing his throat before turning back toward the now awkwardly silent group of competitors.

"As I was saying, before I was... uh, *launched.*" Joe clears his throat again. "We have five minutes scheduled for each of your personal introductions. Say whatever you'd like, the only rule is to be yourself. Chloe Park? You're up first."

I'm more embarrassed than I've ever been. My pulse is basically in my ears and my hands are full of quivering static, but I force myself to look up and see a girl around my age step forward.

She quickly reaches behind her head to release her glossy, pin-straight hair from its bun. Deep, almond-brown eyes meet mine for a brief moment, but she doesn't smile my way. Just casts her gaze on Joe, who's leading the way up the wide floating staircase to the second floor.

The entire group moves to the couches in the living room where we wait for our turn to do our introduction. I plaster a friendly smile on my face, nestling on a cushion between two of the most gorgeous women I've ever met.

A round of rapid-fire introductions is done for my benefit. I smile, nod, and softly repeat each of their names, committing them immediately to memory.

"It's so nice to meet all of you," I say, allowing my gaze to linger on each of their faces. It's important to me that they each feel seen. "I'm Taylor, and I really want to apologize for being late. I'd like to say that it isn't like me, but I also believe in being honest."

That gets a laugh from Jasper, who places a big hand on my shoulder, squeezing gently. "Don't worry about it, you didn't miss anything important. Besides, you got great air on that PA toss. Iconic."

Heat rushes to my face at the memory of the door smacking into poor Joe. That's definitely going to leave a mark. I make a mental note to whip him up a batch of apology cookies during our downtime tonight.

"Sure, don't worry about things like timeliness. That won't be a problem in a baking competition *at all*."

Alex's voice is sharper than I expect. I keep my smile in place, meeting his gaze and taking him in.

Everything about him screams prestige—expensive-looking shoes, perfectly coiffed brown hair, flawless posture. But it's his eyes that hold me: icy, piercing blue, aimed right at me like he's trying to freeze me in place.

If looks could kill, I'd be done for.

Across from me, RaeAnn gives the smallest wince, like she's trying not to react to Alex's retort. A small breath of relief slips through me. At least I'm not the only one who recognized that dig for what it was.

A laugh bubbles out of me a moment later, unsure how else to respond. Obviously, I didn't mean to be late. And even more obviously, I'll be using an *entire army* of timers when I bake.

I'm late, not reckless.

"Alex," Diane chastises in a low voice. "Leave that poor girl alone. She just got here. She did her best, let that be that."

He doesn't respond, instead glowering at her out of the corner of his eye and folding his arms across his chest. I don't understand his hostility.

If I'm late, that doesn't hurt anybody but me.

"It's okay, Diane. If Alex wants to be a crabby patty on day one, let him. No amount of grumpiness is going to change the fact that we're all here! We're on America's Next Great Baker!"

Excitement has me bouncing slightly in my seat.

To my right, Lila perks up. "That's right, girl! Don't let anybody steal your shine!"

Chloe returns with a small, self-satisfied smile. She must have nailed her introduction. All I need to do is keep myself from rambling too much, and I'll consider that a win.

Chatter murmurs through the group, side conversations blooming in small clusters. Everyone is polite enough, but there's a wide variety of personalities on display.

And I can't help but be drawn back to the dark storm cloud in the corner of the room, tapping his foot impatiently and rolling his eyes. What's his deal, anyway? There's no point coming on a show like this if you're just going to waste your time being a jerk at every turn.

New mental note: avoid Alex if at all possible.

"Taylor," Joe calls from the stairs. "Last, but absolutely not least. Let's go."

I pop up quickly, smoothing my hair back from my face. As I approach, I don't miss how Joe takes an extra step to the side to give me ample space, as if I might somehow cause him more bodily harm. Can't say I blame him.

The interview space is way nicer than I ever could have imagined. At the center of the room is a plush, white loveseat sitting atop a bright, citrusy rug. The end tables are adorned with ornate, golden cake stands holding stunning pastries and dripping candles. A warm, sugary vanilla scent swirls through the air.

It's heaven—I want to curl up on that couch with a blanket and never leave.

Joe gestures toward the couch and I take a seat in the center, running my hands over the soft cushions and taking in the lights, cameras, and sound set-up around me.

"Taylor Madden, yes?" A deep voice calls from the shadows across the room, somewhere behind the cameraman. I squint and make out a row of seated figures that I assume are more of the production team.

"Yes, hi, that's me." I smile, though it falters when a woman with neon green hair descends on me with makeup brushes and powder.

"Wonderful."

The voice sounds bored, which makes sense since I'm the last person for introductions and he's probably said the exact same thing a full dozen times now. "We're going to keep this short and sweet. Give us your best shot at your name, where you're from, and why you want to be on the show."

I nod enthusiastically, repositioning myself, and taking a beat before launching into my introduction.

"You have to wait for us to count you in." More boredom, this time tinged with annoyance. I breathe a small, nervous laugh. I'm making the best impression today.

"Three... two... one... action!"

I dip my chin and smile wide, training my eyes directly at the camera. "Hi, my name is Taylor Madden and I'm from Cambria, California. I want to be on the show because I love baking. It's absolutely everything to me."

The room is silent as I stare, blinking into the camera with that same smile plastered onto my face. I shift my eyes around the room, wondering if they're waiting for me to say more.

"Was…" The faceless shadow producer's voice trails off. "Was that it? That's what you want your first impression to be?"

"I'm sorry, did you want me to do it a different way? I was trying to keep it short and sweet, like you said, focusing on the pieces of information you requested."

A low sigh.

"Let's try it one more time. And Taylor? I want you to really shine. Part of the reason we picked you is how you showed your personality in the application. Bring in some of that razzle dazzle, okay?"

A tight ball of nerves has coiled its way into my belly at his correction and redirection. Showing my personality means opening up the possibility that I'll embarrass myself with all my quirks. But, to heck with it. If they want the real Taylor, they're going to get the *real Taylor*.

I'm counted in one more time. I close my eyes and pause for one long exhale to get myself together. When I open them, my smile is genuine and I bite my lower lip quickly before speaking.

"Hey America! My name's Taylor Madden, from the gorgeous coastal town of Cambria right here in California. I decided to apply for this competition because baking is more than just ingredients and timing. It's love, and intention, and magic. And I believe that winning *America's Next Great Baker* is the perfect opportunity to showcase that to everyone sitting at home."

"There she is! That's the Taylor we cast," the producer's voice comes to life. I beam in his general direction before seeing Joe at the door, motioning for me to follow him back downstairs.

"Well done, everyone." He starts as he approaches the group still gathered on the couches. "We need to get everyone over to the restaurant for dinner. We have the vans coming up the drive right now. Friendly reminder, since some of you seem to have already forgotten, we have cameras and mics in every room of this house. Even when you aren't mic'd up, we can still get sound. The network has eyes and ears everywhere."

At that moment, we all flick our gazes to different corners of the room—and there they are. Cameras poised to catch every angle. Not a single moment of this season will go unseen.

I smile to myself. Good thing I'm always on my best behavior.

Much to my delight, the restaurant is absolutely gorgeous. The private room is dimly lit, with flickering candles running down the center of the long, glossy table surrounded by ten chairs. Floor-to-ceiling windows run along the wall, showcasing sparkling city lights beyond.

Totally on par with how my day is going, the seats at the table fill up quickly, leaving me, Alex, and RaeAnn to squeeze together at the far end. I don't miss the tick in Alex's jaw as he sits, unamused that he's on this side of the table instead of at the other end, where Brandon, Ace, and Jasper are already cracking jokes.

But Alex doesn't come off as the cracking jokes kind of guy, so maybe this moody disposition is how he always is. It's unfortunate—if he didn't look so miserable, he'd probably be quite lovely to look at. Almost like Amaury Guichon's younger, hotter brother.

But, alas. That's not the case.

Instead, we get to spend time with the steely version of Oscar the Grouch. Maybe he just needs someone to help pull him out of his shell.

"So, Big Al..." I swing my attention to him, smiling hard at the cheesy nickname I spontaneously bestowed upon him.

"Nope. Absolutely not." He cuts a hand through the air.

"Absolutely not what?"

"Don't call me that." His eyes flare. "Ever."

"Okay, okay... no Big Al. Got it. I was trying to be friendly, but no problem. Big Al is dead to me. RIP." I laugh, raising my hands in surrender.

He doesn't smile.

I keep mine firmly in place, even as it starts to feel a little too tight around the edges.

Cool.

Cool, cool, cool.

Love a man who hates joy and whimsy.

Today clearly isn't my day, I'm batting a thousand here.

Okay, breathe, Taylor. Not your finest moment, but it can only go up from here.

RaeAnn clears her throat before speaking, breaking the tension. "Are you both from here, then? I mean, from California?"

"Yes." I smile.

"Absolutely fucking not." Alex huffs at the same time.

RaeAnn's eyes widen at the disdain in his voice.

"Oh, yeah. Me neither. I'm actually from Kentucky, Pine Ridge to be exact." Her gentle Southern twang comes out stronger when she says it. Joy leaps in my chest at the sound. I want to ask her to say it again, but I know better than to risk any more offense on the first day.

One arch nemesis is enough.

The meal progresses without much fuss or fanfare. Forks clink against plates, and voices rise and fall in overlapping waves of conversation. Brandon launches into a dramatic story about a catering disaster the restaurant he works for encountered last month. Ace interrupts him three times. Jasper laughs loud enough to draw looks from the neighboring room.

I try to focus. I honestly do.

But my attention keeps snagging on Alex.

He eats quietly, efficiently, as if ingesting his medium-rare steak were a task to be completed rather than something to be enjoyed. He mostly keeps to himself, responding with short, clipped sentences only when required. It's deeply unsettling.

I readjust in my seat.

"So," I say, then immediately realize I have no idea where my sentence was supposed to go. "This place is really nice. Like... *really* nice. Definitely not the kind of place where they give you crayons to color on the tablecloth. Which is tragic, honestly. Crayons solve so many problems."

Alex glances at me with a bored stare, brow knitting together in what might be confusion or might be irritation. Hard to tell.

I keep going, though, undeterred, because I can't help myself. Once I get going, I stay going.

"I mean, not that I need crayons. I'm a fully capable adult... Mostly. But there's something super nostalgic about coloring a little horse or playing tic-tac-toe while waiting for food, you know? Or an apple tree. Or scribbling all over one of those little kid menus that has a maze on it that's almost impossible to solve."

I take a sip of water, nodding to myself like I have made several excellent points, and wait for his response. Knowing something like this has to draw out at least a small laugh, even if it's at my expense.

But still, absolutely no reaction comes.

Okay, fine. *New approach.*

"So... where did you say you're from?" I ask, unsure if he didn't answer at all or if I happened to miss it while spiraling.

He looks at me again, slower this time. "I didn't."

"Right. Of course you didn't," I say quickly, deciding to take a page out of Kara's book. "That would require talking, which you are clearly saving for a very special occasion. If you tell me where you're from, I'll gladly send you an official, written invitation to conversation."

RaeAnn lets out a soft cough that sounds suspiciously like she's choking back a laugh.

Alex opens his mouth as though he might respond. Something shifts on his face like he appreciates my sarcasm.

And that is the moment when my elbow catches the edge of my drink and the world slows down around me as the glass tips. Water sloshes and then spills, cascading across the table and straight toward Alex.

"Oh my God," I blurt, grabbing a napkin that is immediately, uselessly soaked. "I am so sorry. I am so, so sorry. I swear I'm not usually this much of a disaster. Well, okay, I am... but not in public. Or at least not on purpose."

I stand halfway out of my chair, dabbing at the table with the already dripping napkin, doing absolutely nothing to help the current situation but not knowing what else to do.

"I don't know why I'm like this. I get nervous, and then I talk, and then I move too much, and then suddenly there's water everywhere and—wow—this is really not making a great first impression, is it?"

I finally look up at him, mortified. Whatever amusement he found for me is gone. "Sorry. I get super chatty when I'm nervous. God, aren't you nervous?"

"No," he replies. "Why would I be?"

"Oh." I blink, a little dumbfounded, and sit back down. "Okay. Well, that must be... nice."

He tilts his head, studying me carefully, and I realize he's waiting for me to go on.

I gesture vaguely between us. "You know. Social situations. New people. The crushing desire to be liked. The constant internal monologue that never shuts up. Oh, and the massively important baking show we all officially start tomorrow. Any one of those would be enough."

He gives me absolutely nothing in response—just his cool, icy eyes that slice right through me. I let out a small huff of nervous laughter.

"Huh. Well, consider my flabbers thoroughly ghasted then. I thought we'd all be a couple seconds away from a panic attack, but I guess it's just me."

Alex's lips twitch.

It's a brief, barely-there reaction that's gone almost as soon as it appears.

But I caught it. And oh, Alex.

Oh, I see you now.

Chapter 6

After what will go down as one of the worst nights of sleep I've ever had, it's barely dawn, and I'm sitting uncomfortably in the first row of the show's passenger van, waiting to be ushered to the set.

The other van already left for our destination, but here we sit, idling endlessly. I lean forward, clearing my throat to address our driver. "Hey champ, what are we waiting for? We should've left with the others."

"Apologies, Mr. Harrington—"

"Alex." I correct him immediately, glancing over my shoulder to see if any of the others heard my last name, but they're too focused on their phones and coffee to care.

The older gentleman winces as he remembers the confidentiality issue.

"Apologies, Alex. We're waiting on Ms. Taylor to come down, but I assure you we aren't behind schedule. Most of you happened to be very, very early. And even if she is running a little behind, like yesterday, I'll get us there on time. You have my word."

"Good man," I say, patting him on the shoulder gently before sitting back against my seat. I crack my knuckles one by one, then jerk my head side to side, popping the tension in my neck. Waiting on people is high on my long list of grievances in this life.

With minutes to spare, Taylor comes barreling into the van and plops onto the only open seat. The one directly next to me.

"Hi, good morning!" she breathes out, smiling warmly. "Almost didn't make it, but I'm right on time today. Score!"

She buckles her seatbelt and lifts her arms to battle her chaotic halo of curls. Strands poke out every which way, sunlight catching the copper undertones like glowing fire.

She's so close I can smell the scent of her shampoo still lingering. Something floral but also bright. I scowl, telling myself it shouldn't bother me how that little detail hits me.

It shouldn't; it *doesn't*.

"Early is on time, on time is late, and late is fired," I mutter, frustrated by her tardiness—and, begrudgingly, by the way her positivity slams into me.

She tilts her head, smile widening. "It's a good thing you aren't my boss, then, right?" She nestles a Tupperware container on her lap, full to the top with cookies.

"Are you bringing baked goods to a baking show? I don't know if you got the memo, but we're supposed to do that *live* for the cameras," I quip, flicking my eyes from her face to her lap in irritation.

I need to keep my mouth shut, but she grates against my nerves in ways I can't explain. She's so bright and bubbly, and damn it, it drives me crazy.

Her head tosses back in a loud, melodic laugh.

Ridiculous.

"Oh, Alex," she murmurs through the giggle, placing a hand gently on one of my crossed arms. "You are so tirelessly cranky. Obviously, I'm going to bake live today. These are a peace offering to Joe for his near-death experience yesterday. I'm making my amends and starting this new day off on the right foot."

The muscle in my jaw ticks as I clench my teeth against a response. She nudges me in the shoulder before adding, "Not too late for you to try it, too."

I scoff, pulling my body away so she can't make such easy contact, forcing myself to focus on the world beyond the window whizzing by.

It's way too early for this much of her.

The van winds up the long driveway, flanked by tall palms and manicured hedges. Early-morning sun glints off the terracotta roof tiles of the manor ahead. The stucco walls glow warmly while arched windows, wrought-iron balconies, and carved stone trim give the house a sense of grandeur.

This place clearly wasn't built for subtlety.

I lean back in my seat, trying to work the stiffness out of my muscles from the ride. Taylor's shoulder brushes mine as she settles in beside me, humming softly under her breath like she's completely oblivious to where we are.

The driver eases the van to a stop at the front entrance, where a small cluster of crew members and assistants move with practiced efficiency, clipboards and walkie-talkies in hand. The polished stone steps and towering double doors feel almost ceremonial, and the warm air carries faint scents of blooming citrus and fresh-cut grass from the gardens beyond.

Inside, the great room stretches ahead. High ceilings and tall windows let in a soft golden sunlight. Folding chairs are arranged in small clusters while tables hold coffee, bottled water, and light snacks. Makeup and wardrobe stations line one wall. A check-in desk sits near the entrance, where producers greet each of us with quick smiles and last-minute instructions.

Taylor nudges me as we step inside. "This is fancy," she whispers, eyes darting around in delight.

I glance at her, trying not to let the corners of my mouth twitch. "Too bad we're not here for the architecture."

Our group moves to a corner of the room where the pre-show prep is happening. Producers hand out schedules and explain the morning's flow, and Taylor leans in just enough for me to catch a whiff of her shampoo again. My jaw ticks. I grit my teeth, forcing my attention back where it belongs—not on her.

Even in this vast, echoing room, buzzing with full-scale network production, Taylor's energy is impossible to ignore. I can't decide if I want to snap at her to tone it down or let it run wild.

Screw her and her infectious positivity, and the way I'm unwillingly, irrationally drawn to it.

"I'm gonna go find Joe and set the world right." Taylor touches my arm again before hurrying across the room. I don't know why she bothers telling me where she's going. I'm not responsible for her, and I don't care.

The more distance between us, the better.

"Alex," a familiar voice booms, stealing my attention. "I've been looking for you!"

Whipping around, I see Julian making his way toward me. He's all smiles as he wraps his arms around me in a hug.

"Surprise, asshole! I'm on this journey with you."

Caught off guard, I stumble back. "What are you doing here? If you're here, who is handling *Prism* back home?"

"Hell if I know, man. Your dad just told me to pack my bags and get here. Something about keeping an eye on his spoiled, pretentious son."

My face contorts, his smile widening at my expense.

I continue toward the door, needing some fresh air, and glance at Julian as he falls into step beside me. His smirk lets me know that he knows he got under my skin.

"What's the plan here? Are we just... hanging out until the cameras roll?"

Before I can answer, one of the producers, a sharp-eyed woman with a clipboard tucked under her arm, intercepts us.

"Alex, Julian—good, you made it. We need to give you a quick rundown before we hit the live prep." She gestures to a table piled with scripts and schedules.

"Don't worry, it's mostly logistics and technicalities. Julian, just stay out of the way of the contestants. And, Alex... try to look a little less, you know, like that."

With a wave of her arm toward me, she's gone.

I snort, crossing my arms. "I don't know what she means. I look great, totally thrilled to be here."

Julian claps me on the shoulder. "That's the spirit."

I don't say anything as I watch Taylor breeze past again, cookies in hand. Guess she hasn't found Joe yet.

Maybe he quit.

My attention drifts to the contestants. It's easier to catalog other people's nerves than sit with my own. RaeAnn is perched in a makeup chair, a stylist fussing over her eyeliner while she chats animatedly.

Khalil is stretched across a couch, headphones on, scrolling through his phone. There's a buzz of quiet nerves and forced excitement everywhere. I can't help noticing the micro-gestures though: Jasper biting his lip, Chloe fiddling with one of her many bracelets, Khalil's incessant shaking of his right foot.

And then there's Taylor. She's zeroed in on Joe, who's seated at one of the production tables. She kneels beside him, offering a cookie with a laugh. He beams at her, running a hand through his hair before cautiously plucking one from the container with a nod.

Her hand brushes his arm. It's the same gesture she used with me only moments ago. A stupid pang of jealousy twists my stomach. I scowl in their direction, forcing myself to ignore the heat simmering under my skin.

I don't get jealous.

There's nothing to be jealous of.

"She's gorgeous," Julian mumbles beside me, noticing my gaze. "You're literally staring, man."

"Shut up," I grunt, though my eyes don't leave her.

The producer from before approaches again and clears her throat, drawing our attention back.

"Alex, Julian, like I said, we need you both over here. We have some last-minute prep notes from the Harrington Group's HR team. It'll only take five minutes. Then we can gather everyone and get rolling."

I didn't realize we were supposed to follow her.

Casting one last glance at Taylor—laughing with Joe like he's the most hilarious person she's ever met—I follow to where I'm needed with an eye roll. Nobody's that funny in real life.

"Stupid," I mutter under my breath. "Stupid. Stupid. Stupid."

Julian grins, clearly catching my internal spiral, biting his lip to hold back a laugh as his shoulders shake.

I grit my teeth, trying to focus on my father's instructions filtering through our producer, but my attention keeps snapping back to Taylor and the way she leans into Joe like he's the only person in the room.

Too bad he didn't quit.

Maybe I should get him fired.

The producer claps her hands, and a hush falls over the great room. "Okay, everyone! Let's get together for a final rundown before we head outside to the tent for the first time."

Contestants shuffle into the center, some chatting nervously, others barely looking up from their phones. I lean casually against a table, arms crossed, with Julian at my side.

"We'll go segment by segment," the producer begins. "You'll walk down the lawn and into the tent in pairs. Cameras will move in this pattern..." she continues, motioning with her hands to illustrate.

"Leave space between you and the pair in front of you. Don't block anyone. Don't touch anything at your stations until instructed, and please, no commentary during the hosts' introduction shots. Timing is key."

Just as she's finishing, the front doors swing open, boisterous laughter ringing through the room. "Hello, my darlings! The talent is here!"

In walks Judy Rhodes, and early-2000s sitcom star turned C-list celebrity whose career has been entirely sustained by appearances on shows like this. Her deep auburn hair is cut in a blunt bob at her shoulders, and she's wearing a faded *Motley Crüe* T-shirt tucked into perfectly tailored pinstripe pants.

A man who is very much the opposite of her steps in beside her. He's awkward; dressed in ill-fitting khakis and a plain navy-blue button-up with the sleeves rolled to his elbows.

"And that talent is all me, folks. Theo Courtman, at your service. You probably recognize me from a handful of *King Mattress* commercials and my cameo on *SNL*. The pleasure is all yours."

His deadpan, bored delivery still manages to pull a laugh from a few of the contestants.

"We are so excited to be here as your hosts this season. It's going to be a blast. I know we only have a few minutes, but we wanted to pop in and introduce ourselves. Get out there, do your best, and we will be right there to cheer you on!" Judy says, a smile crinkling the corners of her eyes.

"Unless you suck, then we'll just send you home!" Theo laughs, waving as he and Judy head out the side door.

More laughter.

I roll my eyes. This man isn't funny. But then again, that tracks because *SNL* isn't funny either.

Fuck. What have I gotten myself into.

"Now that that's over with, find a partner and let's get you all out to the tent."

"Go pair up with her," Julian teases, bumping my shoulder as he heads toward the snack table. "You know you want to."

My face tightens, but my eyes instinctively search for Taylor. She's chatting with RaeAnn. For a brief second, I imagine walking over and telling her to walk in with me just to see how she'd react.

Then I remind myself I don't give a shit about her reaction to anything.

"C'mon, kid." Diane loops her arm through mine, tugging me toward the back door. "Let's get in there and show 'em what we're made of, yeah?"

I blink at her, thrown by the contact. Then I straighten, nod once, and let her escort me into the next ring of Hell.

Chapter 7

The towering peaks of the tent glint white in the bright early morning light, looking more like part of a circus than a TV baking competition.

RaeAnn, my partner for the entrance scene, looks at me with wide, sparkling eyes and we squeal together as we practically skip our way across the lush, green lawn.

Inside, dual rows of workstations line a wide central aisle that slices the tent clean in two. Each station gleams—utensils, ingredients, and appliances perfectly aligned, everything dazzling and new.

For such a plain exterior, the inside bursts with cool blues, rosy pinks, vibrant oranges, and minty greens. A soft breeze drifts through the rolled-up windows, carrying the scent of sugar and vanilla tangled with the unmistakable promise of hope.

The station with my nameplate is one of the stations stocked full of light pink appliances and utensils. It's in the middle of the pack, but I don't mind.

Alex and Brandon occupy the front stations, Lila and Ace just behind them. Chloe and Diane are in the row ahead of me, and across the aisle at the other pink station, RaeAnn gives me a small wave. Khalil and Jasper settle into the final row behind me at the back of the room.

Our charismatic hosts saunter in and stand at the front of the room with their backs to us, chatting quietly to themselves.

"Contestants! Remember, quiet on set while our hosts are doing the cold open. In three... two... one..." The lead producer, Sharon, calls before diving out of the way.

"Welcome to *America's Next Great Baker*, where dreams rise, tempers bake, and someone inevitably burns caramel in the first hour." Judy announces with a flourish of her hands.

"I give it eight minutes." Theo quips, pointing backwards at us over his shoulder.

"Eight? How optimistic of you." Judy teases him, slinging an arm around his shoulders, pulling him into a side hug. "Have a little faith, Theo!"

He gives a dramatic sigh before shrugging into the camera with a guilty expression.

"CUT! That was perfect, guys, let's reset. Keep it pushing to the introduction of our judges and our first bake!"

I can't stop smiling.

My cheeks already ache from the excitement.

Bouncing on my toes, I pull my apron over my head and fasten it tight around my waist. While the production team makes final adjustments, I glance down to find my station fully stocked with everything I need for my lemon-blueberry crème puffs.

Just you wait, judges—you're about to get a blast of sunshine straight in the kisser.

Adrenaline whips through my body, and I wrap my arms around myself, trying to contain the urge to fist pump the air.

"And we're ready in… three… two… one!"

"Contestants, welcome to the ANGB kitchen! We are so happy to have you here for this first season!" Judy exclaims, throwing her arms in the air and wooing as we clap wildly in response.

"But we aren't the only ones who'll be along for the ride here in the kitchen. We have two incredible judges joining us this season. They'll be the judge, jury, and executioner during your time in the tent," Theo says, then turns to Judy. "Should we bring them out?"

"No better time than the present! Our first judge is a Southern powerhouse known for her perfect pies and delectable desserts. Please welcome, Magnolia Beauregard!"

Magnolia *freaking* Beauregard?

No way.

There's no way I'm about to bake for the legend herself.

But sure enough, in walks a very curvy woman with stark white hair, decked out in a lime green cardigan, neon pink shoes, and bright red lipstick. Her smile is wide and perfectly white as she waves with both hands, coming to stand beside our hosts.

"Good morning, y'all. Thank you so much for being here. I can't wait to see what you cook up for us today!"

Her Southern drawl is thick, her tone smooth as molasses—the kind of voice I could listen to all day. I bite my lip and subtly jog in place when our eyes connect, and she winks my way.

"And not to be outdone by our sassy debutante, we have an icon in his own right, at least in his own mind. Please welcome, Garrett Sloan!"

I'm not familiar with the silver fox who walks in, but his presence alone sucks all the air out of the room. His sharp, discerning gaze sweeps over each of our faces. I shiver, barely breathing, when his eyes meet mine. It's like being caught in a mousetrap of judgment. When he looks away, I finally exhale.

"Hello everyone. I hope you brought your best, because if you can't stand the heat, you'll have no choice but to get out of our kitchen."

Magnolia lets out a full, booming laugh before turning to Garrett and playfully scolding him. "Oh, honey, let them settle in before you try to scare the daylights outta them!"

Garrett gives a nonchalant shrug, but there's a quirk to his lips I don't miss. He might mean business, but he's having fun.

Good. That's very, very good to know.

"Now, bakers," Judy starts, clapping her hands together and pulling our attention away from the judges. "Your first signature bake is going to be different from the ones to come. Isn't that right, Theo?"

"That's correct, Judes. This challenge is open to interpretation. Our judges have asked that you create a dessert that showcases who you are. Not only as a baker, but as a person. You will have one hour to create your personality masterpiece." Theo sets aside his dry banter to explain the challenge.

Wait. Did he say one hour? As in sixty minutes?

My fingers flex around the edge of the counter.

No. That's not right.

I've read their email over a hundred times.

They said we'd have *ninety* minutes for this challenge.

Frantically, I glance at the other contestants, butterflies erupting in my stomach. If they're panicking, they don't show it.

Did I misread the email?

"Bakers, for the first time in *America's Next Great Baker* history, ready…" Judy leans forward, bracing her hands on her thighs.

"Set…" Theo mimics Judy's stance.

Do I say something? No—too late for that…

"BAKE!" Both of our hosts shout at the top of their lungs, jumping in the air while all ten of us contestants spring into action at our stations.

I'm going to be fine. Everything is going to be okay. I just have to work a little faster than I did at home. *No biggie.*

I steal ten seconds I don't have to breathe, roll my shoulders, and burst into motion. There's no time to prioritize anything. I have to get everything going at once. With a flick of my wrist, the oven starts preheating.

I pivot, dropping butter and water into a saucepan, listening as it hisses and pops like tiny fireworks. Heat on. Flour in. I whisk furiously as the dough pulls together into a sticky, glossy mass.

My fingers itch to grab the eggs, but I force myself to wait. This is a labor of love. Patience is key; I can't rush this part.

The mixture goes into a bowl. Eggs follow, one by one, coaxed in carefully to avoid scrambling. I stir, fold, and scrape like my life depends on it.

Somehow, it comes together, thick and shiny, and I can't stop grinning at the ridiculous little mountain of potential in front of me.

I reach for the piping bag, but my mind has already sprinted ahead to the lemon curd and blueberries. In my haste, I knock over the canister of flour.

My hands begin to tremble.

Come on, Taylor!

Get the puffs piped and into the oven. They need about forty minutes on their own, and they have to be cool before I can fill them.

Once the oven door is shut, I take a quick breath, adjust my ponytail, and look around the room. The hosts and judges are making their way from station to station, chatting with each contestant as they work.

My apron is already a patchwork of flour and sugar, but I can't bring myself to care. I get blueberries simmering for my compote, half-and-half heating for my pastry cream, and the ingredients for lemon curd in their respective saucepans. The kitchen smells like a citrus-sugar explosion. It's gorgeous.

"Taylor," Magnolia drawls as the group of four approaches my station. "What do you have going on over here? Looks like a little bit of everything!"

"Hi! Oh my gosh, it's so nice to meet all of you." I keep my hands moving, barely containing my excitement as I work. "I'm making a lemon-blueberry crème puff with classic choux, pastry cream, and a lemon curd swirl, topped with blueberry compote."

"Crème puffs in one hour? Aren't you worried about time? Those puffs have to be completely cool before you fill them." Garrett's eyes dance over my station, amused.

"It's ambitious, yes. Truthfully, I thought we had more time. I could've sworn the email said ninety minutes." I laugh nervously, brushing the loose strands of hair from my face.

"You must be mistaken; it's always been one hour," Theo says a little too quickly. Judy glances toward the producers, just as quickly.

I know what that email said.

"Sure," I say, my smile faltering. "I just meant I might have chosen something different if I'd realized the time. But it's fine. I'm going to get it done and it's going to be wonderful. Just you wait."

"Good luck," Garrett says in a low voice.

Magnolia smiles wide. "Just keep your pretty little head down and do your best. I'm sure it'll all come together, sugar."

Judy and Theo give me two thumbs up as they move on to the contestants behind me.

I flip between checking the oven and stirring the curd, whispering encouragement to myself like I'm directing a tiny, flour-covered orchestra. Time flies faster than I expect, but the adrenaline makes me laugh.

Half at myself, half at the ridiculousness of trying to do five things at once and still hoping it all turns out perfect.

When I pull my pastries from the oven, they're perfectly golden brown and puffy. I dance in place as I set them on the cooling rack. No... these babies need to cool as fast as possible, so into the freezer they go.

"Bakers, you have ten minutes left!" Theo calls from the front of the tent.

It's going to be tight, but I might *just* make it.

I spend the next five minutes filling my piping bags with pastry cream and lemon curd, readying myself for the final sprint. I pull my puffs from the freezer; the outsides don't feel too warm, and hope blossoms in my chest.

Holy crap! I'm actually going to pull this off.

After filling my pastries, I spoon the blueberry compote over the top, doing my best to keep it aesthetic rather than messy.

Just as I finish the final crème puff, Judy calls out, "Bakers, your time is up! Please step away from your bakes!"

A bead of sweat trails down my cheek as I take the first full breath since starting. I glance down—and my heart sinks.

A swirling yellow-and-milky liquid is pooling at the bottom of the presentation tray. Those puffs needed another ten minutes in the freezer to fully cool.

Crap!

One by one, we're called to the front to present our personality signatures. I can't hear the feedback over the heavy thud of my heartbeat, knowing I've failed. When my name is called, I pick up my disaster and carry it forward.

The response is exactly what I expect: mortification from Judy and Theo, sympathy from Magnolia, and a self-satisfied smirk from Garrett. Nerves surge through me, but I smile anyway.

"Would you believe me if I told you I was aiming for a crème anglaise?" A few laughs ripple behind me. Glancing over my shoulder, I see Alex lower his gaze, shaking his head.

"Nice try," Garrett says, though he cracks a smile.

"Well, it's obvious there was an issue with timing," Magnolia says gently, "but let's see how it tastes. I've been smelling all that sweet, citrusy goodness all day, and my mouth is watering."

The judges each take a now-empty, soggy crème puff, dip it into the creamy lemon filling, and bring it to their mouths. They chew with intention, studying the flavors and textures.

Magnolia's eyes flutter closed, and she smiles. "Your flavors are divine, my dear. They're perfectly balanced. Not too sweet, not too tart."

"And the parts that weren't bogged down by liquid are really well done," Garrett adds, tossing the puff back onto the tray. "It's unfortunate that timing got away from you."

The walk of shame back to my station feels like the longest walk of my life. My heart races with every step. I keep my eyes on my feet, too embarrassed to look at anyone else.

Plopping onto the stool at my disaster of a station, I drop my head into my hands and just breathe. The disappointment sits heavy in my chest, and I let it settle there for a moment. I've always believed feelings need their time before you send them on their way.

Okay, so with that truly atrocious bake out of the way, it can only get better from here.

Maybe this is the universe ripping off the Band-Aid early—getting the mess and the mistakes out so the good stuff can come next. Maybe this is just the part where things wobble before they take off in the right direction.

I lift my head, wipe my palms down my apron, and straighten my spine.

Sunshine doesn't disappear just because a cloud passes through. And I've got plenty of light left to give.

Alex

Chapter 8

Production calls it a two-hour lunch break, but it feels more like a punishment handed down after our first bake.

Two hours to sit under a pop-up tent with a bruised ego and feedback that still tastes wrong in my mouth.

"Too basic... Lacked risk..."

As if restraint itself isn't a skill. As if execution isn't the whole point. As if anyone else in that damn kitchen—barring maybe Brandon—could've pulled off that same feat at the same level.

What a fucking joke.

Julian sits across from me, legs stretched out, picking at a sandwich he didn't pay for, blissfully unaware that I'm one poorly timed comment away from flipping this folding table. My cousin, not a contestant, was invited solely as a reminder that my father expects my best behavior to win over the American audience.

Diane sits beside him, her Boston accent draping over every sentence as she dissects her bake like she's hosting her own recap show. She didn't get high praise, but somehow, she's happy about it. Either she's unbreakable or she's acting. I respect her for it either way.

Brandon lounges to my right, silent as he listens to our conversation. He clocked my name the second I walked through the door of our shared room. Before he confirmed it out loud, I saw the recognition in his eyes. He hasn't said a word about my bake, which might be worse than the judges tearing into it.

I stab my fork into something unidentifiable and tell myself this is fine. That it's better to get the bad feedback out of the way early. That there's still another bake coming. Another chance.

Still, the critique from my signature echoes.

"Anybody can do something basic with vanilla and almond," Magnolia says with a disappointed smile.

"But it's a gorgeous creation. Absolute perfection from a technical standpoint." Garrett, to everyone's surprise, defends me.

"And if this were a technical, that would matter more. This was supposed to introduce us to who these bakers are. I didn't learn anything about Alex in this bake. This was too safe."

I chew, swallow, and decide the second bake is going to hurt someone's feelings. Nothing about this next one is going to be "basic."

Julian leans back in his chair, stretching his arms high above his head, and grins like he's about to be annoying on purpose. Which, to be fair, he usually is.

"So," he says, too casual to be sincere, "guess playing it safe doesn't really work on reality TV, huh?"

I don't look up as I spear another bite and pop it into my mouth. "Careful," I say, pointing at him with my fork. "I'm not in the mood for your shit, Julian."

Julian laughs, undeterred. "I'm just saying, man. You always do this. You come in hot, pretend you don't care about getting a gold star, then get pissy when someone doesn't give it to you."

He has my attention now.

I glance up, glare sharpened. "You have no idea what you're talking about."

He shrugs. "I grew up with you. I kinda do. You hate being seen trying. Wouldn't want to accidentally let everyone know you want something."

The table goes quieter. Even Diane pauses.

Julian meets my stare, softer now, but not backing down. "You want to win now that you're here, Alex. That's not a crime."

I look back down at my plate before he can see the part of me that knows he's right. While I don't care about this little PR campaign my father is pushing, now that I'm here, I do care about being the best.

Brandon clears his throat. It's subtle, but it slices through my internal monologue. "For what it's worth," he says, calm, measured, "the critique made sense."

"Oh?"

He nods once. "Your bake was flawless. Textbook, even. Anyone with training could see the technique."

Anyone with training.

My jaw tightens, and I steal a glance at Diane to see if she caught his comment. This asshole couldn't be subtle if his life depended on it.

"But this isn't a kitchen," Brandon continues. "It's a show. They don't want to know you can execute. They want to know what you'd bake if you didn't have someone in the back of your head telling you what to do and how to do it."

Diane hums thoughtfully, tilting her head as she rolls that over in her mind. Julian takes a slow bite of his sandwich, watching me carefully. I scoff.

Brandon meets my eyes, unblinking. "You didn't bake like someone who loves it. You baked like someone backed you into a corner and forced you to do it."

The words hit their mark a little too close to home.

I swallow. "You think I don't love this? That food—*incredible* food—isn't my entire life?"

"I think," Brandon starts, voice dripping with that same unearned confidence he carries every time he speaks. He lowers it, just enough so only I can hear. "You're used to your name carrying weight. Here, it doesn't."

Fuck him.

I push my chair back just enough to breathe. He's not smirking. He's not gloating. He's telling the truth.

And somehow, that's worse.

"Bakers, welcome back to the kitchen!" Theo's voice cuts through the tent. "This afternoon is your first technical bake of the season."

He gestures as he speaks, calm and practiced. "You'll be given a set of general instructions. No measurements, no temperatures, no times. You have to recreate the dessert as closely as possible."

"This challenge was set by none other than Garrett Sloan himself," Judy adds, smiling. "Garrett has asked that you bake twelve identical religieuses. Anything you'd like to add to inspire our bakers?"

Religieuses?

This one's mine.

Classic choux with a smooth pastry cream, shiny chocolate ganache, and light, fluffy whipped cream—I'm home.

Garrett's eyes narrow as he crosses his arms. "Religieuses have a very specific structure. If you don't achieve the proper balance, they won't hold."

"Don't give them too much there, Sloan," Theo jokes dryly. "Since this is a blind challenge, we are going to ask our wonderful judges to evacuate the premises."

Theo and Judy gesture toward the door of the tent in perfect unison. The judges give quick waves before exiting.

"Now that they're gone," Judy says with a wide smile, "bakers, you officially have ninety minutes to give your best at the first technical challenge. Theo, darling, would you care to do the honors?"

"Bakers, on your mark... get set... BAKE!"

Paper rustles as everyone scrambles to read the very sparse recipe we were given.

I glance at the card but don't need to read the whole thing to know where to start. Every line is exactly what I've trained for. I've done this a hundred times in kitchens that actually matter.

The others are already whispering to one another and flipping the card like it's a puzzle. It's cute that they're trying to help each other—right up until the dough splits or the cream curdles. That's when they'll panic.

I roll my shoulders, scoop up my ingredients, and start measuring like a man who knows exactly how this ends. This challenge is all about control and precision.

If anyone's going to flinch under pressure, it won't be me. I pipe the first puff with smooth confidence, technique second nature.

I pipe the next puff and glance up, just for a second.

Chloe's pacing, muttering to herself as she figures out the choux. She's overcomplicating everything with a spatula gripped in one hand, eyes darting like she's lost the recipe in the clouds.

Diane is calm, hands steady, lips moving as she quietly recites measurements to herself. She's a respectful mix of focus and determination.

Brandon? The guy is completely stone-faced. It's almost unnerving, which is saying something, coming from me. He's moving slower than everyone else, but with purpose. Everything he touches lands exactly where it should. With his history, I expected more from him, but I'm sure he'll be fine.

I smirk to myself as I watch some of the others already losing it. Then I catch sight of bobbing blonde curls and frantic hazel eyes.

Taylor is moving quickly, leaving a path of controlled chaos in her wake as she furiously mixes eggs into the dough. She should be piping by now if she wants her pastries to cool in time. If she wants to avoid the same fate her cream puffs faced this morning.

But I tell myself that isn't my problem and force my attention back to my station. I take a breath, pipe the next puff, and let the others' chaos blur into background noise.

The ninety minutes fly by, but I'm happy with my perfectly proportioned, balanced, and stacked dozen pastries. When I place my tray in its spot, I steal a glance down the line.

I want to laugh, but I bite my lip to stifle the sound. Dull ganache. Pastries that have fallen over. Melting whipped cream. The pitfalls in this challenge were numerous, and it looks like each of them took out one of the other bakers. It's almost too easy to tell who here is the trained professional.

Turning to take my seat on the stools lined up for judging, I find the only available place is directly next to Taylor. A blessing and a curse.

As I sit, she lets out a small sigh and turns to me. My elbow grazes her arm, sending an unwelcome shiver down my spine.

"How'd it go?"

I don't face her, just slide my eyes her way. "I feel like I should be the one asking you that question."

Her cheeks flush a soft pink, and I have to look away because I like that color on her more than I should. Why is this hurricane of optimism getting under my skin? I'm surrounded by beautiful women all the time, but something about her feels different. That's the problem. And I hate it.

"It went—"

But before she can finish, the hosts announce the judges are returning, and a hush falls over the lineup.

Magnolia looks across the anonymous presentation table, her expression shifting from impressed to pity as she moves down the line. Garrett, on the other hand, remains carefully stoic as he scans our pastries. But his eyes give him away, widening and narrowing as he takes in the best and worst of the bunch.

Garrett clears his throat. "We have a pretty wide range of religieuses here. Some are on point, and others are, well… a disaster. Religieuses roughly translates to *nuns* in English, because the pastries should be assembled in a way that resembles tiny nuns on the plate."

"It looks like we have a few promising ones, but let's not forget; they also have to taste amazing," Magnolia adds, doing her best to give hope to those who missed the mark on presentation.

Too bad it won't matter; mine look perfect, and they'll undoubtedly have the right flavor to match.

One by one, the judges try the pastries, speaking in voices too quiet for us to hear. After a few minutes of private discussion, they return to announce the lineup.

The worst of the bunch is Ace—puffs undercooked, pastry cream lumpy, whipped cream dripping down the sides. There was no saving him.

When they reach seventh place, Garrett calls Taylor's name, and she lets out an audible sigh of relief. My lips quirk into a small, rebellious smile before I can stop them. I wouldn't be happy with middle of the pack, but after the disaster of her signature this morning, I don't blame her.

"Taylor, this morning was rough. But you really redeemed yourself with this one. You can make a filled crème puff, and you should be proud of that." Magnolia offers her a warm smile.

When it comes down to the top two, it's Brandon and me. He smirks in my direction. I roll my eyes in response. This challenge was made for me. There's zero chance he's taking it.

"Our runner-up for this challenge is this one," Garrett says, gesturing to Brandon's tray. His expression tightens as he raises a hand to claim his place. I mirror the smirk he sent my way moments ago. "This was a very close decision. Brandon, your pastries are nearly perfect. We just felt your proportions were slightly off compared to our top selection, which is Alex."

At the sound of my name, Taylor slips her arm through mine and squeezes tight. My head snaps toward her, caught off guard.

"Congratulations. You deserve it." Her smile is bright, warm in a way that seeps in whether I want it to or not.

After thanking the judges, the producers call cut, and we begin packing up to head back to the house. Joe—who unfortunately still works on the show—approaches me, steps quick and purposeful.

"Alex, we're doing contestant feedback shots. We need you on the lawn."

Stepping outside, I see they've pulled me, Brandon, Ace, and RaeAnn. The top and bottom two for interviews. I'm led to the side of the tent and positioned with the house behind me before they ask for my thoughts on the other contestants.

"They're fine, but they're not what I'm concerning myself with while I'm here." I tuck my hands into my pockets as I respond.

"That's it?" Joe asks. "You aren't going to give us more than that?"

I scoff, raising my palms in irritation. "If there's something specific you're looking for, I'd really prefer you ask directly. I'm not good at filling in the gaps. Be direct. Or pick someone else and leave me alone."

"Okay, that's fair. Let's try this then. What are your thoughts on Taylor?"

Of course, he asks about Taylor. She didn't just get under my skin, she has everyone in the room melting into her goodness.

"Taylor is..." I pause, searching for the right word. "Ambitious, to say the least. She's reckless and disorganized, and she needs to make sure she doesn't bite off more than she can chew if she wants to survive this competition."

Joe leans back slightly at my honesty, but a slow smile plays at his lips, like he can see through my words to everything I didn't say.

That Taylor's brand of chaos is intriguing. Magnetic.

That everyone loves her, and her laugh is an infectious melody that lingers in my head against my will.

That what she lacks in technical skill, she more than makes up for with charm and charisma.

That she is dangerous to me—far beyond this competition.

Chapter 9

If I thought the tent was loud with frantic bakers and whirring appliances, I was wildly unprepared for the volume of our shared house at night. Music blasts from the open-concept space below, the bass vibrating through the floor beneath my feet.

The suitcase I tossed haphazardly next to my bed sits half-unpacked when my roommate, Lila, sets up a ring light in the middle of our shared bedroom.

"You don't mind, do you?" she asks, already clipping her phone into place.

I smile her way. "Not at all. You record a lot, and I love that for you. Do you have a big following?"

"You could say that," she says brightly, flashing a smile at her screen. "Hey guys! Day one in the Bake-Off house and I'm already obsessed."

She pans the phone around the room, narrating everything. The exposed beams. The trio of beds, where hers is aesthetically staged with decorative pillows she must have brought from home, a notebook, and a rainbow of pens. Then there's me, sitting cross-legged on my mattress with my hair in a messy knot and a bag of pretzels open beside me.

"This is Taylor," she says, plopping down on my bed beside me. "She's literally sunshine in human form."

I laugh, giving the camera a small wave. "I don't know about that, but hi, everyone. *Holy crap*, Lila, there are already over a thousand people in this live!"

Lila beams, her eyes sparkling. "I know, and we are just getting started! But seriously, guys... this girl right here is constantly smiling. When I walked past her this afternoon, when all hell was breaking loose in the kitchen, she was just humming to herself in her own little world. How cute is that?"

"I didn't even realize I was doing that," I admit, glancing away from the camera, suddenly a little embarrassed.

"Exactly. That's why it's adorable. And we all love you."

Our third roommate—Chloe, quiet and observant, already curled up with a book—snorts without looking up.

"It's going to be a long few weeks," she mutters, earning a scowl from Lila.

"You can always go home, Chloe. Nobody's forcing you to be here. Sign the withdrawal form and trudge back to San Francisco. Don't forget to take your bad attitude with you. We don't need that kind of negativity in our lives, am I right, lovelies?" She wiggles her eyebrows at her now five-thousand viewers.

Who *is* this girl, and what does she do that this many people pay attention to her?

Chloe rolls her eyes and shifts on her bed until her back is to us. Lila returns to her own bed, still chatting away about the first day of baking.

Moments later, there's a knock on the door. Someone from below yells that drinks are happening downstairs *right now* and that if we don't come immediately, Ace is going to drink all the good stuff.

"That man does *not* need encouragement," Chloe mutters, closing her book.

Lila quickly says goodbye and ends her livestream before bounding over to my bed, grabbing my wrist, and dragging me out of the room.

Downstairs, the entire vibe of the house has shifted from calculated competition to electric camaraderie. Everyone's clustered around the kitchen island or sprawled across the furniture, red cups and wine glasses already in circulation. I bite my lip as I take it all in. I feel like I've been dropped into a house party scene from an early 2000's teen movie, and I love it.

Ace is exactly where you'd expect him to be; in the center of it all, leaning against the counter, sleeves rolled up, mixing drinks for everyone.

"I'm just saying," he announces to no one in particular, "these shows are elite because you get to bake and meet fun, beautiful women. It's like... orchestrated flirting."

"Orchestrated flirting isn't a thing," RaeAnn says, sipping her wine.

Ace grins at her. "Everything's a thing if you believe in it hard enough."

She rolls her eyes, but she's smiling, too.

Even Mr. Grump is mingling with the group. Our eyes meet across the room, and I beam his way with a quick thumbs-up. His icy gaze stays locked on mine as he tips his red Solo cup back and drains it. His Adam's apple bobs as he swallows, and shiver dances up my spine under the weight of his attention.

The man is terrifying in a beautiful way, and even though he's done very little to encourage me, I find myself drawn to him.

I can't seem to stay away.

"Taylor!" RaeAnn drawls, already tipsy, wrapping her arms around my waist in a tight squeeze. "I'm so happy you're here. Let's get another drink."

"Maybe you should pace yourself, Rae. We have a showstopper tomorrow, remember?"

The effort is futile—the chance for good decisions is already so far behind us it's basically a speck in the rearview.

"Come on, Taylor! Live a little, one of us is going home tomorrow!" Jasper cups his hand around his mouth as he calls out to me across the room.

"Yeah, Taylor, live a little," Alex smirks as he approaches, a new drink in hand, echoing my own words from this morning back at me. "*It's not too late for you to try it, too.*"

His expression is a mix of challenge and something I can't place. But the challenge is the only part I need to see.

Oh, it is on. It's on like Donkey Kong.

Giving the large, sarcastic grouch towering in front of me my sweetest smile, I snatch the cup from his hand and chug the drink.

Alex's eyes go wide.

And *oh my God*, it burns the entire way down. I sputter, doubling forward as I try to catch my breath.

"Holy cannoli," I wheeze. "What was in that? Lighter fluid?"

That's when it happens. A full, deep, rumbling sound explodes out of Alex. It's rich and melodic and hits me somewhere low in the belly. My eyes snap up just as he drags a hand over his face, trying to ride out the laugh.

I freeze as I take him in.

His smile is absolutely unreal. The lines of his face soften, his blue eyes sparkling in the light, and I immediately know I will be chasing another one of his laughs for the rest of this competition.

A slow smile spreads across my face, a giggle bubbling up as I share this brief, unexpected moment with him.

"Jesus, that was straight bourbon. And it was mine." His voice still carries the edge of a laugh.

"Sorry, I thought you were bringing me a drink. I'll refill it for you and find something a little less, uh... *abrasive.*"

He shakes his head, another quiet laugh slipping out. "Let's do it together. Can't risk wasting good bourbon on one of your special, grace-filled moments."

"Shut up," I laugh, swatting his arm, but I don't stop him when his hand settles at the small of my back, guiding me into the kitchen.

Joe slips in through the side door and steps up beside me, lowering his voice. "We need you upstairs in the confessional."

"Right now?" I ask, glancing around at everyone still caught up in the moment.

The easy look on Alex's face disappears as he sizes Joe up. When Joe guides me away, I hear an exasperated, unmistakably irritated, "Of course."

The upstairs confessional is just as warm and inviting as before. I settle onto the couch, sipping from the wineglass I brought with me.

"So." Joe clears his throat, and I notice it's just the two of us in the room this time.

"So?" I echo, taking another sip.

"We want to get everyone's reaction to the other contestants. We got a few earlier, but I thought we should do yours tonight, given how the day went. Tell me about Alex. You seem to have cozied up to him pretty quickly."

I choke a little on my wine. "Oh! Um..."

"Be honest," he says with a smile. "There's no right or wrong answer here. Just the truth."

"This feels like a trap of some kind."

Joe laughs again. "It's curiosity. *The audience* is curious."

I glance down at my wine, turning the glass slightly as I think. I doubt they want to hear about how his laugh feels like sunlight cracking through a storm. They're asking about him as a competitor. Not *that*.

"Okay," I relent, understanding what they're looking for. "Alex is..." I trail off, searching for a truthful word that won't sound mean later.

"Terrifying." I land on finally.

Joe perks up. "Terrifying how?"

"He's just... so serious. All the time. But he's also unshakeable. I swear a bomb could go off at the station next to him, and he'd just be standing there, calmly folding egg whites into his cake batter."

Joe snorts, motioning for me to continue.

"And he's incredibly talented. Like, unfairly so. But he never looks like he's having fun, you know?"

Joe tilts his head, eyes glinting. "Interesting."

"He's kind of like a robot in an apron," I add, smiling into my glass as an image of Alex moving methodically around his station surface. "Which I mean affectionately, of course."

Joe's grin turns knowing. "That's good TV."

"Is it?" I ask, looking up past the camera at him.

"Oh yeah."

When Joe escorts me back downstairs, the party has carried on without me, like it didn't even notice I was gone. He casually refills my wine glass before grabbing a beer from the fridge, flashing me a quick wink.

"Have fun tonight. I'll see you bright and early tomorrow."

I don't notice Alex watching us. But when I say goodbye to Joe and glance his way again, his eyes flick away too fast. I sigh, deflated. Back to cold indifference, I suppose.

The night stretches on, drinks loosening tongues with every passing minute. Chloe starts a debate with Kahlil over whether brownies should be fudgy or cakey, which gets surprisingly heated. Ace flirts with *everyone*, indiscriminately, like he's been training his whole life for this very moment. He even flirts with Diane, who could easily be his grandma.

"I'm telling you," Ace says, arms stretched wide across the back of the couch, "I thrive in environments with attractive women and low emotional stakes. This is way better than when I was on *The Love Gauntlet*."

"Is that why you're here, then?" Diane asks, clearly not enamored by his charm.

He winks at her anyway. "One of many reasons."

The night begins to wind down, and I settle into an oversized chair in the corner with RaeAnn and Jasper, both of whom have had more than their fair share to drink.

"I don't know if I should be saying anything," RaeAnn whispers, leaning in, "but I recognize Lila. She has a massive following on social media. That's weird, right? Not exactly a home baker at that point."

"I mean," Jasper murmurs, "Brandon definitely isn't, either. Did you see his bakes? No way he learned that on his own."

The thought sparks something in me—low, buzzing speculation. Who trained where? Who's worked professionally? Who's pretending? Between the timing "mix-up" and Joe prodding me about Alex, I'm starting to wonder if this show is less about baking than I thought.

I shrug it off, grasping for neutrality. "Does it matter?"

Their attention turns to me, confusion etching across their faces.

"We're all here to bake," I say, flicking my eyes to the nearest camera, hoping to end the conversation on a positive note. "Everyone's got a story."

Later, upstairs, I curl into bed with a slight buzz in my head and the thought that I need to be on my game tomorrow to make up for my performance this morning. My technical was decent, but I don't feel safe in this competition. Tomorrow will come fast. Another bake. Another chance.

As I drift off, I picture piercing blue eyes and a dazzling smile. I wonder, briefly, if Alex ever hums to himself when he's alone.

Alex

Chapter 10

"Welcome back to day two of your first week here at *America's Next Great Baker!*" Judy beams into the camera, slinging an arm around Theo's shoulders and pulling him in close.

"Big day," Theo says. "High stakes."

"High stress," Judy adds.

"High chance I say something I'm not allowed to say on national television." He wiggles in Judy's tight grip.

Judy smiles at the camera. "And, that's why I'm holding him, folks."

They record the cold open three times. It shouldn't be that hard, but Theo has a talent for overestimating how funny he is.

Production shuffled our station locations. I'm no longer in the front row but the second, and Taylor is right behind me. Her excited, frenzied presence buzzes at my back. I clench my jaw against the contagious energy, refusing to admit I kind of like it.

"Your first showstopper challenge is a cake—any cake, so long as it has three tiers," Judy explains, hands clasped in front of her in a polite gesture. "With three distinct flavor profiles."

Magnolia hums approvingly. Garrett slides his gaze over each of us, alert, listening.

"Unity without sameness," Magnolia elaborates. "Each tier should stand on its own, but the cake must still feel cohesive. We want something that stands out."

"Exactly, Mags." Garrett agrees. "A showstopper should make us stop in our tracks and take notice. So, make us notice."

In other words: don't be boring. Don't play it safe.

But I've built my entire career on safe.

Safe is how you get a perfect crumb. Safe is how you avoid surprises. Safe is how my parents talk about success, earned one careful step at a time. Safe is how I learned everything in the kitchen. You master the rules first, then maybe, someday, bend them ever so slightly.

I picture two different cakes immediately. Elegant lines, flawless execution. Predictable flavors. Cakes that would impress back home, but would be a disappointment at that judging table. Cakes no one would remember.

My jaw tightens. I flip my notebook closed before I can sketch them, like the ideas might poison the page if I give them ink. This is exactly what Magnolia meant yesterday. This is what Garrett called out.

I didn't come here to prove I can do what I've already done a hundred times before.

Pressing my lips together, I close my eyes for a beat, frustrated with myself. *Why the fuck do I default to boring?*

I didn't come here to be safe. I came here to make people remember me.

After gathering my composure, I glance over my shoulder

at Taylor, who is already vibrating at a frequency that could shatter glass.

She's pacing in a loose little circle, hands fluttering as she talks to herself, eyes bright as her ideas come together. She's chaos incarnate. Whimsical. Untethered. Free.

The opposite of me in every possible way.

And somehow, it works.

"Bakers," Theo calls, "you have eight hours. Your time starts... NOW!"

The tent erupts into motion once again.

I move automatically, gathering my ingredients and setting my station up for success, but my thoughts keep snagging on the instructions. Three tiers. Three profiles. Something unexpected.

I force myself to pivot from my original idea, letting my thoughts wander into unfamiliar territory. There's no hiding when it comes to a showstopper, and I refuse to disappoint the judges again.

A trio of citrus. Spice. Dark, milk, and white chocolate. It's a riskier balance than I'd usually attempt, but still grounded enough to feel intentional. I start pulling ingredients, measuring by weight instead of feel, but allowing myself to adjust where I normally wouldn't.

Halfway through creaming butter, I smell it.

Something bitter and unmistakable. *Burnt sugar.*

I look back just in time to see the first curl of smoke rising from Taylor's station. Her eyes are wide, spatula frozen midair, like she isn't sure what she's seeing.

I shouldn't step in.

That's the unspoken rule in a game like this. You don't help or interfere. You focus on your own bench and let everyone else succeed or fail on their own merit. Anything else could get misconstrued on camera.

And the cameras are absolutely on us.

If I help her and she recovers, it doesn't benefit me in any way. If she doesn't, it could look like I distracted her. Either way, there's risk.

I've won competitions by being disciplined enough to ignore moments like this. By minding my own business, letting mistakes happen because they weren't mine to fix.

But the smoke is thickening, and I know that smell all too well. I know exactly how fast sugar crosses the line from golden to ruined.

She's seconds away from scorching the entire batch.

I swear under my breath and move closer, keeping my voice low. "Taylor."

She jumps, startled, but her eyes meet mine.

"Kill the heat," I say quietly. "Now. Pour that top half into a bowl and stir it off the burner."

She blinks once, then lunges for the dial, dragging the pot away just in time. The smell fades immediately—it just might be salvageable.

"Oh! Oh my god." She laughs, breath uneven, one hand pressed to her chest. "I was *this close* to committing a sugar hate crime."

I nod. "You caught it early."

"No... you caught it early."

Taylor takes a deep breath and drags a hand through her hair to steady herself. The way she's looking at me right now is as if she's seeing me for the first time. "Thank you. Seriously. I don't have time to remake the candy shell for my jumbo cherry."

A jumbo cherry? What the *hell* is this girl making?

I shrug, already stepping back, but the look on her face holds me captive. A jumbled mix of confusion and appreciation. I caught her off guard. And fuck, flustered looks good on her.

"No problem."

But she's still staring at me, studying me. Then she squints, leaning over her station to get a little closer.

"Wait." Her mouth tilts. "Was that... another smile?"

I stop. It takes me a second to realize she's right. My lips are turned up in the corners. I didn't even feel it happen. I run a hand over my mouth, thumb brushing beneath my lower lip.

"Jesus," she says, grinning wider now. "Okay, well, we'll work on that. Thanks again, Grumpy."

I should scowl. I should say something dry and walk away.

Instead, I feel the corner of my mouth twitch again.

Before she notices, I go back to minding my own business.

The hours blur together in a mirage of mixing, baking, filling, and assembling. I fight my instincts every step of the way, pushing flavors a little further than I'm comfortable with. Letting the cake be bold instead of restrained.

This cake is nothing like the delicate ones I've mastered throughout my career. The dark chocolate is rich and bold. The bursts of citrus are punchy and bright. Cinnamon and cayenne enhance the overall profile.

This is more than a cake; it's a declaration that I do, in fact, want to be here. I've left the presentation simple, hoping my flavors will stand out in protest to the judges' critique from yesterday.

Behind me, Taylor is humming to herself again, and I can't help but turn to watch as she builds something unhinged and perfect.

An ice cream sundae cake—*no, I saw her with bananas*—a banana split cake?

Her three tiers are stacked, waiting to be frosted. Chocolate, strawberry, and pineapple with a caramelized banana filling. Something I never would have thought of. She's either an absolute genius or completely insane.

She coats the whole thing in smooth vanilla frosting, unapologetically classic, but adds a glossy fudge drip that cascades over the edge. She crowns the top with a bright red candy apple, standing in as the cherry.

It's absolutely incredible.

She bites her lip as she studies her work, the soft curve of it disappearing from view. Heat floods my system. Her eyes flick up, and she catches me staring.

"We did it."

I nod, swallowing hard, just as time is called.

Judging is full of polite nods and careful examination. Most of the feedback for the other contestants leans positive, neutral at worst. A pang of unfamiliar unease carves its way into my chest as I lift my cake and carry it to the judging table.

"This is very elegant. I appreciate the gold leaf accents and sugared lemons as decor. What should we expect inside?" Magnolia asks as Garrett picks up a clean knife.

"You have a trio of chocolate, each enhanced with a citrus pairing and spices. The top layer is a white-chocolate cake filled with zesty lime curd. In the middle, you'll find a lemon cake with a milk chocolate cinnamon ganache. And the base layer is a dark chocolate cayenne cake, paired with a blood orange filling."

Garrett's eyebrows shoot up. "That's a very different approach than you took yesterday."

"It is." I widen my stance, clasping my hands behind my back. "I heard what you said about playing it safe. It's been a while, but I know how to take criticism and correct it."

Garrett nods, a flicker of respect in his expression. I force myself to remain still as they taste each layer, waiting for their verdict.

"This is lovely, Alex. Your cakes are the perfect texture, and those flavors are exceptionally balanced. I'm proud of you for getting out of your comfort zone on this one." Magnolia forks another bite of the top tier into her mouth.

"I agree," Garrett says, placing his fork down. "It has the same precision as before, but it's more thoughtful. Nice pivot."

I tilt my head in response, then move to retrieve my cake and return to my station.

Theo helps Taylor carry her bake to the front. Garrett's eyes sparkle with amusement, and Magnolia audibly gasps in delight. As they take it in, they laugh with her. Actually laugh.

"This tastes like childhood," Magnolia says, eyes lighting up. "Playful, but well-executed."

"It's a little messy, but that candy apple cherry on top is so creative. You know exactly what it is the second you look at it." Garrett adds. "I do think your cakes needed a little longer in the oven, but they're close to perfect. You should be proud."

Taylor shrugs easily and thanks them, already heading back toward her station. As she passes, she offers me a small smile, tucking a curl behind her ear with a dip of her head.

I raise an eyebrow, unsettled by the look. I don't know what it means, but another flare of heat surges in my chest anyway. My pulse betrays me. *Fuck.*

The production team lines us up so the judges can announce week one's winner. We stand there for so long it's uncomfortable, pretending not to watch each other, wondering who will be going home first. No one speaks. The tent is overflowing with residual heat and nerves.

Taylor rocks gently on her heels, hands clasped in front of her. She looks calm, but her fingers twist together, giving her away. I realize, distantly, that I don't feel much of anything. I know that I'm not the one going home. There's no chance of that.

But I'm also not remotely concerned with winning.

Because I'm proud of the cake I made, regardless of the outcome. Huh, that's new.

When Star Baker is announced, it isn't either of us. Diane takes the win with a boozy cocktail-inspired cake that took the judges' breath away. It was impressive; she deserves it.

Brief disappointment flickers when my name isn't called, but it fades quickly. The feedback today is significantly better than yesterday. And I'm still here.

But Ace isn't.

When Theo says his name, the tent quiets in that heavy, inevitable way. Ace takes it with grace, smiling bright even as his shoulders slump.

"Baker fam, it's been fun. As much as I wish I could stay here longer, especially with all you beautiful ladies, when it's your time, it's your time."

"We are going to miss you, Ace!" Judy says with a sad smile. "Losing someone from the group is never easy."

Ace smiles, then flexes both arms next to his head. Ever the showman, the house is going to be quieter without him. "Keep your heads up, guys, and have some extra fun for me. Remember, it doesn't matter if you win or lose; it's how you play the game. Peace!"

He flashes peace signs with both hands as he leaves.

I notice Taylor watching him go, her joy dimmed by empathy. Her eyes travel back to me, and I notice something else behind her gaze. She's analyzing my expression for something. It's almost like she expects me to be angry that I didn't win.

I'm not.

While that surprises me more than anything else, she's clearly pegged me as the type who needs to win. Who expects it, no matter what. The kind of person who treats anything less than first place as failure.

And before this challenge, she wouldn't have been wrong.

Watching the group mingle, it dawns on me that I broke one of my own rules today. I stepped in to help when I didn't have to. Not on only that, there was no benefit to me in doing so.

With her infectious smile still aimed in my direction, I realize something else uncomfortable and undeniable.

There's far more to Taylor Madden than she lets on.

And I want nothing more than to find out what that is—even though experience has taught me that wanting answers like that never ends well for me.

Chapter 11

In the middle of a sprawling green lawn, a lone table for two sits beneath the open sky, draped in a red-and-white checkered tablecloth. Magnolia and Garrett are seated across from each other, mid-conversation, each holding a glass of red wine.

"Dinner is served," Theo announces in a painfully exaggerated Italian accent as he strides into frame, setting down a platter of spaghetti and meatballs between them that's comically oversized.

He's in black slacks and a black-and-white striped shirt, complete with red sashes tied at his waist and neck. A curly mustache is scrawled across his upper lip in what is very clearly permanent marker.

Judy enters from the opposite side, dressed nearly identically—minus the mustache—with a full-sized accordion strapped to her chest.

"A little music to set the mood," she says, her accent just as terrible as Theo's.

The accordion wheezes to life in what might generously be called a traditional Italian tune. Theo sways dramatically, clutching his chest as though he's witnessing a masterpiece.

At the table, the judges do their best to maintain composure. They lift their glasses and clink them together.

"Let's hope our bakers are better equipped for this challenge than our hosts," Magnolia says, laughing.

Garrett turns directly to the camera, a knowing smile tugging at his mouth. "And with that, welcome to *Italian Week*."

Who doesn't love Italian food? Pizza, spaghetti, minestrone, garlic bread—you name it, I'm here for it. But Italian desserts feel a little trickier to place. Aside from tiramisu and gelato, what else even counts?

Since my experience with Italian baking is limited, I opted for mini tiramisu cups for our signature this morning. It was risky given the time constraint, but I stabilized the mascarpone cream as much as I could so that I didn't serve them creamy coffee soup.

Thankfully, it worked.

Magnolia appreciated the intensity of my espresso, but Garrett called out my presentation. The layers weren't perfect, which isn't the worst critique I could've gotten, but it still stings since I took my time with them. I'll just have to try that much harder next time.

There were a handful of other tiramisus. I guess a lot of us were unsure how to tackle the challenge of *celebrating classic Italian flavors*.

Alex and Brandon were the standouts, each making different Italian cookies. Both batches were flawless, but Alex received high praise for his precise layers in his Italian Rainbow Cookies. It doesn't surprise me that a man who moves with such intention across his station has flawless execution with something like this.

We took a brief lunch break and have all reconvened in the tent for our second technical challenge. Lila, who is directly in front of me, turns around to flash me a quick smile.

"Let's do this, Taylor!" She exclaims, raising her hand high for a high-five over my workbench. I smile back, smacking my hand into hers, catching the glint of her phone screen on her station. I wave, then slide to the other side of my station to be out of frame.

I don't fault Lila for filming every moment she can here, but I also don't want to be on her live when I'm doing my best to swallow all of my nerves. Just in case, I swipe my hands over my hair to smooth it down anyway.

God, I'm so nervous for this one.

The judges consistently love my flavors, but Garrett always finds fault with my execution.

There's no room for error today.

"For this challenge," Garrett announces. "We would like you to make twenty-four identical pizzelle. They should be thin, crisp, evenly colored, and delicately flavored. Twelve with anise, and twelve with citrus. You have one hour to accomplish your task."

Same as last week, the judges leave the tent, and the hosts immediately announce that our time has begun. Since they don't waste any time, neither do I.

I set the iron to what I assume is the proper temperature and mix my batter while I wait for it to heat up. There's some trial and error in finding the right amount of batter and the exact timing to achieve that perfect golden shade, but it only takes a couple of oopsies before I figure it out.

Pizzelle are deceptive like that. Simple enough to look easy, unforgiving enough to punish every lapse in attention or judgment. Good thing I have a little extra of both today.

Once I find that magic ratio, I lean into the rhythm of the process, reminding myself that I don't have to be the best. I just have to avoid being the worst.

Across the tent, Alex barely looks up from his station. His movements are efficient as always, almost bored, like he could do this in his sleep.

Who am I kidding? He probably can.

When he lifts the lid of his iron, his expression gives away nothing. He just checks the color, adjusts the heat, and moves on with no wasted thought or effort.

In front of me, Lila is having the opposite experience. She opens her iron and winces. The pizzelle droops over the edge, too pale in places, too dark in others. She peels it off with her fingers, already shaking her head before it's fully free.

"Ugh," she mutters, glancing toward the cameras.

I refocus on my own station, but my eyes keep drifting forward to Lila's growing discard pile, then sideways to Alex's neat row of cooling cookies. He lines them up without thinking, adjusting one that's barely off-center.

He seems different today, almost content in a way I don't recognize on him. The scowl that usually guards his face is gone, replaced by a soft peacefulness. It makes him look younger, or maybe, more his age. Less android prodigy, more compelling artisan.

I bite my lip and smile; *it looks really good on him.*

As if he heard me, he inclines his head in my direction. He smirks, eyes darting from my face to the iron on my station before mouthing, "Pay attention."

Silly, Alex. I *am* paying attention.

When time is called, I look down at my plate of cookies, proud of what I accomplished. They're relatively close in size, with good design definition from the iron. The shade isn't exactly identical, but they're in the same window. Definitely more cousins than sisters, but hey, at least they're in the same family.

Somehow, I'm the last to bring my bake to the judging table. The rest are already exiting the tent, waiting.

I move to place my pizzelle behind my name tag, which happens to be right next to Lila's disaster. When I set my plate down, the impact shakes the table, and a few of Lila's pizzelle jiggle in response.

Oh no, that's definitely *not* good.

Curiosity overrides any sense of urgency to go meet up with the others, so I linger and survey the rest of the cookies on the table.

Movement from the side entrance to the tent startles me.

A production assistant I don't recognize approaches the table and replaces Lila's plate with one filled with beautiful pizzelle. The replacement is flawless, easily the best on the table and not something that comes out of a technical challenge under this much pressure, and definitely not from Lila.

"Hey," I say, keeping my voice light. "What's going on?"

The assistant hesitates, eyes shifting my way. "Just helping things along."

"That wasn't what she turned in."

She exhales through her nose, like I'm being difficult. "Lila's got a big audience. Viewers like her."

"Okay, but what difference does that make?" My stomach twists. "She messes up and gets a do-over? I'm sure people loved Ace, too."

Out of nowhere, Joe steps up behind me before I can say more, his smile already in place. "This isn't the fight you want."

"But it's not fair," I say as I turn to him. The word feels childish as soon it leaves my mouth, but it needed to be said because Lila shouldn't get special treatment just because she has a social media following.

That's not how competition works.

Joe leans in, voice low. "This is television, Taylor. Not a meritocracy." Then, softer, like advice: "Don't make waves if you want to stay in this."

He subtly angles his body, blocking me from the cameras without drawing attention to it. His gaze meets mine, imploring me to keep my mouth shut. I see the warning for what it is as he steps aside, clearing the path to the exit without looking at me again. Unsure if I've been dismissed or saved, I take a step back.

"Okay..." My voice trails off as I stumble in that direction.

I'm distracted when I join the others.

How can they just replace Lila's bake with something better? Every single one of us has struggled with something here. She's no different, no better than the rest of us. I don't care how many followers she has; the most talented bakers should be the ones moving on.

But what am I supposed to do with this information? Clearly, the production team knows about it since they're the ones doing it.

Is there any point in telling the others?

Probably not, it won't change anything. I press my lips together, brows furrowing.

"If you were concentrating any harder, you'd have smoke coming out of your ears," RaeAnn says as she nudges into my shoulder. "Penny for your thoughts?"

I shake my head, deciding in that moment not to tell her what I saw, and force a smile. "Just reliving that whole technical, you know? Just when you think you know what's coming, it's something else entirely."

She hums her agreement. "You looked like you did okay."

"I've definitely done worse, that's for sure."

We laugh together at that because almost nothing could be worse than my first bake in the tent. It isn't long before we're called back in for judging. And, to everyone's surprise but mine, Lila wins the technical.

Her shriek of excitement hits me like a punch to the chest. She knows that wasn't what she turned in to the judges.

She knows, and she doesn't care.

The house is quieter than usual when we get back, the kind of quiet that only happens when everyone's drained and pretending not to think about judging. Lila's already in our room when I push the door open, sitting cross-legged on her bed with her phone propped up.

She's smiling wide, effortless and camera-ready.

"Hey, bestie," she chirps, eyes flicking to the screen. "We survived *Italian Week.*"

I hover just inside the doorway, suddenly unsure how to start. Kara is usually the one who confronts people. I'm the "nice" one.

"Hey."

She taps something on her phone, the smile softening but not disappearing. "Okay, guys, I'm gonna hop off for now," she says, blowing a kiss. "Love you all. Lila out!"

The smile drops the second the phone goes dark.

She tosses her phone onto the bedside table, rubbing her temples in deep circles. I step farther into the room, setting my bag down a little too carefully. "Congrats on the technical."

"Thanks." She smooths her hair over one shoulder, not missing a beat, already reaching for a makeup wipe. "It was wild, right? That technical was brutal."

I hum, noncommittal, and sit on the edge of my bed. I don't look at her when I speak. "Can I ask you something?"

"Sure," she says with a casual shrug.

I sit back, resting my weight on my hands. "Did you actually turn those pizzelle in?"

The air changes, and her eyes flick to mine.

"I just—at the table, I noticed something weird. And maybe I'm wrong, but—"

She tosses her wipe in the small garbage can near her bed, leaning back against her pillows. Her expression is pleasant enough, though a little condescending. Like she's humoring a child.

"What are you talking about, Taylor?"

I swallow, pressing on, afraid I'll lose my nerve. "Those pizzelle... they weren't *yours*."

Much to my surprise, she just laughs. It's not loud or defensive. Just a small, surprised sound as a hand flutters to cover her mouth.

"Oh my god," she says. "Are we really doing this?"

"I'm not accusing you of anything." I amend quickly, though it definitely feels like I am. "I just thought maybe there was a mistake, or—"

"Or what?" she asks, tilting her head. The motion is almost predatory, making me swallow hard against the lump of nerves forming in my throat. "You think I cheated."

"I'm not saying that. I think production stepped in."

Her smile sharpens as she stands, crossing the room toward me at a pace that suddenly feels territorial. "You know how this works, right?"

"I thought I did."

And that's the truth. I genuinely thought this show was a bunch of home bakers coming together in good faith. We'd all show up, do our best, and the most talented among us would win the grand prize.

"It's a show, Taylor. *Entertainment*. People want stories. They want faces they recognize." She gestures toward her phone. "I give them that."

"And the rest of us don't?" I ask, a little offended.

She studies me for a beat and chews the inside of her cheek like she's deciding how honest to be. "I don't know," she says at last, her tone clearly over this entire conversation. "It sounds to me like you're just jealous because you're irrelevant."

Her words land between us, stark and ugly. No, the only *irrelevant* thing in this room is her. She isn't talented or special; she just spends a lot of time pretending to be someone likable online.

I blink a few times before plastering a smile on my face, because that's what I do when I'm surprised. "Irrelevant?"

She shrugs again, already turning back toward her bed.

"I mean, no offense, but no one's tuning in for you, babe. Not yet, anyway."

Heat crawls up my neck, my heart pounding harder than it ever has in the tent. But I just sit there on my bed, staring at my roommate in complete disbelief.

I think I just met the real Lila.

"Goodnight, Lila," I say, because if I try for anything else, I might crack.

"Night," she replies lightly, already lounging on her bed and scrolling her phone again.

The soft material of my pillow is cool beneath my cheek, soothing the lingering embarrassment there. I curl into myself on the bed and face the wall, wishing I could ignore Lila's presence the way Chloe seems to do.

But I can't; her incessant static vibrates against my spine from across the room. Hot tears threaten to fall.

Maybe I *am* irrelevant in all the ways Lila cares about.

But there's another showstopper coming tomorrow. Another chance to make something good with my hands and win over the judges.

There'll be flour under my nails and cakes rising in the oven and a clock ticking down, whether anyone's watching for me or not. I know how to do that part at least.

I close my eyes, already running through flavors in my head, and let that be enough for tonight.

Alex

Chapter 12

No one cheers when Jasper's name is called as the baker going home this week.

Jasper nods, smiling in that stunned, gracious way people do when they're trying not to ruin the moment for everyone else. He presses his lips together, lets out a slow breath, and files the disappointment away for later when he's alone.

I clock our resident optimist immediately.

She's standing a few feet behind him, hands clenched at her sides, eyes already glassy. When he turns to hug her, she breaks.

"I'm so sorry." Her usual cheery voice wobbles, muffled against Jasper's chest. "It really shouldn't have been you. I'm so, so sorry."

Jasper laughs awkwardly, pulling back just enough to look at her. "Hey, kiddo. It's okay. That's the game, right? Someone's gotta go home. I get to see my kids tomorrow, so it ain't all bad."

Taylor shakes her head. "No. It's not—"

But she stops herself, swallowing hard, shifting on her feet like she's weighing whether to say something she can't take back. "I'm just… I'm really sorry."

Her reaction throws me.

Taylor's empathetic, sure. That's nothing new. Kindness is practically built into her. But this isn't that. This sits heavier, the kind of feeling that makes your hands tremble when there's nothing you can fix.

Jasper makes his rounds, hugging everyone, thanking the judges, promising to bake again. When he finally disappears through the exit, the tent exhales. The cameras cut.

But Taylor doesn't recover.

Her usual soft, smiling face is gone—replaced with something sharper, eyes cutting across the room. I follow her gaze to… Lila?

I narrow my eyes, scrutinizing her, trying to piece together what Taylor sees. What I'm missing. What's already taken root right under my nose.

Lila is smiling too wide, already talking to the camera about how happy she is to still be here, her voice wrapping around the loss of Jasper like it belongs to her.

My jaw tightens. I don't like her.

Taylor drifts through the aftermath like she's underwater. Her beautiful hazel eyes remain unfocused, her smile nowhere to be found.

When I catch her eye, she looks away too quickly.

Usually, she lingers, smiles, or throws me a dorky thumbs-up. Now, she's avoiding me, and everyone else, entirely.

As she silently tucks herself into one of the window seats of the van, she curls toward the window and closes her eyes, shutting the world out. I tentatively take the seat beside her, not sure what to say, so I don't say anything at all.

That's when it hits me—I don't have a clue what in the hell just happened.

Because whatever Taylor is carrying right now is more than just losing a fellow baker. And she's carrying it alone.

The ride back to the house passes in a blur of cracked jokes and forced laughter all around us. Diane, I think, starts talking about what she'll bake next week for *Southern Classics Week*. Khalil jokes about carbo-loading after *Italian Week*. It all drifts past me.

Taylor doesn't move from her spot, arms wrapped tight around herself. A low pang of unease unfurls in my chest as I sit there, completely useless.

Fuck.

Taylor is the last one out of the van and the first one inside the house. She doesn't look at anyone as she barrels through the front door. I linger in the foyer, watching her disappear up the stairs before a door clicks shut in the distance.

"Don't," Julian says quietly, appearing at my side.

His hand lands on my shoulder, grounding me. "You don't need to fix everything you notice."

I huff out a breath, still not looking at him. "I wasn't going to."

He gives me a look that says he knows better.

Inside, the house hums with that uncomfortable post-judging energy. Everyone searches for distractions to avoid replaying the same three moments in their heads. A champagne bottle pops somewhere, and music rises to fill the silence.

Julian steers me toward the kitchen under the guise of grabbing a beer. "Walk with me," he says. "I want to know where your head's at."

I don't fight him this time because a beer sounds perfect.

"You look like hell," he taunts, smirking.

I grunt in response and grab the bottle he offers. My hands are still faintly tacky with sugar and citrus oil despite the scrub I gave them before we left the tent. I press my fingertip against the glass a few times, focusing on the slight pull.

"Good showstopper?" he asks.

I take a long drink. The cold steadies me. "Yeah."

"That's all I get?" Julian arches an eyebrow.

I shrug, leaning back against the island. My body aches in that deep, satisfying way it only does after hours of standing, repeating the same precise motions. A sign of a day well spent and a job well done.

"I got star baker this week," I say.

He breaks into a wide grin. "That's a *good* thing, right?"

"It is."

"You should tell your face that." His grin shifts into another smirk when my exhausted gaze meets his.

"I don't know," I reply after a beat. "It's hard to be excited when someone else's dream was destroyed in the same sentence."

That earns me a look. Julian twists the cap off his beer and takes a sip, eyes never leaving mine. "That's new."

I let the silence stretch. The house creaks softly around us—footsteps overhead, someone laughing down the hall. The others are decompressing in their own ways. I don't feel like joining them yet.

"The judges really liked it," I admit. "They said it was great. I've been working with bolder flavors, and they're responding to that. They gave me all the words you want to hear in a competition like this."

"But?" Julian prompts.

"But that's not the part that mattered."

He waits, completely at ease, while I sort through the feeling that has been lodged in the back of my head all day. I glance down at my hands, flexing my fingers.

"I had fun today."

There it is. The thing I haven't said out loud in years.

Julian's expression changes. The look isn't exactly surprise, but something close to it, mixed with a healthy dose of relief. "You had *fun*."

"Don't make a big deal out of it." I take another drink, looking anywhere but at the smirking asshole standing in front of me.

"I'm absolutely making a big deal out of it."

I scoff, shaking my head.

"I wanted to impress the judges, but I also knew I wouldn't be going home today no matter what. I just... got into it. Lost track of time. Forgot about the cameras, the clock— everything—and just baked something I wanted to bake."

"And how did that feel?"

I close my eyes briefly as I recall the day. The memory is still warm in my mind, fragile as glass. "Like something I didn't realize I'd been missing."

Julian nods, and I can see the gears turning in his head.

"You remember when you were sixteen, and you ruined that batch of croissants at three in the morning because you stayed out too late at Homecoming?"

I snort. "You mean the batch Chet made me redo over and over again until sunrise?"

"You cried," Julian reminds me, a softer smile on his face.

"I was exhausted."

"You cried because you thought you'd ruined everything for the restaurant," he corrects. "And then you did it again the next night. And the night after that."

"Your point?"

"My point is, you used to love this. And then someone taught you that having fun and being good at what you do are mutually exclusive."

The words land harder than I expect, because he's not wrong. I straighten my shoulders, but I don't answer right away.

Because the truth is, standing there in the tent today felt like I was stealing something back for myself. Like joy was contraband, and I'd managed to smuggle it out without anyone noticing.

"I hate that he gets to take that from me." The admission is bitter on my tongue, so I wash it down by chugging the rest of my beer. "Even now."

Julian presses a warm hand against my shoulder.

"He doesn't get to, not if you don't let him."

I let out a humorless laugh. He doesn't push.

"So," Julian says, lightening again. "Aside from baking revelations. Anything, or *anyone*, catch your eye?"

I glare at him, already seeing where this is going. I don't know why I thought my attention on Taylor would slip by him unnoticed, but I'd be lying if I said I wasn't hoping it would. Not only is Julian my cousin, the asshole's my best friend and has some kind of sixth sense about these things.

But that doesn't mean I'm in the mood to talk about it.

"Don't start."

"Oh, I'm starting. You haven't been this... *human* since before starting with *The Harrington Group* back in the day."

I push off the counter and head for the stairs, refusing to entertain this back and forth. I'm too tired. Too preoccupied by the pretty girl upstairs, sulking and alone.

"Drop it, Jules."

He doesn't drop it, though, per usual. Instead, he saddles up next to me, egging me on further. "It's Taylor, isn't it?"

I stop short on the first stair. "What?"

"It's Taylor." His grin widens at whatever reaction flickers across my face, and *fuck*—I instantly know I've given myself away.

"Absolutely not, that's ludicrous."

"Is it, though?"

The arrogant way he cocks his head in challenge makes me want to take him to the ground like we're kids again. I size him up out of habit, head to toe.

He isn't bigger than me.

I could definitely still take him.

"Of course it is."

"You watch her like you don't believe she's real, man. If I didn't already know how much you hate relationships, I'd bet anything you're working up the nerve to make a move."

"I watch everyone," I argue, crossing my arms, conveniently ignoring the second half of that. I don't hate relationships. I just don't think most people are worth the effort.

"You *observe* everyone. You *linger* on her."

I open my mouth to defend myself, then close it again.

Julian hums at my silence, like he knows he's got me.

"She's just... different than everyone back home."

I sigh as I think about all the little ways Taylor shines that others could never compete with. "And she actually *likes* being here, no matter what the judges throw at us."

"And you don't?"

I hesitate.

Do I like being here?

I don't know. I didn't ask to be on the show. All I know for sure is that I didn't want to come, but now that I'm here, I'm having a good time.

"I didn't."

"But now you do."

His words aren't a question but a declaration. He's thoughtful for a minute before continuing. "You know, it's hard to miss when you smile because it doesn't happen often, but it's been happening a lot more since you've been here."

"I don't smile."

"You did today. And I saw one yesterday too."

I scoff and head upstairs, putting distance between us before he can say anything else. His laugh chases me down the hallway.

I did smile today smack dab in the middle of the tent.

The catalyst is clear in my mind—Taylor across the tent, hair escaping her ponytail, laughing at something one of the hosts said.

It wasn't performative or contrived for the cameras.

It was just pure, unadulterated joy.

And so was mine.

Dinner consists of Thai carry-out that we eat directly from the cardboard containers. Some of us remain standing around the kitchen island while others lounge across the living room furniture. Our conversations overlap, laughter edging with exhaustion.

I keep catching glimpses of tension I can't quite place between Taylor and Lila. Taylor is quieter than usual, and Lila is chatting with everyone a little too loud. She's animated and bright, the way she usually is when the cameras are on. It's a facade that feels brittle if you look too closely.

When Lila laughs, it doesn't reach her eyes.

Taylor notices it too. I see it in the way her smile falters, the way she keeps trying to reframe her focus on RaeAnn instead of interacting directly with whatever Lila is saying.

Okay, what the fuck happened here?

The tension in the room is almost suffocating, coiled beneath the surface like a rattlesnake.

If anyone else knows why, they don't show it. Would Taylor tell me if I asked her directly? Maybe it's personal and she's planning to leave the rest of us out of it.

Truthfully, I don't need the details to know I'm on Taylor's side. She loves everyone on sight, so if she has a problem with anybody in this house, they must deserve it.

After an hour of forcing myself to be part of the group, I slip out onto the back porch, drawn by the need for air and a break from the incessant chatter in the house.

For solitude.

The night is cool for LA, and crickets chirp an a cappella rhythm in the grass. It immediately makes me think of summer nights back home, and I sink into one of the lounge chairs with a sigh, tipping my head back, staring at the dark outline of the balcony above.

Propping my arms behind my head, I recline with my eyes closed. I must doze off because an indeterminate amount of time passes before I'm jolted awake by the slide of a glass door closing above me.

A voice drifts down between the cracks of the balcony.

"Mom, it's okay. Really."

I freeze on the spot—it's Taylor.

Is her room directly above the shared living space?

Too busy minding my own business, I never thought to scope out the other rooms. A mistake I plan to remedy immediately, because for some reason it feels like something I should know.

"I know... I know you tried." Her voice drips with exhaustion, and something heavier. Resignation. Her footsteps are light as she paces the balcony.

"No, don't apologize," she continues. "No, Mom. No, it isn't your fault that they don't have overtime available right now. I can make it work, it's fine."

My chest tightens, guilt slamming into me for eavesdropping. I shouldn't be listening to her private conversation, but I stay rooted in place, needing to know more about the girl who's been running through my thoughts all day.

"Yeah, I'll just drive back after judging every Sunday. It's not that bad. Traffic should be better this late at night anyway."

Another pause. Longer this time.

"I don't know," she admits. "I guess I thought... I thought the show would help more. How else is everyone affording this?"

Doesn't this show give a living stipend?

My brows furrow in confusion. I guess I never asked or paid attention to the financial implications of the show. It didn't matter to me either way, but now that it's hurting Taylor, I care more than I should.

I wonder if I can get Julian to look into it for me.

"Monday through Friday," Taylor says. "I can be back in time for the weekend bakes if I leave straight from work."

That's insane.

That's *hours* of driving every week. Exhaustion layered on exhaustion, topped with a generous helping of stress.

Where did she say she was from again?

"I'll be fine," she insists, but her voice dips. "It's just like Gram used to say, nothing worth having comes easy."

Silence stretches for a while. I assume it's her mom's turn to speak on the other end of the line.

"Love you too," she murmurs.

After the call ends, I hear it.

A single shaky intake of breath and a soft cry. Soon, her footsteps pad across the balcony, and the heavy glass door slides shut, sealing her back inside the house.

I sit there long after, heart pounding, staring up at the now-empty balcony.

It clicks into place then—the unfairness of it all. The invisible advantages people like me have, where we get to focus solely on the bake, while others here are juggling survival.

And suddenly, winning doesn't feel as clean as it did an hour ago. I thought coming here meant bringing home the win for Chet to drape around his shoulders like a victory flag, when in reality, I'm taking a win from someone who needs it way more than we do.

Fuck.

What do I do with that?

Still on the patio, lost to the ethical war playing out in my mind, I hear a door open and close, the drag of a suitcase across pavement, car keys jingling, and tires crunching over the driveway.

Taylor leaves immediately, in the middle of the night.

And I hate how it unsettles me. I don't have a name to place on the feeling, but it's a lot like losing something I never actually had.

Chapter 13

I don't remember most of the drive back to the house in LA as much as I remember the moment it ended.

The headlights cut across the driveway just after midnight on Friday, my hands aching from gripping the wheel for three straight hours after a full shift at my day job.

This week has been one of the hardest of my life.

Trying to focus on client calls at work while my head was back here in the house with the other contestants was next-level taxing. But I did it, and I'm back.

I kill the engine and sit there for a second longer than necessary, forehead resting against the steering wheel, telling myself I at least made it. That I didn't fall asleep at the wheel and die in a fiery highway explosion, and that counts for something.

Easing open the front door as quiet as I can, I slide into the dark foyer and slip off my shoes in an effort to make as little noise as possible. The door clicks shut, and I gently pad through the living room toward the stairs. In my exhaustion, a silent laugh surfaces because it feels like I'm fifteen again and sneaking back into the house after curfew.

Someone clears their throat.

I jolt, heart lurching, and look up to find Alex on the couch, legs stretched out, a book open in his hands. He looks up at me with tired eyes, but there's something else there too. Relief maybe? I don't know, that doesn't make sense. Any social awareness or EQ I may have had seeped out of my body hours ago.

"Oh," I whisper-laugh, pressing a hand to my chest, because apparently that's all the vocabulary can handle right now.

"You made it."

He doesn't look up from his book when he speaks, but there's something about the way he says it that jumps out at me. But, again, too tired to figure out why.

I smile, clumsy and half-asleep on my feet.

"Yeah. Long week."

He nods like he understands more than I said, though it's doubtful since I'm sure he spent all week lounging or relaxing in whatever way someone as rigid as he is does.

"Get some sleep," he says, keeping his voice low.

I don't even make it through a full reply. I just hum in agreement and shuffle toward the stairs.

Lila and Chloe are both asleep when I slip into the room, collapsing into bed still wearing my hoodie. I don't so much fall asleep as I succumb to unconsciousness.

The next day passes in flashes, which is problematic since I'm quite literally baking for my life.

The signature goes fine, I guess.

About as good as it could have gone, considering I didn't get to practice as much as I wanted to throughout the week. My bake wasn't great, but it wasn't a disaster either, so I'll take it. The judges said my flavors are there, but my execution is still struggling.

The technical, however, is a completely different story.

I place near the bottom—second from last—and, at this point, it just feels like insult to injury. One week back home, trying to manage this new schedule, and everything is already falling apart.

I knew this was going to be rough. I just didn't expect it to be this rough this fast. Internally, the walls are closing in because I know I'm blowing my only chance at making my dream come true, but I'm apparently helpless to do anything about it.

Somewhere far away, Magnolia says something encouraging. Garrett, on the other hand, does not. As we are leaving the tent, Lila gives me a once-over, followed by an eyeroll.

I've never had an enemy before; it looks like this show is bringing all the new experiences my way, whether I want it to or not.

Normally, I'd care about someone not liking me.

I'd at least feel *some type of way* about it.

But right now, all I can think about is coffee and a nap.

Waking up the next day feels like coming out of a fog. I stretch my arms above my head and blink against the light filtering through the windows. My body is still heavy with sleep but my mind is a little clearer than when I went to bed last night.

Yesterday's disappointment threatens to resurface, but if I've learned anything in my life, it's that if I let negative thoughts linger too long, they'll turn into something much harder to shake. So I roll out of bed, take a deep breath, and decide whatever challenge the judges have planned, I'll meet it head-on.

Tired or not.

Just as we're walking down the lawn to the tent, my phone vibrates in my back pocket. I slip it out and glance down to see a text from Kara.

KARE-BEAR:
break a leg! or whatever
the baking equivalent to
that phrase is 🧁🍫

What would that be—*break an egg?*

The pun makes me laugh. I chew my lower lip as I tap out a quick reply, then look up and slow to a stop just inside the entrance.

Something is immediately off.

There are only four stations set up inside the tent. Not eight like you'd expect, considering we have eight contestants at this point in the competition. Not even six with some kind of trick lighting or TV magic.

Four.

What the crap is going on?

Confused whispers ripple through our group. RaeAnn laughs nervously as she links her arm through mine. Theo grins at the front of the tent like a man who has been waiting all morning for this exact moment. Judy is bouncing on her toes next to him, looking like she's ready to burst. Cameras are already circling to catch every one of our reactions.

"Welcome to your showstopper challenge for the day," Judy begins. "As you probably noticed, the tent doesn't look the same as it has for the past couple of weeks."

"That's right, Judy. It sure doesn't. And if any of you are also math nerds in addition to bakers, you'll see that we have exactly half the number of stations we need. Can anyone guess what that means?" Theo asks, glancing between Judy and us, the camera trained on him.

"We thought it would be fun to do something a little different today to keep things interesting with a *pair* challenge!" Judy's exclamation hits my ears, my stomach churns at her words. "We toyed with the idea of having you draw straws to pick your partner, but that felt a little juvenile, so instead, we just chose for you."

Brandon and Lila.

Diane and RaeAnn.

Khalil and Chloe.

Which leaves me paired with the prickliest man to ever come out of the Great White North.

Biting my lip, I chance a look his way to gauge his reaction, and my stomach goes on another tilt-a-whirl ride. Maybe anxiety and nerves are rearing their ugly heads. Or maybe it's excitement? I'm getting to work with one of the most talented bakers in the competition.

I don't understand my own feelings or reaction to the announcement, and I don't have time to mull it over. I just know that when our eyes meet, he doesn't look thrilled.

As we scramble to our new, combined stations, the hosts and judges line up across the front of the tent. I trail my fingers over the edge of the workstation, standing a respectable distance from Alex, who radiates what I can only assume is irritation over our current predicament.

He refuses to look at me.

"Now that you are all settled, last week we announced this week's showstopper as a Southern celebration spread that includes a cake, a pie, and a cobbler."

Magnolia's smile is absolutely radiant as she speaks.

"You each went home and came back with a plan. Part of this pair challenge is that you have to blend both partners' plans together. We need to see elements from each of you, no boycotting one entire idea in favor of the other. As bakers, we need to be able to pivot and adapt when necessary."

"Oh!" Theo exclaims like he just remembered what he was about to say. "Because you will pass or fail as a team, this is going to be our only double-elimination of the series."

"Good luck, bakers!" Judy croons. "Make us proud!"

When we're released to start baking, my tall, brooding partner turns toward me. I mirror him, and we end up face-to-face. He inhales slowly, his pale blue shirt pulling taut as his chest expands.

"Before we jump into this, we need to take a beat and figure out how we're going to merge our bakes together."

"No," I say, shuffling to the far end of our station where the ingredients are set. "We need to get *moving*. Time always runs out faster than it should. Pie crust is pie crust, and a cake base is a cake base. We'll figure out the details as we go."

A series of emotions flashes across Alex's face in rapid succession: confusion, disbelief, calculation, and annoyance.

"Taylor, come on."

Something in his tone snags in my brain. He's not angry, but clipped, like this one conversation is already a setback for him. It brings me to an abrupt stop, and I turn to listen.

"I know you like to wing it, but we can't. We can't risk moving in different directions. Especially since it's a double-elimination, and you—"

I take a step forward, squinting and crossing my arms, as he trails off. His eyes hold mine briefly before looking away.

"And I what?"

He leans forward, bracing his hands on the work station with another deep breath, and drops his head down between his shoulders. *Is he counting to ten?*

"You've had some really great feedback," he starts, forcing his voice into a smooth, calming tone. It's almost the kind you'd expect from someone that's coaxing a scared animal out of a corner.

"But there've also been some really tough critiques, and I don't think it's fair for you to risk a swing and a miss when my fate in this competition is also tied to it. Okay?"

Even though he's not technically wrong, the words sting as they slide under my skin. I've not been the greatest, but I'm also not the worst baker here. I know what I'm doing. My instincts are usually pretty good.

But, he's right—this isn't just about me. This paired challenge directly affects him too, so I give in without putting up any more of a fight.

"Okay," I answer softly, uncrossing my arms. "I hear you."

He looks up at that, surprised.

"I know I haven't had a perfect run," I continue, hoping my voice doesn't betray the confidence I'm pouring into every word. "But I'm not reckless. I don't come in here trying to blow things up for fun. If I say something will work, it's because I genuinely believe in it."

I shake my head, lifting a small smile that doesn't quite land. More than a little sad that I'm having to defend myself to my partner.

"I promise you I'm trying just as hard to stay here as you are."

Something shifts in his posture, his shoulders squaring like he's taken my words as a sign that things are going his way. "Okay great, so you'll just listen to me for this challenge, and we'll both make it through to next week…"

A laugh explodes out of me. He's so full of himself.

His brow furrows.

"We plan enough to make you comfortable," I counter, stepping closer and laying a hand on his forearm. "And we leave enough room for improv so it still feels like me, too. Deal?"

He gives a small nod and pulls out his notebook.

By some miracle, we're able to come to an agreement on our spread without too much fuss. And much to my surprise, Alex takes my advice on how to jazz up our peach cobbler to make it stand out, and a giddy tingle dances across my chest.

Peaches are such a classic Southern flavor, but I talked him into trying a cornbread-based topping and brown sugar bourbon glaze. The last thing we need is to be one of four identical cobblers—and our Southern belle judge is not going to forgive boring.

We both assumed that the other bakers would do a traditional pie, maybe apple or strawberry, so Alex planned to do pecan pie instead. Which is perfect, because I decided to do a hummingbird cake.

The compromise for our collaboration on the cake is simple: we keep all my flavors, and I let him elevate the presentation.

Easiest deal I've ever made.

Our movements are awkward at first, as we try to work around one another. No matter where I stand, I always seem to be in his way. It becomes immediately clear that this man is used to commanding his own space.

"If you're going to hover," he says, not looking up, "can you at least make yourself useful and add some more flour to the bench? This crust is too sticky."

"Bossy," I tease, nudging him as I step closer.

Reaching across him for the flour, I bite my lip to hide a smile while he struggles with the sticky dough, webbing his fingers together.

My arm brushes his chest on the way back. Startled, he sucks in a quick breath and takes a small step back—somehow straight into me.

"Sorry," I murmur, already sprinkling flour where he asked. "Just... trying to make myself useful like you said. Occupational hazard of teamwork, you know?"

His eyes flick to mine, amused. We're still standing too close, and I'm suddenly very aware of my own breathing. With my face tilted up toward his, I'm close enough to see the lighter blue flecks sprinkled across his irises. The shadow of stubble along his jaw.

Alex's gaze slides down my face, registering the distance between us. He turns back to the crust, but the corner of his mouth stays tilted up, and neither of us rushes to adjust the space between us.

Our bake is going really well, we're so close to the finish line, I can almost taste the win.

The glaze for our cobbler is my responsibility, which means I'm working without a recipe and trusting my gut. Brown sugar goes into the saucepan first, followed by cornstarch, a splash of lemon juice, and a sprinkle of cinnamon. I stir the mixture, watching it all melt down into something glossy and thick as I add in the bourbon and some diced peaches.

Alex moves in behind me, close enough that I feel his energy pressing between my shoulder blades, sharp and restless.

"How confident are you about that ratio?" he asks, trying—and failing—to sound casual. This man might be a phenomenal baker but he does *not* do well with giving up control.

"Medium-high." I laugh, giving the spoon a swirl before lifting it to my lips, blowing lightly, and tasting it.

It's good. Rich and decadent. Almost perfect.

I discard my licked spoon into the sink, reaching for the bourbon to pour another measure.

"Let's maybe not get too reckless with that," Alex coaches. "We want finesse here."

I glance over my shoulder at him, eyebrows lifting. "This *is* finesse. We agreed I could have fun with this part, remember? It's all about the vibes."

He exhales through his nose, obviously unimpressed. "I trust precision, Taylor. Not vibes."

I roll my eyes, grab a clean spoon, and dip it into the sauce before pivoting toward him, holding it out between us. "Then verify."

He freezes. He's so still it's like staring at a painting. I'm not even sure he's breathing at this point because how does someone breathe without moving at all?

His eyes flick from the spoon to my face, back again. For a second, I think he's going to refuse on principle alone. But then he steps closer, jaw ticking as he leans in and opens his mouth.

He doesn't rush the moment.

His tongue slides in a slow drag along the curve of the metal before his lips close around the edge.

Something low and unfamiliar twists in my stomach, my body reacting before my brain can make sense of it.

Alex swallows, expression carefully neutral, but his eyes have gone darker. "Okay," he says quietly. "That's... really fucking good."

Everything is in slow motion, and I blink slowly, momentarily forgetting how to breathe. "Yeah?"

He takes the spoon from me, his fingers brushing mine. "Yeah. Just, uh..." He clears his throat. "Don't add any more."

I nod, turning back to the stove before he can see the blush creeping up my neck, across my cheeks.

Because watching him *lick* the spoon was not something I was prepared for. And my response is definitely not something I'm ready to unpack on a reality baking show.

When time is called, Alex and I step back from our presentation to assess our work. It genuinely looks beautiful, like it jumped off the pages of *Southern Living* magazine.

"We make a good team," Alex says, bumping his elbow into mine like he's daring me to look at him.

I glance down at the spot where his arm touched mine—still tingling from the contact—then back up to his face. He's already watching me, that familiar, arrogant smirk in place.

"Careful there, Alex." I waggle my eyebrows, smiling. "I'm starting to think you might actually *like* working with me."

Our gazes hold for longer than they need to as something shifts further between us. His smirk softens, giving way to a real smile. It's wide and bright enough that it steals the air from my lungs.

Garrett claps loudly at the front of the room, snapping us back to attention. We immediately face forward, focusing on the judges. Alex's arm brushes against mine again but this time it stays pressed there, keeping the contact between us, his warmth seeping into me.

I catch him looking at me out of the corner of his eye. I smile, and he mirrors it briefly, just for me, before smoothing his expression back into his usual stoic default and leveling his stare on the judges.

Alex

Chapter 14

It's late, the sky is dark, and I can just barely make out the Big Dipper through the haze of light emanating from the city below. Back home, I'm higher up in the mountains, where the stars burn sharp against an endless black sky.

I stretch back against my pillow, folding my hands behind my head and closing my eyes, reliving every second with Taylor in the tent.

Over and over, I replay my favorite moment—her wide hazel eyes lighting up when, on impulse, I licked the spoon in her hand instead of taking it.

The memory sends a jolt of electricity through me.

Fuckkk…

I groan, shifting restlessly against the mattress.

Frustration coils tight under my skin.

Swinging my legs over the side of the bed, I pace the length of the room. Back and forth. Trying to burn off energy that has nowhere to go.

I thought I could ignore Taylor. I was wrong.

That firecracker's taken a wrecking ball to the control I usually have.

"Man, if you keep this up, neither one of us is going to get any sleep," Brandon mumbles from beneath the covers of his bed. "Don't be a dick."

"Sorry," I grumble, taking the hint. I grab my sweatshirt and head out to pace literally anywhere else.

There isn't much to distract me on the main floor, so I take the stairs down to the basement where the production company has recreated an entire commercial kitchen for us to practice in if we so choose.

Maybe I can whip something up that releases some goddamn endorphins and finally relax a little.

I was under the impression no one else was down here, but I stand corrected.

Light spills through the open doorway, catching on stainless steel and the ceramic tile floor.

In the middle of the room, standing with her back to me, is a familiar silhouette, shoulders hunched in concentration. Whether I want to or not, I'd know those curves anywhere.

Of course, it's her—the reason for all this pent-up tension coiled inside me.

Her hands move across the dough, and I can barely think past the sight of her.

"Hey," I say gently, closing the distance between us slowly so I don't startle her.

Taylor glances my way, and all I can focus on is the exhaustion in the swirling gold and green of her eyes.

"Hey."

"You aren't going home tonight?"

The question feels stupid as it slips out, but she should be on the road already if she wants enough sleep to tackle work in the morning.

She shakes her head once, her eyes still trained on the dough in her hands.

"Not tonight. There was some kind of building emergency that started Friday afternoon, and they're finishing up repair tomorrow, so I have until Tuesday to figure out how to make decent bread. No pressure, right?"

She laughs, though it's a little strained.

I shouldn't notice the difference in her laughs, but I do.

Without realizing it, I've moved closer to her. I can feel the warmth of her skin radiating through the thin fabric of her T-shirt when I lean forward to look at the dough she is working with.

"What's going wrong? Maybe I can help."

"I just don't know what I'm doing wrong. I've never baked actual bread. Just quick breads like banana bread. No matter what I do, I can't seem to get this to pass the windowpane test. Is that even a reliable measure?"

Her admission surprises me. Never done actual bread?

How is that possible? All bakers learn how to make bread.

Actually... No—*not* all bakers learn that. Trained bakers would be forced to learn, but home bakers? They might never have tackled it on their own.

I clear my throat. "Yeah, the windowpane test is reliable. The whole point of working the dough is to build up the gluten strands. Show me what you've got so far, and I'll read it."

"Read it?"

"Your dough will tell you what it needs. You just have to know how to analyze what you're seeing and feeling. May I?"

I reach out and take the dough into my hands. Her shoulders relax a little as she watches me stretch it out. It immediately tears.

"Okay, see that? It tore right away, which means there isn't enough gluten built up. It's also not perfectly smooth. If it had stretched but not thin enough to see through, then it might just have been overworked and tight. In that case, you'd let it relax for a little and try again."

She leans in, watching the dough in my hands.

"So what you're saying is I need to rough it up a little more?" she asks, rewarding me with a genuine smile.

Fuck—I swallow hard, the way she says "rough it up" doing something I don't have the patience to unpack right now. I nod quickly.

She plops the dough on the counter and starts kneading. I immediately see the problem. She's being too gentle.

She'll be here all night if she keeps handling it like that.

"Right." I interrupt her with a hand on her wrist. Her skin is so soft and smooth beneath my palm. "That's the issue right there. You need to work it harder than that. Let me show you."

I smack the dough against the workstation, firm and decisive. Rolling my sleeves up to my elbows, I press the heel of my hand into the dough, pushing it away before pulling it back toward me. I repeat the motion a couple of times, letting muscle memory take over.

My attention shifts to Taylor, watching her reaction instead.

First, her focus is on my hands. Then her gaze drifts up my arms, lingering for a moment before settling on my face. Her cheeks are flushed, that soft pink I've come to notice.

Fuck, she's beautiful.

"Your turn," I direct, my voice tighter than I intend.

She does her best to mimic my movements, but it's still too gentle.

"That's still too soft, Taylor. Here... can I help you?"

She nods once, and that's all the permission I need to move behind her. I cage her in, one arm on either side of her, my chest just behind her back.

Her breath catches.

I close my eyes for a split second, holding onto the sound like it's a gift meant for someone else. Someone who deserves it.

My fingers trail a slow path down her arms. My hands dwarf hers as I guide her movements, hand-over-hand, showing her the pressure she needs.

But it's hard to focus on the task.

It's the feel of her instead—soft and warm, pressed against me—that keeps pulling my attention away.

Unable to resist, I lean in, my face brushing into her hair, and inhale her scent.

Citrus blossom.

Bright. Clean. So perfectly Taylor.

I breathe in again before I realize I'm doing it.

"Alex..." Her voice is a breathy whisper. She leans back against me, and I have to swallow hard against the sound rising in my throat.

Move.

Move now, before you do something you regret.

I step back, clearing my throat.

One hand slides across her back as I pull away, my fingers lingering for just a second too long before I force distance between us.

I'm too wound up around Taylor. I need space. But even now, I can't seem to put enough distance between us.

"Try the windowpane test again."

She complies without hesitation, and the dough gives easily, thinning into a cloudy, flimsy membrane we can see right through.

"We did it!"

Taylor squeals, bouncing on her toes before turning and wrapping her arms around me, her cheek nuzzling against my chest.

Slowly, I lower my hands to her back, rubbing in small circles.

"Alex, I've never been able to do this on my own before. I thought I had my ratios all wrong. Oh gosh, thank you so much."

Her excitement spills out in an unrestrained, carefree ramble. I don't try to stop the smile that pulls at my mouth. Instead, I rest my chin against the top of her head as she clings to me.

We stay like that longer than we should.

Her pressed against me. Me, memorizing the feel of her beneath my hands, the softness of her curls brushing my jaw, the warmth of her against my chest.

Taylor shifts, pulling back just an inch, her face tilting up toward mine.

Fuck—her pupils are blown wide, and the sight knocks the wind out of me. I clench my jaw against the sharp jolt that goes straight to my core.

I shouldn't be looking at her like this, but I am.

And I don't think I could stop, even if I tried.

I don't want to.

Her gaze drifts between my eyes and lips, a slow smile creeping across her face. She slides her hands from my back, circling around to my stomach, then higher, over my chest.

Goosebumps spread across my body at her touch.

I catch her by the wrists, halting her exploring hands.

Her smile falters a fraction.

"Taylor, we can't," I whisper, tipping my head toward the camera.

She glances over her shoulder, then back at me. The rejection and disappointment on her face threatens to crack my resolve.

Stepping back, I put more space between us.

"I don't care about the cameras, Alex," she says. "I like you. And I think you might like me, too." Her voice wobbles at the edges, another attack on my self-control.

"That's the problem," I confess. "I do like you, Taylor. And that's exactly why we can't do this. Not here. Not with an entire production team watching, waiting to twist whatever they want for their own agenda."

She takes a small step forward, closing the distance I just created.

Oh, my bold, brave girl.

"People meet in crazy ways every day. We wouldn't be the first two contestants on a show to start something outside the competition."

My father's words war with my growing need for Taylor.

I'm here to win over the American audience. Making a move on this incredible woman and letting *FluxTV* turn us into a spectacle could backfire. That wouldn't live up to "Harrington excellence".

No—I'm here on a very specific mission, and Taylor can't be part of it. I need to win the competition, establish a face and rapport with the viewers, then get my ass back to my real life in Vancouver.

That's the plan.

Nothing more. Nothing less.

Her hands clench, brows knitting together in a small scowl. I bring her knuckles to my lips, pressing a gentle kiss to her skin before letting go and stepping back toward the door.

I need to leave while my head is still clear.

Taylor stands there, one hip pressed against the counter. She glares down at her hands, then back up at me. I turn sharply, fully intending to hightail it back to my room, take a cold shower, and force myself to sleep.

Just as I reach the threshold, her small voice stops me.

"*Alex.*"

My eyes slam shut, and I grip the doorframe, trying to hold the line. But her voice—my name, soft and full of something like need—slips under every layer of logic I've built.

I turn, really looking at her. Taking her in.

Beautiful. Talented. Passionate. Funny. Everything a person could want.

She's all gentle curves and full, pouty lips. Her wild, untamed mane is one of the most tempting things I've ever seen.

But it's her eyes that do me in—big, round hazel eyes that say everything she isn't brave enough to admit out loud.

My breath hitches on a final, sharp breath.

"Fuck it."

I cross the distance between us in a few long strides. Her eyes light up. My hands slide up her neck, thumbs tipping her chin back, fingers tangling in her hair at the base of her neck.

A small gasp escapes her before I'm crushing my mouth against hers in a hungry kiss. Her lips move against mine, and they're just as soft as I imagined they would be.

"I should stop." I murmur against her lips.

She hums in quiet disagreement, sliding her hands up my chest, tracing light patterns as we move together. I press closer, pinning her against the counter. She brushes her tongue across my lower lip.

An invitation to deepen the kiss that I'm more than happy to accept. My hands slide down to her waist, lifting her onto the flour-covered counter in one smooth motion. She wraps her legs around me, pulling me in closer without breaking the kiss.

Her body presses into mine, and a quiet sound escapes her as she shifts against me.

Fucking hell.

Her fingers tangle in my hair, pulling me closer as my tongue teases hers. She opens for me, and the kiss deepens.

Kissing Taylor is everything and not enough at the same time. I can't get close enough, can't touch her in all the ways I want to. The way her body responds to mine feels like she was made for me.

I don't know how long we stay like that, but when I finally pull back, we're both breathless. She's smiling a lazy, dreamy smile that looks way too good on her.

Leaning forward, I catch her lower lip between my teeth, then brush my tongue against it. Another small moan slips from her.

"God, I knew you wouldn't disappoint," she says, laughing under her breath.

I smirk. "As I said before, I aim to please."

Another quick kiss.

"Clearly," she murmurs, running her hands down my chest. "Look... I don't want to be *that* girl, but... I have to ask—what does this mean?"

I hum, resting my forehead against hers and closing my eyes, searching for the right answer. Because what *does* this mean?

"I think it means that you're right. We do like each other."

Her hand comes up to my cheek, and I lean into her touch. When I open my eyes, she's watching me closely.

"I don't think we have to define this right now," she says softly. "But I want you to know, whatever this is, I want it with you."

Her words are vulnerable and sincere. I lick my lips, holding her gaze, and just nod.

Because I don't have the words.

I don't think I have ever felt the way kissing Taylor makes me feel.

My fingers twist into her curls, absently rolling the silky strands as I look at her.

This feels different.

I want to sit down and hash out every detail from every angle, but I know it isn't the time.

Instead, I kiss Taylor again with long, unhurried strokes.

Doing my best to memorize everything about this moment, because I don't know if I'll get another one.

God, I really hope I do.

Right now, the only thing I know with absolute certainty is that my plan for a cold shower has officially become my top priority.

Chapter 15

Holy crap.

I can't believe yesterday actually happened.

Apparently, the baking gods were on my side, because Alex and I took the top spot. That win was definitely the turning point between us—if the spur-of-the-moment make-out session in the basement last night is any indication.

I bring my fingers to my lips, remembering the heat of his kiss pressing against me. I should be embarrassed by how readily my body responded to him, especially since before that moment, I was pretty sure he just barely tolerated me.

But, I'm not.

Alex showed me a new side of himself. A side that runs far deeper than the dismissive, sarcastic, standoffish persona he uses most of the time. I kick my feet under my blankets, stifling a giggle at the thought of getting to pull back all those broody layers and finding the soft, gooey parts of him underneath.

And make no mistake about it, I'll do exactly that.

I reach for my phone to check the time and find it's a little after nine a.m. I haven't slept in this late in...

I don't know how long.

Leisurely, I stretch my arms and legs, enjoying the tingling happiness of waking up on my own instead of to a screaming alarm.

Pulling on a pair of comfortable sweatpants, I shove my sleep shorts into the already packed duffle bag at my feet. Before crashing into bed last night, I took a few minutes to cram all my belongings into my bag to save time and stress today.

Thank you, *Past Me*, for looking out for *Future Me*.

I swing my duffle bag over one shoulder and head downstairs to find something to eat before hitting the road back to Cambria.

I'm freaking starving this morning.

My brows pull together as I try to recall when the last time I ate was. It honestly might have been the chocolate chip muffin I snagged from one of the production tables yesterday morning.

The main floor is unsettlingly quiet compared to how loud it was in the beginning of the season. But I guess that's what happens when half the house has already been sent home. My heart aches, remembering the devastated look on Chloe's face when she and Khalil were announced as the casualties of the double elimination.

I turn into the kitchen and find Alex sitting on a stool at the counter with a coffee mug in hand, scrolling through his phone. He doesn't notice me at first, and I take the opportunity to appreciate this relaxed, off-guard version of him, with tousled hair and the same hoodie on that he was wearing last night.

Alex always looks good. He's usually very put together, dressed in business casual attire even while baking inside a canvas tent with ovens blasting in the middle of a California summer.

But phew, he looks even better dressed down, casual.

"Aw, Alex," I say, voice chipper, reaching for his coffee mug playfully. "Super nice of you to make a cup of joe for me!"

He looks up, his sharp blue eyes softening as he takes me in. What used to be a cold, icy stare is now an inviting pool of crystalline blue.

"Take a seat, I'll make you a cup."

I shake my head with a soft laugh. "I was joking, I can make my own coffee."

"I know you can," he responds with a simple shrug of his shoulders. "But I don't mind."

"No, really. You're already comfy-cozy with your own cup. Besides, it's just a Keurig, right? I can totally handle that on my own."

I take a step toward the coffee machine, but Alex rises, blocking my path across the kitchen.

"Taylor," his voice is a low command. "I said, sit down."

The authority in his voice hits low in my belly, and I have no choice but to comply. When I sink down onto the nearest stool, he quirks his eyebrow at me, then smirks over his shoulder as he turns and reaches for the Keurig.

Making out with Alex in the practice kitchen and waking up to him preparing coffee for me the next day wasn't on my bingo card for today, but I'm totally here for it.

And it's actually really nice being taken care of for once. I've been on my own for so long, struggling to make ends meet, and the guys I sporadically spend time with are definitely not the "sit down, I've got this" type.

Maybe that's the difference between a guy and a man.

Minutes later, steam from a mug of hazelnut coffee that's been swirled with the perfect amount of cream curls toward my face while Alex leans on the counter across from me with a lazy smile.

I never told him how I take my coffee—he just knows.

Butterflies ping-pong in my stomach, and I wrack my brain for something to say, because chatting over coffee is a totally normal thing people do.

"Only a few more weeks left before the finale. Are the nerves setting in for you at all yet, or do you plan on being unmovable and unshakeable for the whole season?" I ask, propping my chin in my hand.

His lips quirk. "I planned on the latter."

"Of course you were." I tease, rolling my eyes.

"I don't know, Taylor. Baking doesn't make me nervous anymore. I've done it for so long that it's just second nature at this point."

I hum in response, unsure how to answer, because I've been baking for a long time too, but the competition part of this whole experience is static in my veins.

He cocks his head, studying me and it's like he can see right through my optimistic exterior.

"You don't think you're good enough to be here?"

The question surprises me. I straighten where I sit. Do I think I'm good enough to be here? In theory, I believe that I am. In practice, I haven't done as well as I thought I would, and that stings.

I can't bear to tell all of that to Alex, though, so instead I beam a smile his way and shrug dismissively before turning the question around on him.

"You've had a good run here. You're freaking amazing, so you have a really good shot at winning the whole show. What are you going to do with the money if you take it all?"

I'm not sure what kind of answer I expect, but I'm hoping he gives me something whimsical. If he says he's going to pay off student loans, I might scream.

He eyes me warily, expression suddenly guarded. "I don't know. Haven't thought much about it."

My face scrunches up. Somehow, that's worse than wanting to pay off debt. "What do you mean you haven't thought about it? Don't tell me you're here because you just *really* want that platinum rolling pin."

"The what? I don't know what that means. But no, I don't care about that either." Three lines crease between his eyebrows as he frowns.

"What other reason is there to be here?" I sigh, confused, sipping from my mug and letting the warmth swirl across my tongue before swallowing.

Alex runs his hands along the counter as he straightens but doesn't speak. His expression has gone completely unreadable in the silence. Back and forth, his fingers trace the edge of the marble. The shift unsettles me, and weight of everything he isn't saying is claustrophobic.

"Winning is important to my family. My father is the one who signed me up and insisted I come on the show. My being here wasn't optional, so here I am." His tone is clipped. "My answer is boring. I'm far more interested in what you would do if you won."

I stare into the coffee mug that's now clutched between both hands, wanting to push Alex to tell me whatever he's holding back but not willing to risk this moment with him. Taking a deep breath to steady myself, I decide that the only way he's going to trust me with the secret pieces of himself is if I go first.

"I want to open my own bakery," I start, lifting my eyes to meet his and praying I don't see judgment in them. His entire body relaxes, and an encouraging smile plays on his lips, so I keep going.

"Picture an old-fashioned ice cream or soda shop, with the checkered tile floors, chrome bar stools, the whole shebang. The awnings outside are a bright neon pink, and there's an accent wall of the same shade behind the bar." My eyes crinkle at the corners as I squint, envisioning *Taylor's Treats* in my mind's eye.

"Keep going," Alex whispers, eyes dancing over my face.

"I see my bakery as a place of happiness for the community. A bright spot in the neighborhood where people come because they know they're loved and welcome. I want to put my own flavor spins on all the classic pastries and create incredible custom orders for birthdays, baby showers, and all the best moments in people's lives. I want to make the world feel a little lighter, you know? Help people believe things can be good again."

Alex stays quiet, that small, reserved smile on his face, during my entire TED Talk. I realize I'm smiling so wide that my cheeks hurt, and heat floods my face. I'm sure he didn't want to hear all of that, but once I got started, I just couldn't stop myself. I bite my lip, tucking my hair behind my ear, and look away.

"Sorry, that was a lot. The short version is that I'd like to start my own business."

Alex shifts, coming around the counter and using two fingers under my chin to guide my gaze back to his. "Hey, don't do that."

"Don't do what?"

"Don't hide from me after you just shared your dreams. It's a beautiful idea, Taylor. I can see you doing all of that. You won me over, and I hate everybody. If there's anybody out there who can make that dream a reality, it's you." He says it quietly, nodding to emphasize his words.

When I don't respond, he uses his thumb and forefinger—still under my chin—to move my head in a small nod.

Emotion swells behind my eyes, and I blink back the tears threatening to fall. It feels good to be validated by someone like Alex. If someone so put together and talented believes in me, then there's no reason I shouldn't also fully believe in myself.

"Thank you," I whisper, my voice catching.

He rubs his thumb along my cheek, then presses a quick kiss to my forehead. I close my eyes, savoring the feeling.

When I open them, I catch movement out of the corner of my eye and notice Joe and one of the camera crew hovering nearby. They weren't there when I sat down, but based on the satisfied look on Joe's face, they definitely caught our entire interaction.

Maybe they'll take pity on me and this scene won't make the final cut.

If Alex notices them, he doesn't say anything as he quietly takes his place next to me, brushing his hand over my thigh before returning to his phone.

It's a small gesture, but it sends electricity skating down my spine at the gentleness and intimacy of the touch. I dip my head and press a kiss to his cheek before pulling out my phone, silently scrolling next to him. Just two people sharing a quiet morning together before the insanity of the week intrudes.

By the time I badge into the building, the glow of the weekend has completely abandoned me.

The sky outside is still a pale, early-summer blue, but inside the call center is all washed out under buzzing fluorescent lights. The rows of gray cubicles stretch out in front of me, identical and endless, each one containing someone already logged in, fully resigned to ten hours of customer service calls.

The difference between the lively baking tent and my drab daily job has never been more apparent or offensive than it is right now.

I pause for a second just inside the door, letting the atmosphere wash over me: the low murmur of voices speaking in practiced customer-service tones, the rhythmic clicking of keyboards, the occasional sharp ding of a call connecting from someone's too-loud headset.

It's amazing how quickly this place can drain the color out of you. I suck in a sharp breath. I can't believe I've survived this long in such a joy-crushing job.

Less than twenty-four hours ago, Alex was standing across from me in the kitchen with hazelnut coffee steaming between us, his attention focused fully on me like there was nowhere else he needed to be. Like I was worth being seen.

I exhale slowly and force myself to move.

My cubicle feels more suffocating than it used to. The walls are just a little too close, the screen of my computer a little too bright. I set my bag down at my feet and start to log in to the *Elite Connections* client management system.

My fingers move on autopilot through motions I've performed hundreds of times before.

Kara rolls toward my cubicle in her chair until her elbow rests casually on the low divider between us. She watches me intently for a minute before speaking.

"Okay, Sunshine." She squints. "Whatever it is, spill it."

I smile despite myself. "Good morning to you too."

"Yeah, yeah, yeah," she replies, gesturing with a hand. "Good morning. Now spill it—something's different, but I can't put my finger on it."

I glance down at my screen, pretending to read the login confirmation, ignoring the fact that I could recite it from memory.

"Different how?"

She tilts her head, studying me again. "You look... lighter, somehow. Which is saying a lot, because you've always got your head in the clouds anyway. Which I *love*, by the way. But you also seem distracted. Which is a suspicious combination."

I hesitate, then lower my voice. "Things with Alex have taken a turn. He made me coffee yesterday morning before I left."

Her eyes widen.

"And?" she presses.

"And..." I trail off, flicking my gaze around the room to make sure nobody is eavesdropping. Which is silly, of course nobody is listening in. Having a camera crew around all the time is creating some strange reflexes.

"We kissed on Sunday."

One hand clutches her chest, the other snapping loudly before pointing a knowing finger my way. "I knew it."

"Kara," I hiss.

"*I knew it*," she repeats, quieter this time, grinning. "You don't look like that unless something *really good* happens."

Warmth spreads across my cheeks as I replay the kiss in my head—his hands, his mouth, the way everything else seemed to fall away. "It wasn't planned," I say softly. "It just... happened."

"Those are usually the best kinds," she murmurs.

Before I can dish out more details, the ones I know my best friend is dying to hear, a familiar shadow falls over my shoulders.

"Clock-in time is nine sharp."

The Trunch's voice cuts through the air behind me, clipped and cool. I straighten instinctively. "I'm logged in."

She peers over my shoulder at the screen, lips pursed. "Mmhmm. Just barely."

Kara swivels back to her desk, her expression carefully neutral. I don't blame her for retreating. I'd wheel myself away from this conversation, too, if I could.

The Trunch lingers at the threshold of my cubicle longer than necessary, her presence compressing the small space.

"Your call times were up last week."

"I stayed late on Thursday," I explain with a sigh. "Some of the accounts needed more attention."

She hums, unimpressed. "Efficiency matters more than empathy here. You know we don't do unapproved overtime."

I wince as her words land, though I've heard versions of them before. No matter what I do, The Trunch will always find something to complain about when it comes to me. I don't know why I bother at all, sometimes.

"I resolved everything," I amend in what I hope is a pleasant tone, knowing I need to keep this job. At least until I find time to line something else up.

"I'm sure you did." Her gaze flicks up to my face. "While that may be true for last week, you seem... out of sorts today."

"I'm fine."

"Are you?" She crosses her arms. "Because bad moods tend to show in performance, especially when people start getting the wrong kind of ideas."

My stomach tightens.

"What kind of ideas?" Kara interrupts, unable to keep the edge out of her voice or mind her own business any longer.

Our boss smiles thinly. "The self-obsessed kind that come from being on TV."

The floor threatens to drop out beneath me.

"I'm still doing my job," I say carefully, choosing each word with precision. How have I gone from doing too much to doing not enough in a matter of seconds?

"For now," she quips with a shrug. "But I've seen this before. People get a little attention, then think it means they're special. Let me be very clear, Taylor. We uphold certain standards here. No exceptions."

It's impossible not to think of Alex's hand under my chin, his voice steady as he reassured me I could make my dream come true. That my vision wasn't silly or small. That he thinks I *am* some kind of special.

"This is real life," The Trunch continues, cocking her hip. "Running a business takes dedication. We can't all be out there playing around in a baking fantasyland."

Kara's jaw tightens. "That's unnecessary."

"Maybe. But, it's true."

She looks back at me, a cruel smirk curving her lips. "Focus on your calls, Taylor. This isn't the place for daydreams."

Then she turns and walks away, heels clicking sharply against the floor. I stare at my screen, the cursor blinking patiently, waiting.

She's right. This isn't a place for daydreams. It's the abyss where dreams go to shrivel up and die.

Kara leans closer again. "She doesn't get it."

"Maybe she does." My throat is tight. I swallow hard.

"No," Kara says firmly. "She just doesn't want you to want more. She clearly gave up on her own dreams a long time ago. Don't let her get to you, okay? You're doin' the damn thing."

The phone chimes, signaling an incoming call, and I slip my headset on, accepting it. My voice automatically smooths into something polite and pleasant.

But inside, everything feels off-balance.

Between calls, my mind drifts back to the kitchen. To flour-dusted counters and heated kisses. To the way Alex listened as I gushed over pink awnings and checkered floors like it wasn't ridiculous to imagine something so vibrant.

My boss's voice echoes faintly in my head, heavy and dismissive.

Focus on your calls, Taylor.

I glance down at my hands resting against the keyboard. The same hands that knead dough and shape pastries and ache in the best way after a long day in the kitchen. Hands that feel wrong typing repetitive responses into our system about strangers who will forget my name the second the call ends.

When my break finally comes, I stand and stretch, my spine cracking with every inch my hands rise above my head. Kara catches my eye and gives me a small, encouraging smile.

"You okay?" she asks.

"I think so," I reply, though I'm not entirely sure.

Because something has shifted.

Being seen—really seen and heard—has a way of changing your perspective on things. And now that I know what it feels like, this place feels colder than it ever has before.

I don't know exactly what comes next.

I just know that the life waiting for me outside these gray walls suddenly feels closer than it ever has. Even if the next step isn't starting my own bakery, my time at *Elite Connections* is coming to an end.

And that scares me almost as much as it excites me.

Alex

Chapter 16

It's only ten a.m., and the sand is already too hot.

I shift my weight, adjusting the mic pack clipped to the back of my shorts as I stare out across the ocean, arms crossed. Camera operators jog past me with lenses lifted, like we're filming the climax of an action movie instead of a glorified reality show beach day.

When production stormed the house this morning and announced we needed a change of scenery and some good, old-fashioned team building, I didn't realize that meant stripping us down to swimwear and forcing enthusiasm under a cloudless sky.

I should've known better. That one's on me.

The sky is an obnoxious shade of blue that feels unnatural for real life. Seagulls shriek overhead. A production assistant flits between us, chirping about the importance of sunscreen and hydration.

I scrub a hand down my face—I'd rather be anywhere else. Anywhere *she* is.

The thought catches me off-guard, but damn. I miss her.

Taylor would've rolled her eyes at the cameras circling us but run straight for the water anyway, daring me to follow. She would've splashed me first. Laughed when I pretended to be annoyed. She would've turned this into something almost fun without even trying.

Instead, she's hours away, burning the candle at both ends for another week in this circus of a show.

The other night replays in my mind without permission— the heat of her pressed against me, the soft give of her body beneath my hands, the way she melted into my touch like she's never wanted anything else. My jaw tightens. I exhale a slow breath through my nose.

I chew the inside of my cheek, wondering what she would've worn today.

Would she be bold about it like Lila—wearing something small and bright that clings in all the right places, pretending not to notice the way every head turns. The thought sparks something ugly and possessive in my chest.

But fuck, I'd give damn near anything to see my girl in something like that.

Or maybe she'd go softer, like RaeAnn, in something vintage. Something that makes her look sweet until you get close enough to realize there's more lurking below.

I'd probably lose my mind watching her tuck her hair behind her ear and look up at me through dark lashes like she doesn't know exactly what she's doing to me.

Or maybe she'd be more like Diane, keeping it simple. Black. Clean lines. Understated. The kind of suit that wouldn't scream for attention—wouldn't need to—because she'd own every inch of it just by being herself.

My hands curl at my sides. It's a fucking crime I don't get to know what she would've chosen, since she isn't here at the beach with us. With me.

A speaker crackles to life, a thumping beat vibrating the sand at our feet. Someone whoops. Within minutes, the beach transforms from a cliché TV set into a lively party.

Diane slathers sunscreen over her shoulders, walking along the water's edge. Lila poses for a drone shot like she's done this before.

Who am I kidding? She probably has.

Brandon immediately recruits Joe and Julian from the sidelines to toss a football around. A bright red cooler appears. Then another.

"We deserve this," RaeAnn laughs, cracking open a seltzer before settling into one of the beach chairs set up for our group.

I stay rooted in place, watching everyone around me as the warm sun and chilled alcohol dissolve whatever lingering tension remained from the competition.

It's so easy for them to relax. I don't think I've relaxed since I was ten years old.

A football crashes into the sand at my feet, granules scattering against my shins. I bend, pick it up, and straighten, meeting Julian's gaze as he jogs my way.

"You going to stand there brooding all day?" He grins.

"Considering it." I twirl the ball in the air.

"That's no way to be." Julian slows to a stop and grabs the ball from my grasp. "Come on, we need a fourth. Maybe you'll even get a shot in on Joe—ya know, for all those times he's gotten close to your girl."

He's teasing me, I know he is. But it grates.

"She's not my girl." I hold his gaze, even though the words don't feel entirely true. Still, I don't like Julian talking about her like she's a thing instead of a person.

"Don't talk about her like that."

Julian's grin falters, just a fraction, like he hears more in my words than I intended. He gives a small nod before jogging backwards and motioning me forward.

"Whatever you say, man."

It takes less than a second for me to take off after him. Blowing off some of this pent-up energy is the best thing I can do for myself right now. I'm wound so tight, one minor inconvenience and I might snap.

"Maybe I'll get one in on you instead!"

The shit-eating grin on Julian's face only spreads as he runs at me, faking left before spinning around to the right.

"Do your worst!" He taunts, before Brandon comes out of nowhere, tackling him to the ground and tossing the ball my way.

"Harrington's with me!"

Everything in me cringes at the casual use of my last name, but a quick glance around confirms no one's paying attention. I rake my lower lip between my teeth, clench my jaw, and sprint toward the guys. Because sometimes it's easier to tackle something I can get my hands on.

Twenty minutes later, sweat drips down my chest, and my breath comes in shallow pants. My muscles buzz with the fading adrenaline and exertion. It feels good. I feel good.

I grab a bottle of water and gulp it down in one shot, then swipe a beer from the cooler. Dropping onto the sand with my knees bent, I scan the group, all of them in varying states of relaxation or entertainment.

That's when my gaze finds Lila.

She's already staring right at me.

I scoff and look away, uninterested in whatever it is she's thinking or planning. But I've clearly pissed off the universe, because when I chance another look, she's already smiling and walking toward me.

My gaze locks on the waves licking the shoreline. Maybe if I don't make eye contact, she'll course-correct on her own.

But she doesn't.

Lila shakes out a towel beside me, then sits and edges a little closer. "You looked good out there, Alex."

Heat from her sun-drenched skin bleeds into my side. I instinctively lean away. This isn't a game I'm playing.

Her smile doesn't falter. If anything, it sharpens into something harder, more calculated. "Relax," she says lightly, brushing sand from her thigh. "It was just a compliment."

The breeze kicks up, carrying the scent of sunscreen and salt between us. Her knee nudges mine. It's brief enough to be dismissed as accidental, intentional enough for the cameras to catch.

I take a slow pull from my beer, letting the silence stretch. If she's going to force me into this conversation, then I'm going to make her work for it.

"You've done well for yourself here. Everyone thinks you're the frontrunner," she says, softening her voice to something breathy, her nails tracing lightly along my forearm. "I think you're going to win it all."

I roll my eyes. Lila is a carbon copy of every pretty, vapid girl back home—looking for attention, opportunity, a leg up. And she knows exactly how to play this game.

I set the beer down, straighten my legs, and lean back on my elbows just enough to create distance between us.

"You don't have to make this about me," I say evenly, letting my gaze drift to the waves.

Her lips twitch, but she doesn't retreat. "Oh, I'm not. I'm just... noticing. People notice winners." Her voice drops, it's just loud enough for the cameras, and her knee shifts again, edging closer still.

"You could have anything," she continues, brushing a strand of hair behind her ear. "If you wanted. You just have to reach out and take it."

I tilt my head, measuring her. "I don't want what isn't already mine."

She pauses at that. Her half-smile tightens in acknowledgment, and maybe a little surprise, but she doesn't push further. She's tested the line, found the boundary, and recalibrated.

"Hmm," she hums, letting the sound drift into the wind. "I suppose that makes sense. Wouldn't want to be too evenly matched or anything."

I shrug, keeping my posture loose. If she thinks she's getting under my skin, she better try a lot harder than that. I'm steady, totally unfazed, and completely uninterested in taking the bait.

I don't care about her, and I definitely don't have anything to prove.

She tilts her head, studying me like she's seeing me clearly for the first time. Then she leans back on her hands. "Fine," she says, tone easing into something more casual. "We'll see how long that stance holds."

And just like that, she's done testing me for now. The cameras are still rolling, the beach still hums with laughter, but for a moment, the only game that matters is the one she can't control: me.

Julian bursts out of the waves, hair plastered to his forehead, water streaming in every direction as he jogs toward us. He spins, shakes his head like a dog—and before either of us can react, sends a curtain of droplets arcing straight at Lila.

She squeals, jerking sideways as the water catches the sunlight and scatters across her.

"Julian!" she snaps, standing up and brushing frantically at the sand clinging to her legs. Her expression is a perfect mix of outrage and annoyance. She steps back, glaring at him, towel clutched in her fists like a shield.

My lips twitch. Julian looks entirely pleased with himself, grin wide. Lila's sharp retort gets swallowed by the thump of music and the laughter echoing down the beach, but I catch enough to know she's fuming.

Well-played, Julian.

He drops down onto the sand next to me, seemingly unbothered by how it clings to his wet skin. "You looked like you needed saving," he says, loud enough for the cameras to hear.

That earns a quiet laugh from me. I wouldn't say I needed saving, but I appreciate his intrusion all the same. And it would be really great if the cameras caught it, so Lila can't twist this conversation into something it isn't when Taylor's back in the house.

He props himself up on one elbow and grins after Lila's still-retreating figure. I shake my head as my cousin openly ogles the girl he intentionally just pissed off. There's something clearly wrong with him.

"Hey, so I got a call from your favorite parent earlier today," he says, a smirk tugging at the corner of his mouth. "He's curious how his son is doing. Asked me to check if you're still alive or if you've run off into the ocean permanently."

I raise an eyebrow, amused and irritated at the same time. "Smart move calling you. I don't have anything to say to him."

It isn't fair to put Julian in the middle as the go-between, but I'm not ready to face my father. Or hear his opinion on everything I'm doing here. I'd rather stick my hand in a fryer than answer what I'm sure would be tedious questions about optics and reputation.

"You need to call him. He's been getting updates from the producers, but he needs to hear your version of things, too." Julian shifts closer.

"My version of things? What the hell does that mean?"

"I don't know everything that's been said, but I do know they've told him you haven't exactly been winning. And they've hinted that you're involved romantically with someone on the show. He thinks you're distracted."

A dry scoff escapes me. "He can fuck right off with that."

"I'm serious. He's threatening to pull funding from Northern Flame. You need to call him."

I roll my eyes and meet Julian's gaze. He's right. Avoiding Chet Harrington isn't a long-term solution. And the longer I put it off, the more pissed off and petty his response is going to be.

I nod. "I'll call him soon."

Julian's shoulders loosen, visibly relieved.

As much as I don't want to speak to my father, I can't risk losing everything Julian and I have been working toward this year. Our one real chance at making a name for ourselves, outside of the family's restaurant group.

At the water's edge, Brandon decides it's his moment to shine. I watch him sprint toward the surf, chest puffed up like he's the star of some slow-motion commercial. Someone had tossed a football too close to the waves, and he's determined to claim it, diving headfirst into the shallow water.

The first few steps look promising. Then his foot catches a patch of uneven sand—and physics wins. Brandon slips, flailing, arms windmilling, and crashes into the water with a spectacular splash. Waves tumble over him, sand flies in every direction, and for a second I can't tell if he's laughing or screaming. The football plunks into the water beside him.

"Brandon!" Joe yells. "You okay, man?"

He pops up sputtering, spewing water like a human fountain. His hair is plastered to his forehead, water streaming down his chest. Lila, who is still drying off from Julian, bursts out laughing, clutching her stomach, while Diane just shakes her head, smirking like she saw it coming.

Even the drone hovering above dips, trying to follow the chaos. Julian howls with laughter. "Nice one, Brandon! Nailed the landing, bud!"

I lower my head, bracing my arms against my knees. They're all absurd—every one of them, performing for cameras, for fun, for nothing.

And me? I feel like I'm on the outside looking in. Watching it all unfold, completely untouched. Some days you get to participate. Some days you just sit back and watch.

Today, I'm definitely in the latter camp.

Chapter 17

At the front of the tent, a single colosseum-pillar podium topped with a golden loaf of bread sits beneath a spotlight. Magnolia and Garrett are positioned on either side, pretending to bow solemnly to the baked centerpiece.

"Behold... the power of gluten!" Theo declares, striding into frame with a flour-dusted apron. He brandishes a giant wooden rolling pin like it's Excalibur.

Judy follows, equally dramatic, carrying a wicker basket overflowing with baguettes, sourdough boules, and petite rolls. She gives a deep, exaggerated sniff, eyes rolling heavenward.

"Ahhh, ze aroma of victory, and yeast," Theo intones, speaking in another painfully overdone French accent. He spins on his heel, narrowly missing the podium, and flour explodes from one of his hands into the air like a tiny snowstorm.

A drumroll booms from the sound system as Judy taps a baguette like a baton, conducting an imaginary orchestra. Theo throws a sourdough boule into the air, catching it with dramatic flair, and somehow, miraculously, not smacking anyone in the face.

The camera pans to the judges, who carefully tiptoe away from the hosts' antics, trying to keep a straight face. Garrett leans toward the camera with that signature half-smile. "And with that, welcome to *Bread Week*."

"Buongiorno, bakers!" Theo bellows as we clap politely. "Today, we honor the noble art of one of my favorite substances on Earth... bread!"

Judy pipes in, lifting a giant proofing basket up for all of us to see. "This is about as serious as it gets when it comes to bread, guys. We mean business here. This bread has a cult-like following for good reason."

She sets the basket down with a flourish, letting the wobbly dough slump exaggeratedly over the edge. "Your challenge," she says, voice low and mock-ominous. "Is simple. And intimidating. And very sticky."

Theo claps his hands. "Bakers, you have in front of you sourdough that's been bulk fermenting for ten hours. It is alive! It is breathing! And it is very, very temperamental."

"You have the rest of the afternoon to bake the perfect sourdough boule. You'll decide when it's ready to shape, proof, and bake into the loaf of your dreams," Judy finishes.

A drumroll from an off-screen camera operator adds unnecessary gravitas as Theo leans in. "This is *Bread Week*, people. The flour will fly, and the loaves will rise, or deflate, but only one will come away as the victor."

"May your proofing be precise, and your patience intact. But if not, there's always toast and croutons to be made!" Magnolia announces cheerfully.

Garrett lifts a hand to his chin, shaking his head. "Not for this challenge there's not."

Theo twirls, tossing flour like confetti, and Judy lets out a triumphant whoop. "Let the baking begin!"

I take a deep, steadying breath before uncovering the container on my workbench. With sourdough, it's important to know how much the dough has risen during bulk fermentation, but there's no mark showing where this dough started.

It's the only method I've ever used, the only way to know if the dough has risen enough.

Is there another way to know? How can you tell?

Panic erupts in my chest as I realize I don't know what to do. Wide-eyed, I turn to Alex, who's calmly seated on a stool at his station. The moment our eyes meet, he rises to his feet.

"What's wrong?" he asks, worry lacing his tone.

"I don't know how to tell when it's done. I've always just measured rise percentage for sourdough. There's no way to know how much it's risen, though. They didn't mark it."

A small smile ghosts his lips. He runs a gentle hand up my arm. "First, breathe."

I suck in a sharp breath through my nose. The tang of sourdough and spearmint from Alex's gum fills my lungs. His warm, strong hands linger on my biceps.

A few stations down, Lila pauses her work, watching us. Technicals are usually silent. They're meant to be independent and competitive.

A camera moves in closer to focus on our interaction. The baby hairs at the nape of my neck prickle with awareness. No one says anything, but they're all watching.

"Good," he soothes without a care in the world.

"You have to read the dough, Taylor. You're looking for a domed surface, bubbles along the top and sides, and for it to pull slightly away from the container. It should also wobble a bit if you jiggle it. Then it's business as usual: final shaping, proofing, and baking. You've got this."

"And what if it's over?" I swallow hard, glancing at my dough again.

"Then you shape it gently and pray," he says lightly with a shrug. "But it's not. Just do what you do best."

"And what do I do best?"

"Flash one of those gorgeous smiles and wing it," Alex says with a wink before crossing the aisle back to his station. A blush heats my cheeks, and I duck my head to hide my smile. Then I turn back to my dough and give the bin a careful jiggle.

It takes forty-five minutes before all the telltale signs of properly fermented dough appear. Shaping and the final proof go off without a hitch. I've chosen to bake my boule in a Dutch oven, which has been preheating in my oven the entire time.

Now it's just a game of timing—baking it covered, then uncovering it to achieve that perfectly golden crust.

Just as I slide the oven door closed, Joe approaches. "Hey Taylor, since you're just waiting on the bake for now, can we grab you for a quick interview?"

Production has never pulled us mid-bake to film soundbites, and that alone makes me nervous. Can't they do this afterwards, like they usually do? I glance from Joe to my oven, then back to Joe. He smiles, gently nodding his assurance.

"Oh—uh, yeah, sure. I've got about twenty minutes before I need to be back to finish up. I guess I could step away…" My voice trails off. I really don't want to leave my bread baking, but I also can't tell production no. This is all part of it.

Alex catches my eye as I walk past. "Go. I've got it."

I reach out, squeezing his hand in thanks. Joe eyes it before placing a hand on my back and guiding me out the front of the tent.

We walk across the lawn to a makeshift patio under a pergola, staged with a basket of bread and a crisp, icy pitcher of lemonade. I perch on one of the chairs, shaking out my curls. My best attempt at being camera-ready in this heat and under this pressure.

Anxiously, I pick at the dry sourdough that's clinging under my fingernails.

Joe settles into the chair across from me while a camera operator named Cameron adjusts a reflector to bounce light onto my face. The pergola offers shade, but the heat still clings to my skin. The pitcher of lemonade sweats onto the glass table between us.

"You good?" Joe asks lightly.

"Yeah." I smooth my apron over my knees. "As good as you can be during a sourdough technical."

He chuckles. "*Bread Week.* No pressure."

"Right, no pressure," I echo, smiling tight.

"Okay," he says, glancing toward the camera. "So, we saw a little hesitation earlier when you uncovered your dough. What was going through your head in the moment?"

I exhale softly, tracing a finger through the pool of condensation on the table. "I usually measure rise percentage during bulk fermentation. Without a marker on the container, I couldn't tell how much it had grown. For a second, I just... blanked."

"You don't usually blank, you're the queen of improv here in the tent."

"No, you're right," I admit, shifting uncomfortably in my chair. "Technicals are supposed to be about precision, but they're also about instinct. I just had to trust mine."

"And did you?"

I hesitate, not trusting his line of questioning. Is the plan to corner me into admitting Alex is the only reason I was able to move forward?

"Eventually."

Joe nods like he's waiting for me to go on.

When I don't, he presses harder.

"You went to Alex."

My fingers curl together in my lap.

As always, this is a sidestep into talking about Alex. Every time the production team pulls me, the conversation circles back to him. Which isn't surprising since he's one of the best bakers in the tent, but it's odd they only seem to want to talk about him. I need to choose my words strategically.

Be smart, Taylor.

"He noticed I was panicking."

"And you trust him?"

I glance toward the tent without thinking, already knowing I can't see inside from here. "I trust his read on dough."

Joe tilts his head, eyes glinting. "Just on the dough?"

Heat rises up my neck. The look in Joe's eyes and his underlying tone put me on edge. It's almost as though he's trying to lead me into a conversation I have no intention of participating in.

"He's always very poised and calm. I'm not always calm, so his perspective helps."

There's a beat of silence before Joe clears his throat.

"Do you worry that leaning on him could hurt you in a technical? It's supposed to be every baker for themselves."

"We're all competitors. But we're also human. If I can give someone a tip, and it doesn't cost me anything, I will. I'd hope they'd do the same." I swallow hard, knowing Alex has saved me more than once by now.

"Even if it's your biggest competition?"

"Especially then." I smile faintly, raising an eyebrow at the camera. "If you want to be the best, you have to beat the best."

"If it came down to you and Alex in the finale... who deserves it more?"

The question lands heavier than the others. He was saving this one for the end on purpose.

"I don't think baking works like that," I say carefully. "On any given day, one of us could have the better bake. That doesn't mean the other doesn't deserve it."

"That's not what I asked."

My gaze snaps to Joe's, and all I see is cool indifference where warmth used to live. He isn't usually this pushy. What's his problem?

"I deserve to be here." I inhale slow through my nose. "But, so does he."

Behind the camera, Cameron checks his watch. Joe follows the movement with his eyes, then looks back at me. "We'll only keep you a few more minutes."

My gaze flicks toward the tent again.

"My loaf's in the oven, I'll need to get back and uncover it soon."

"You've got time," he reassures me smoothly. "How are you feeling about your bake overall?"

"It looked good going in," I say, though unease pricks at the base of my spine. "Strong structure. Good surface tension. If it springs the way I think it will, it should be really beautiful."

"And if it doesn't?"

I let out a small breath, half laugh and half sigh. "Then it'll be perfect for Magnolia's croutons."

"You're calmer than you were earlier." Joe smiles at me. His friendly demeanor has returned, and the back-and-forth threatens to give me whiplash. I thought Joe was my friend, but right now, I don't trust him.

A brief silence stretches as Cameron checks his watch again and gives a small nod. Joe straightens in response. "Okay. Last one. You said Alex calms you down and helps your focus. What do you think you do for him?"

What do I do for him... how should I know?

"I don't know," I admit, suddenly self-conscious. "Maybe I remind him that he doesn't have to be so serious all the time."

"Interesting." Joe's smile sharpens just a fraction, and he stands. "Alright. That's perfect. Thank you, Taylor."

I push to my feet, adjusting my apron and pulling my hair back into a ponytail. "Can I head back now?"

"Of course," he says, stepping aside with an easy gesture. "You've still got plenty of time."

Plenty of time.

Dread pools low in my stomach. Call it intuition, but something inside me knows something bad just happened, even if I can't quite explain why.

I step inside the tent and the air immediately feels wrong. It's heavy and thick with tension. What did I miss?

Nobody meets my gaze as I walk down the main aisle to my station. Instinctively, I check my oven. There's still a few minutes before I have to open it up. Hopefully, I'll see a perfectly formed ear along my score line—the judges will love that.

I smile to myself as I drop onto my stool.

Looking over at Alex's station, I realize he's nowhere to be found. He probably stepped out to eat something or run to the bathroom. When I uncover my boule and he still hasn't returned, I step over to his station to do the same for his loaf. His ear has that perfect curl I can never achieve, but instead of silently hating him, I feel a surge of pride on his behalf. It's a perfect loaf.

He's still missing from the tent when my final buzzer goes off. I pull both loaves out and set them on their cooling racks.

I slide the extra scrunchy off my wrist and wrangle my unruly ponytail into a messy bun. It's too hot and sticky to have my hair down anymore. The cameras are off now, so it doesn't matter what I look like.

Fanning myself with the bottom of my apron, I step into the comparatively cool air outside the tent. RaeAnn rushes to me, wide-eyed and frantic.

When she reaches me, she clutches my wrists in her trembling hands. I search her face, hoping she can clue me in on what's going on. She's vibrating with nerves.

"Oh my God, Taylor, you're not going to believe what happened—"

Chapter 18

"Go. I've got it." The words slip past my lips before I've even decided to say them. When she reaches out and squeezes my hand, my heart lurches in my chest at the contact.

Fuck, I'm so far gone for this girl already.

Joe notices. His eyes flick between Taylor and me, and a flash of jealousy crosses his face. I smirk in response, but it fades just as quickly when he presses his palm firmly against her back, guiding her away from me.

My back molars grind together. It takes everything in me to stay seated at my station when what I want is to pry each of his fingers off what's mine. The thought of him touching her like that makes something dark and territorial flare in my chest. I don't want anyone's hands on her.

Except for mine.

I crank my head side to side, cracking my neck and rolling my shoulders to release some tension. Taylor took my advice and ran with it. From what I could see across the aisle, her boule looked promising. I hope so, anyway, because I don't want to imagine what this competition would be like without her.

Pacing the length of my station, I clench my hands into fists, glancing over at Taylor's station again and again. It's only been a handful of minutes, but the urge to check is already needling under my skin. When I can't resist any longer, I cross the aisle, keeping my distance so it can't be misconstrued as tampering.

400°F?

I automatically convert to Celsius in my head. It's lower than I'd like, but not concerning. But as I stand there, the display drops—395°F.

Seconds later, it's down to 385°F.

I dash back to my station and check my oven's temperature reading, finding it right where I left it.

Quickly, I make a lap around the tent, stealing glances at the other contestants' ovens. They're all steady, too.

Just hers, then.

My eyes dart to the entrance of the tent as pieces begin slotting into place. These ovens can be controlled remotely. Production has to be behind this.

Motherfuckers.

Without a second thought, I stalk to the corner of the tent where the producers are huddled, walkie-talkies in hand. One of the senior producers notices my approach and meets my gaze without hesitation.

"Taylor's oven is off."

They don't even have the decency to feign concern. "Must be a display glitch. We tested the ovens this morning."

"Turn it back on," I demand, widening my stance. I cross my arms and narrow my eyes, leveling them all with the full weight of my accusation. "*Now*."

Silence.

"Alex, there's nothing wrong with Taylor's oven. Everything is working exactly the way it's supposed to. Go back to your station."

Un-fucking-believable.

A slow burn rises from deep in my chest as I take in their blank expressions. Fury begging to be unleashed, I lower my voice. "Exactly the way it's supposed to? I don't think so. First, you pulled her. Then her oven fails while she's gone. That's not a coincidence. Fix it."

My final words are punctuated by two steps forward. I can feel the stares of the other bakers burning into my back. The cameras circle in, capturing the moment. Fuck the optics, and fuck this production crew. I've kept my mouth shut through all their manipulations, but I won't be quiet when it comes to Taylor. They can do whatever the fuck they want with anyone else—just not her.

Never her.

I don't blink, and the producer folds under my glare. She nods once, then gestures behind her. Two fingers flick upward.

I breathe a sigh of relief, but I'm still seething.

"Call your boss and tell him I'm on my way in. Trust me, you don't want me making the phone call we both know I can make. Because if I do, we won't be discussing oven calibration— we'll be discussing contract violations." I grind the words out before storming out of the tent.

Loose rocks crunch beneath my shoes as I pound up the steps to the main house on the property. I keep my eyes fixed on the terracotta building, afraid that if I glance back toward the tent, I'll catch a glimpse of Taylor returning from her interview. If I see her, I might soften. And I need all my hard edges right now.

The back door crashes open with enough force to make a PA near the entrance flinch, her phone clattering to the floor.

"Where is he?"

I don't raise my voice—I don't need to. I also don't need to clarify who I'm looking for, which means the degenerate producer down in the tent did exactly what I told her to do.

The girl in front of me doesn't break eye contact as she reaches for the phone lying at her feet. "He's in his office. It's—"

"I'll find it."

I don't wait for permission. I ascend the stairs, taking them two at a time. The hallway feels narrower than it is. It's too quiet compared to the whirring chaos of the tent. My pulse hammers a furious rhythm in my ears, but my hands are steady.

I shove open the office door without knocking.

The executive producer, Hal Gordon, looks up from behind his desk, irritation already forming in his expression.

"You're supposed to be baking."

I pull the door closed behind me. The click of the latch sounds like a lock sliding into place.

"You pulled her in the middle of a bake."

Hal leans back, propping his hands behind his head.

"We conduct interviews throughout the day all the time."

"And while she was gone, her oven dropped fifteen degrees." I continue, stepping forward.

He smiles, but it doesn't reach his eyes. He folds his hands on the desk before responding. "We tested the ovens this morning, but you know how temperamental technology can be. Glitches happen."

"You expect me to believe that, Hal? Come on now, don't insult me."

I move closer to the desk with measured steps. My palms settle flat on the wood as I lean in just enough to invade his space, but I don't raise my voice.

"You don't get to manipulate the conditions of a timed technical challenge because you want better footage."

His jaw tightens, and he leans forward in an attempt to reclaim some of the ground he's lost. "Careful with your accusations, Alex."

I cock my head to the side. A slow smirk quirks into place. "No. You be careful."

That's when the room shifts. I'm not posturing or bluffing, and we both know it. He knows my family and the influence we carry. The connections we maintain.

"You're very invested," he says lightly. Too lightly given the circumstance he's found himself in.

I bark a dry laugh. "You have no idea."

Images of Taylor flash through my head. Soft, golden curls glinting in the light. Her hand squeezing mine. The determined set of her shoulders. The way she chews on her bottom lip when she's thinking. The musical laugh she uses to cover any hint of her nerves.

They don't get to mess with that.

"You interfere to see if you can get someone to crack. I'm sure it's great for editing and ratings."

I straighten to my full height and step around the desk. I'm close enough now that Hal has to lean back in his chair to maintain eye contact.

His eyes narrow. "No one sabotaged anyone."

"I checked every oven in that tent, Hal. They were all fine—except for hers. Try again. Maybe the truth this time."

Tension crackles between us. A beat of silence passes, and then he caves and speaks first.

"Let's say something was adjusted," he says carefully, "that's within production's discretion. It's our show."

That's the moment something in me goes completely still. Rage doesn't explode out of me, it simmers into something white hot. Liquid fire coursing through my veins.

"You intentionally altered the conditions of a technical after the challenge was already in progress."

He doesn't answer. There isn't anything he can say to absolve himself of this monumental fuck up.

I reach into my pocket and pull out my phone, placing it on his desk between us with the show's contract open.

"I know exactly what's in that contract."

He scoffs. "You're just a baker."

"And because of that, you were counting on me not reading the fine print." I hold his gaze. "But you must have forgotten who my father is."

My eyes don't leave his as I rattle off part of the contract.

"Section four, bullet three: you are required to provide equal, functioning equipment to all contestants. Section four, bullet seven: you are required to avoid any and all interference that materially affects the outcome of a bake."

Hal exhales slowly through his nose.

"Are you threatening us? Legally, I mean."

I ignore the question, cracking my neck as I continue to stare him down. The air between us is razor-sharp.

"We're going to bury you in the edit," he says through gritted teeth, and a slow smile curves my mouth.

"You think I care?"

It isn't a real question. I don't care what they do to me. I don't care if they cut every decent moment I've had on this show and turn me into public enemy number one. I don't care what *The Harrington Group* has to say about it, either.

If Taylor loses because she wasn't good enough, that's an honest competition. But if she loses because *America's Next Great Baker* stirred up drama for tension and footage...

A shudder skates down my spine.

"Let me be perfectly clear, Hal." I lean down, bringing my face inches from his. "I will burn this entire production to the ground. I don't care. Taylor's off limits from here on out. You understand me?"

Hal's throat works as he swallows. Even as the executive producer of the show, he shrinks back from my words. Men like him make me want to puke.

"You'd tank your own career over a girl you met a few weeks ago?"

There's zero hesitation. "Yes."

The answer lands harder than I expect. Surprise flickers in my chest at how absolute it feels—no mental math, no weighing options. Just yes.

Between late-night prep sessions and quiet glances across workbenches, Taylor stopped being a distraction. She became inspiration.

"You're being irrational right now, Alex. Think this through." He studies me differently now, his eyes tracking every movement.

"I'll call Standards and Practices. I'll call our contact at *FluxTV*. And if I have to, I'll call the financial team that helped fund this entire show."

I push off the edge of his desk and tap my phone once with my finger, drawing his attention to the screen.

"Touch her oven again," I continue, my tone controlled but deadly. "And see what happens."

Silence stretches for a beat before he leans back in his chair. "You've made your point."

"Good." I turn toward the door.

"Alex."

I pause, hand on the knob.

"You escalate this, you're declaring war."

I glance over my shoulder.

"Then don't give me a reason to." I walk out without waiting for his response.

The hallway feels cooler. My pulse is still pounding, but underneath it there's a clarity sitting heavy and solid in my chest.

FluxTV controls the narrative. They control the footage. They control this entire game. But they don't own me. And if it ever comes down to it—if they try to interfere or push Taylor to see if she'll break—I'll make them wish they hadn't.

I'll choose her over the optics, the title, the exposure. Over the version of my life that's always been about reputation and expectation. I meant it when I said I'd burn it all down for her without a second thought, and I wouldn't regret it.

I push through the main door and head toward the vans parked out front. I'm done with today and everything it's offered me.

All that matters is that Taylor is still in there baking. And I'm heading back to the baker's house. I've given them enough footage of me for the day.

The bedroom door slams harder than I intend. Everything in this house is too fragile for the kind of energy vibrating under my skin right now.

I drag both hands through my hair and pace the length of the room—back and forth, back and forth. My jaw aches from clenching it. I flex my fingers, working out the tight fists that have left my knuckles bone-white.

I should feel victorious, but all I feel is wound tight and ready to snap. Something coils low in my chest, bracing for impact. I threatened a man who could bury me professionally, but he backed down from me.

My slacks and fitted button-up feel suffocating. I need to change into something that lets me breathe. Since I have no plans of leaving this room tonight, I grab a pair of loose pajama pants and head to the bathroom.

I brush my teeth a little too hard. The minty foam turns pink, and I swish with water until it runs clear.

Dropping onto the bed, I toss one arm over my face. I need to calm down and let everything from earlier go. It's over. I handled it. Consequences be damned.

A sharp knock rattles the door, and my eyes fly open. I sit up, scrubbing my hands over my face.

How long have I been lying here?

Another series of knocks—faster this time.

"Alex," Taylor calls through the door, breathless.

My pulse spikes so hard I feel the muscles in my neck twitch. I cross the room in three long strides and yank the door open.

She's standing there flushed, curls wild around her shoulders, chest rising and falling like she sprinted the entire way up the stairs.

Her eyes are bright, and a little frantic, as she speaks.

"RaeAnn told me everything," she says between breaths.

Her words hit me square in the chest. For half a second, I just look at her, unsure how she's going to react. I hope she understands I was just looking out for her, but you never know.

I brace for anger. For distance. For her to tell me I was out of line and I shouldn't have said anything. Nobody likes an asshole, but I did it *for* her. That has to mean something.

Without hesitation, she steps forward, fisting her hands in the front of my shirt as she closes the distance.

"Taylor—"

She cuts me off, rising onto her toes, hooking her arms around my neck and wrapping her legs around my waist with surprising confidence. I steady her automatically, hands gripping her hips to keep her from sliding.

Her mouth crashes into mine, and I stumble backward into the relative privacy of my bedroom, caught in a kiss that threatens every ounce of restraint I've been pretending to have.

Yeah. She's definitely not mad.

Thank fuck.

Chapter 19

The cool surface of the door presses into my back as Alex lifts me, his hips rolling against mine, dragging a soft, involuntary whimper from my throat.

His hands move quickly after that, one sliding beneath my jaw to tilt my face where he wants it.

Oh God. This is happening.

His mouth finds mine, warm and insistent, and I meet him without hesitation, matching his rhythm as the kiss deepens. Another quiet sound slips from me, swallowed by the heat of his mouth, by the way he doesn't give me space to think.

I catch his bottom lip between my teeth and tug, just enough to feel the shift before I let go. My head tips back against the door as I release him, and the groan he makes in response sends a sharp, heated thrill through me.

"You went to war for me," I breathe.

Alex opens his eyes, the love-drunk haze sharpening into something so intense I almost look away. He leans in, nose brushing the curve of my throat, his voice a low murmur against my skin, dark and full of promise.

"You have no idea the hell I would raise for you, Taylor."

A gentle bite at my earlobe draws a soft inhale from me, my lower lip catching between my teeth in response. Heat unfurls low in my stomach as his mouth moves, tracing along my jaw, then back to lips.

This is more than a kiss. It's worship. It's reverent.

It's everything and still not enough.

If I could, I'd hold onto this moment, tuck it somewhere safe for the hard days waiting back home. Something to remember when things feel too heavy, too loud.

Because this isn't just physical, not for me.

It's the way he's holding me, the way he's choosing me like there's no other option. And it sinks into me deeper than anything I can name, deeper than anything I've felt before, like I was always meant to end up here, with him.

My hands find his hair, fingers tangling in the soft waves as I tug him closer. I can't help it and I don't want to. Stopping what's growing between us would be impossible now.

With a low grunt, Alex carries me toward his bed and lays me down gently. I make room, and he fills it instantly, settling beside me on his side, propped up on an elbow.

His other hand traces slow, teasing circles across my chest, then feathers over my collarbone.

My eyes grow heavy as I watch his fingers move over my skin. I've never paid attention to hands before, but my God— Alex's are beautiful. My gaze drifts higher, following the movement of his forearms. I want to run my tongue along the perfectly sculpted muscle there.

He hums softly, like he's heard every thought, then trails his hand upward, tilting my chin with his finger so I'm looking straight into his ocean eyes.

Tension crackles between us.

Alex licks his lips. A slow, intentional tease that floods my senses. A devilish smile cuts across his face before he closes the distance again.

I'm floating.

Drowning, lost in every sensation he's pulling from me. Our kiss is heat and pressure, sharp edges and swallowed sounds. My hands slide up his arms, press over his chest, and trace their way down his back

I break the kiss first, chest rising too fast as I focus on the steady movement of his hand gliding up and down my belly. Each pass drifting a little lower than the last.

Hot breath brushes my lips as I look up at him. He's watching me closely, searching my face for something. Hesitation or maybe permission.

"Can I touch you?" His voice breaks slightly, rough with restraint. "I want to touch you—*fuck*, I *need* to touch you—but only if you want it too."

A shaky breath slips out of me as I nod, pulling him closer instead of answering right away. My hand cups his jaw, the faint scratch of stubble grounding me, holding his attention.

"I wouldn't be here if I didn't."

His eyes flick between mine, searching one last time for any doubt. When he finds none, his expression softens into relief, quiet and unmistakable.

"Okay," he murmurs, voice rough. His hand moves with new certainty, like my answer was the most precious thing in the world. And in this moment, maybe it was. "Okay."

My breath catches as his fingertips slide beneath the waistband of my shorts, warmth meeting the heat already pooling low in my stomach. I moan at the first brush, as he traces over the thin lace covering me.

"Fuckkk..." Alex groans against my neck. "You're already so wet for me, Taylor. *Holy shit.*"

Whatever restraint he had left snaps.

His hands tighten on my shorts and panties, pulling them down my legs and letting them fall to the floor beside the bed. In one swift motion, he's over me again, kissing me with deep, deliberate strokes. His lips, his tongue, all intent, all claim.

Goosebumps pebble my skin as he slides his middle finger through my wetness, circling my clit with a slow, deliberate tease that makes me want to scream. My hips roll into his touch, and Alex grins against my lips.

"Oh, my beautiful girl," he murmurs. "You like that?"

"Just like that, please." I moan, rolling my hips again as I crush my mouth against his. His hand works me into a frenzy, and my kiss turns sloppy as I climb higher.

A rumble from Alex's chest lets me know he doesn't mind.

Just as I'm inching toward the edge, he pulls back, removing his hand entirely.

"What—"

The protest dies on my lips when I open my eyes to find Alex maneuvering down my body, settling between my legs. I fall back against his pillow with a breathy moan.

This man. Where has he been my whole life?

"I'm not done with you yet." His voice drops even lower. "There's no way I'm wasting the chance to finally have your taste on my tongue."

He presses his forehead just below my belly button and inhales deeply, exhaling on a low, unmistakable sound.

"Not a fucking chance."

With that, he lowers his head and peppers kisses along my inner thighs. I try to keep them open, but it tickles, and I let out a breathless giggle. He nips at my skin, sending a jolt of pleasure racing up my spine.

When his mouth finds my center, he presses a flat tongue against me and drags a slow, deliberate stroke upward.

Stars explode behind my eyes.

He alternates between licking and sucking, slipping a finger inside me and moving with slow, steady intent. A second follows, stretching and filling me as his mouth works in tandem with his hand.

My thoughts scatter completely.

"Alex—oh God, I can't... I'm going to—" The words fall apart on my tongue, spilling out broken and incoherent anyway.

Piercing blue eyes meet mine as he pulls away just enough, his fingers still moving at a steady, deliberate pace.

"You can. And you will." He drawls with a smirk. "Be a good girl, Taylor. Come for me, baby."

He lowers his head again, working me in the same rhythm he's already figured out. With his words still ringing in my mind and the steady curl of his fingers, my body gives in.

"Alex!" I cry out as pleasure crashes through me like lightning. My body tightens, then releases in a fierce, trembling wave that leaves me shaking, curling in and then melting back with a breathless moan.

But Alex doesn't stop.

He licks through it like a man starved, like my taste is everything he's ever needed. As I lie back, coming down from the peak, a deep groan rumbles against me.

"Fuckkk…"

Alex drops his head against my lower belly, breathing hard. His shoulders rise and fall with the effort as he stays there, grounding himself, not rushing the moment.

He stays there a little longer than is comfortable.

"Hey," I whisper, propping myself up into a sitting position. "Are you okay?"

Alex sucks in another long breath, then pushes up onto his knees, settling back on his heels to face me. His chest rises and falls fast, a faint pink flush staining his cheeks.

My grumpy storm cloud blushing might be the cutest thing I've ever seen.

His expression, however, is off. I narrow my eyes, trying to figure out what's happening. He looks away quickly, then bites his lip. Confused, I glance down… and clap a hand over my mouth to hide my growing smile.

On the front of Alex's thin, light gray cotton pants is a dark, unmistakable spot, right where the tip of him is still pressed.

My eyes widen, and I reach for him. He's as human as he is impossible, and somehow, I like him even more for it.

He braces his hands on his thighs, dropping his head between his shoulders. "I swear, this is not a problem I've ever had before," he mutters. "It's just… been a while."

He lifts his gaze to meet mine, the look almost pleading, and I cave immediately, moving toward him.

I cup his face in both hands, then kiss him sweetly on the lips. He tastes like me, and him, and every bit of trust that's growing between us.

I can't get enough, so I do it again.

"It's okay, really." I nudge his nose with mine. "But you know what this means, right?"

He gives me a wary look. "What does this mean?"

"This means you definitely, absolutely, totally like me and can't pretend otherwise anymore."

I beam at him, his shoulders relax, and then we're both laughing, because this was definitely not on either of our bingo cards for today.

"I'm going to go get cleaned up. And, you know… change my pants," Alex grumbles, scrubbing both hands over his face.

I smile to myself, nodding, and press my lips together. They're warm and swollen in that just-kissed way that makes my heart jump.

As Alex slips into the adjoining bathroom, he leaves the door ajar. Which I take as an invitation because I also need to clean up after baking all day and, well… after what we just did.

I don't bother with the clothes on the floor. I just head into the bathroom, where Alex is at the sink, his hands gripping the waistband of his pants. His surprised expression meets mine in the mirror.

I trail my fingers across his back as I slide past him toward the shower. With my back to him, I pull my shirt off over my head, then toss it in his direction before turning the water on and stepping inside.

A mumbled, "Fuck me," reaches my ears as I slide the glass door shut behind me. Through the textured glass, I see Alex's silhouette—still, watching—with my shirt draped over one shoulder.

His shower is immaculate. Organized in a way I could never achieve. A neat row of dark amber bottles with cream labels in... French, maybe?

I pick one up, carefully unscrewing the lid, and inhale deeply. Spiced bourbon. Oaked vanilla. Perfectly Alex.

The consistency makes it clear that it's body wash, and I can't resist pouring some into my hands, working it into a rich lather and smoothing it over my skin.

As I angle my face under the stream of water, eyes closed, I hear the glass door slide open.

Warm hands travel up my arms, settling between my shoulders where strong thumbs begin working out the tension that's taken up residence over the past few weeks.

I groan, tilting my head to the side to give him better access to the tight muscle at the base of my neck. Alex obliges immediately, focusing on exactly where I need him.

After a few minutes, I turn to face him and inhale a sharp breath as I take him in.

Water slides over him, tracing the lines of muscle as he moves. His chest is solid, defined with a light dusting of hair, his breath rising and falling in a way I can't ignore. When he reaches for one of the bottles, his stomach tightens, the movement revealing a quiet strength as his body flexes around mine. Not model-perfect—*thank God.*

He obviously takes care of himself. But he also lives in his body, not denying himself the things he enjoys. He's real and that makes him completely devastating.

His hands find my hair, guiding my head under the water, snapping me out of my thoughts. His knowing smirk makes my cheeks heat. *Busted.*

"You know," he starts, voice low, pouring shampoo into his hands before working it into my hair. "I could get used to this. And I really fucking love that you'll be walking around all day tomorrow smelling like me."

His lips find mine in a sweet kiss that contrasts the hunger that existed before. My eyes flutter closed as his hands continue their careful work.

We don't rush the shower, taking our time as we wash each other, kissing under the water as steam gathers around us.

When my fingers are wrinkled and my skin is flushed, Alex finally leads me out. He wraps me in a fluffy white towel, drying me off before pulling one of his T-shirts over my head.

He presses a kiss to the tip of my nose, then dresses himself.

"Stay with me tonight, yeah?" His voice is warm and unguarded. This intimate version of him settles deep in my chest, right between my ribs.

I nod.

We slide into bed, and he immediately pulls me into him. One strong arm wraps around my waist, drawing me back against him with a quiet hum.

Everything smells like him. The pillows. The blanket. Me. And it's quickly becoming a scent I don't think I could live without.

My eyes drift closed, rehashing everything that's happened today.

But Alex turned it into something else entirely—standing up for me, saving my bake, and showing me a side of himself I didn't know existed.

I'm asleep before I even realize I'm falling.

Alex

Chapter 20

The tent feels smaller today.

It's the same white canopy. Same polished benches. Same too-bright lights reflecting off gleaming countertops. But the air is heavier than it should be, like static before a storm that hasn't decided whether it's going to break.

Or maybe that's just me, still ruminating on my confrontation with Hal and the production team yesterday.

I roll my shoulders once, flexing my fingers against the edge of the counter. Dough rests beneath a linen cloth in front of me, proofing quietly, indifferent to everything else happening around it.

Bread doesn't care about narrative arcs.

But cameras do.

"Alex."

I don't need to look up to know who it is. Theo's voice has that taunting lilt to it, like he already knows how this conversation is going to go.

When I finally lift my gaze, both hosts are already closing in on my station. They wear matching smiles—small, calculated, and entirely too pleased with themselves.

"Just the man we were hoping to catch," Judy singsongs. "You really stirred things up yesterday. Anything to say for yourself?"

I scoff, barely resisting the urge to roll my eyes.

My movements are neutral, controlled in a way that doesn't betray anything, as I wipe my hands on the towel tucked into my apron.

I don't owe them an explanation. And I'm definitely not going to give them something they can twist later.

"I stood up for something," I say evenly. "For someone that matters."

They tilt their heads in unison, a practiced, almost rehearsed reaction. A pause stretches between us, the intentional kind that lives for editing rooms.

"Would you do it again?" Theo asks.

My first instinct is simple: tell them to go straight to hell.

My second is far more strategic. Deflect. Smile. Give them something clean they can package into a soundbite. I guess all the PR training wasn't a complete waste of time.

Instead, Taylor flashes in my periphery.

Flour covers her station like it spontaneously exploded, her hair slightly undone, cheeks flushed. She's laughing with RaeAnn, completely unaware of how quickly I'd escalate if anything threatened her again. Of how far I'd go.

A smile tugs at my mouth before I can stop it.

"Yes," I say, without hesitation.

I lift the linen from my dough, checking the surface, even though I already know it's fine. The motion gives me something to do with my hands.

Theo's smile sharpens and Judy crosses her arms, expression shifting, subtle but satisfied. Like they've pulled something out of me they can use.

"Even if it puts a target on your back?" Theo presses.

My jaw ticks at the implied threat, and I press my fingers into the dough, feeling its resistance.

"If fairness puts a target on my back," I say, voice even, "that says more about you than it does about me."

The second it leaves my mouth, I know it was a mistake. And now they know exactly where to aim when they come for me.

Across the aisle, Taylor glances over. She catches my eye and offers a small smile, and the tension lodged in my chest eases. I drag a hand across my chest, fingers pressing lightly over my sternum as I hold her gaze a beat longer than I should.

"Fair enough," Judy says, too quickly. "Tell us about your showstopper."

Her smile returns like a switch flipped. It's warm and welcoming, like the last minute never happened.

The shift is disorienting.

I inhale a sharp breath, then launch into a safe, automatic explanation. A whole lot of technical details that most people don't pay attention to and are way easier to talk about.

To their credit, the hosts nod along, listening like I'm saying something meaningful. Then they move on, redirecting their attention to Diane as if I'd already been filed away.

I drop my head and let out a slow breath, tension bleeding out of my shoulders.

Out of the corner of my eye, I catch Taylor again, completely absorbed in her work. I hold the sight for another second, then square my shoulders and get back to mine.

The rest of the time in the tent flies by. Judging goes as expected. Brandon and I land at the top. Taylor and Diane take the middle. RaeAnn and Lila fall into the bottom two.

Our resident influencer smiles like she's in the top, not at risk of going home. It's the same bright, polished expression she's worn every week she's survived when she shouldn't have.

I watch the judges speak, hands folded loosely in front of me, my expression neutral. Inside, however, irritation coils low and familiar.

Not at her, necessarily, but at the machine itself.

Production and the network have been protecting her. I should have noticed it sooner. I mean, for fuck's sake—I grew up in this. Different industry, sure. But same mechanics.

Marketability, retention, leverage, relevance.

It's the same beast hiding behind a different face.

When her name is finally called, the tent stills.

For a fraction of a second, Lila looks genuinely shocked. Like she believed she was safe again this week. If there was any doubt before, it's clear now that she knew what they were doing, and expected it to keep working.

Then her face collapses, and she puts on a different kind of performance for the cameras, full of crocodile tears and breathless hiccups.

It takes everything in me not to roll my eyes at her.

Her elimination is long overdue.

Applause swells as people gather around her, offering hugs and promises to stay in touch, to call, to meet up after this is all over. The cameras move in closer, hungry for every second of it.

I clap because it's expected, but my attention drifts.

Not to Lila or production, but to something else entirely. A thought I can't seem to shake. Nothing here goes untouched. Not the judging. Not the narratives. Not the way conflict gets shaped into episodes.

My stomach drops, a sickening realization settling in.

Not the way I handled things yesterday.

All day, I've been telling myself I did the right thing by defending fairness and protecting the integrity of the competition. Making sure production didn't hurt Taylor. And that's true.

But it isn't the whole truth.

It was also instinct, a reflex as natural as breathing.

Power and influence, applied without hesitation. I didn't stop to consider alternatives, didn't weigh consequences.

I just reached for the most effective tool I had and used it. Just like *him*.

The realization is a hard pill to swallow.

I don't regret defending her. I don't.

But I can't ignore how easy it was. How quickly I defaulted to a version of myself I've spent years trying not to become. I didn't hesitate to throw my weight around, didn't stop to think—I just acted, because I knew it would work.

Even if the outcome was justified, the method feels… uncomfortably familiar. Uncomfortably close to the man I've spent my life trying to differentiate myself from.

"You okay?"

Taylor's voice pulls me out of it, her fingers brushing up my bicep, over my shoulder in a light, grounding gesture.

"Yeah." I nod. "It's just been a long weekend."

It isn't a lie. It's not the whole truth either.

I'm not ready to give her the parts of me she doesn't already know. Not yet. Because right now, I'm just Alex to her. Not Chet Harrington's son, heir to Canada's most influential culinary empire.

She studies me for a beat like she might push—and for one terrifying second, I think she will and I'll cave because the thought of lying to her makes me sick—but then she smiles instead, her fingers playing with the hair at the nape of my neck.

"Coffee later before I head out?" she asks.

Something in my chest softens despite everything.

"Deal."

I watch her walk away, my gaze locked on her as she heads toward interviews. She reaches up, undoing her hairclip. Golden curls spill loose as she disappears through the tent opening.

I drop my head into my hands, the thought comes back louder now. I need to tell her everything, and soon.

Because the longer I wait to tell her the truth, the harder it's going to be to say.

And harder still for her to hear.

I wait until the noise dies down to do what I know I need to do. Until interviews pull most people away. Until the tent feels temporarily hollow, like an empty shelf of a space between performances.

My phone sits heavier in my palm than it ever has before, and I stare at my father's name in my contact list, dread gathering in my chest.

Chet Harrington.

I exhale, hitting call before I can second-guess it.

"Alexander."

My father answers on the second ring. There's no greeting. Just acknowledgment and annoyance, which means he already knows what's happened. Fucking perfect.

My jaw tightens. "You heard."

There's a pause, followed by an exasperated sigh on the other end of the line, like he's counting down from ten before responding.

"I heard you threatened production with legal action on a televised competition," Chet says, too calm for comfort.

I crack my knuckles one by one.

"I didn't threaten anyone." The accusation needles under my skin. "I set a boundary."

I exhale sharp through my nose, familiar frustration creeping up my throat. Every conversation with my father makes me feel like I'm seventeen again instead of a grown man capable of making his own choices.

"They crossed a line. They're sabotaging—"

"You are not there to manage production ethics." His voice sharpens. "Get in your lane, son. Your purpose there is bigger than being a regular contestant."

Don't I know it. I've been a piece on a board since the moment my father decided to send me on the show.

"You chose this, now get it done."

"No," I say, more firmly this time. "You forced me to come here. You threatened to pull funding from *Northern Flame* if I didn't."

There's another brief pause on the other end of the line, the kind that isn't hesitation so much as recalibration.

"You agreed," he replies. "Which means you chose the exposure and the visibility that come with it."

"I agreed because you backed me into a corner," I push back, my grip tightening around the phone. "If I didn't come, you walk, and the restaurant I've spent the last year building disappears with you. That's not a choice—that's leverage."

"You're choosing to frame it that way," he says calmly. "I presented you with an opportunity. You should be grateful."

A quiet, humorless breath escapes me. "A threat dressed up as an opportunity is still a threat, *Chet*."

My father sighs over the line, I know the conversation is all but finished by the tone.

"You don't get to forget who you are."

My eyes close.

"I'm not trying to forget," I say, quieter now. "I just wanted something that was mine. Something I did without it being... this."

"And I allowed that," he replies. "Because there was strategic value in your participation."

Of course, because everything I do has to serve his dream, not mine. Because everything I have, I owe to him. Being his son is both a blessing and a cage.

"I know why I'm here."

"Then act like it." His voice hardens again before softening, just slightly. "Don't let distractions cost you something meaningful in the end."

The line goes dead.

As if he were standing right outside the tent—Julian steps in. He studies me for half a second, before pressing his lips into a straight line.

"How bad was it?"

I huff a quiet breath. "Predictable."

He leans against the counter, arms crossed, waiting, and I stare out toward the garden, words heavy on my tongue.

"He heard about what I did with production, and felt the need to remind me why I'm here."

My cousin glances sideways, warily. "And?"

"And I don't know if I care anymore."

The admission hangs there, but Julian doesn't react immediately. Just nods slowly, dark eyes blinking in thought.

"That's not new for you."

"No. But it's getting harder to play his game."

I drag a hand through my hair, frustration bleeding through. "He didn't mention pulling funding this time. I think *Northern Flame* is safe."

Silence stretches.

Julian watches me, then nods again, more at ease. The lines between his brows smooth out on a heavy exhale.

I let out a slow breath, too. "I'm tired of being... useful. Just a means to an end."

"That's a loaded sentence."

But he knows exactly what I mean. Love is a four-letter word in our family. The only thing that matters is how every choice benefits our legacy.

"Everything is leverage. Everything is positioning. Even this." I gesture vaguely at the tent. "Especially this."

"And what does Taylor say about all of it?"

Her name lands hard. I drag my gaze back to Julian. He knows the PR plan was to keep my identity and ties to *The Harrington Group* a secret.

"She doesn't know anything about any of this."

Julian nods like he expected that.

"I don't want her to know," I admit. "Because everything changes when people know. It always does."

Julian doesn't interrupt, understanding flashing across his face, and he gives me a sad smile.

I toss my head back, eyes on the ceiling, searching for words that don't sound as bad as they feel. "I just wanted something that was real without context attached to it."

Blowing the air from my lungs, I stare at the ground as guilt eats away at me. Taylor's one of the kindest people I've ever met. If anyone was going to take this information in stride, having it change nothing, it would be her.

"I shouldn't have let it go this far."

The silence that follows feels different. There's a shift before I understand why. Julian's eyes flick past me, and I spin around to see Taylor standing a few feet away.

Her big hazel eyes are locked on me

And I know.

I know exactly which part she heard.

Fuck.

Fuck. Fuck. Fuck.

Everything in me goes cold as ice. My hands shake as panic and adrenaline surge through my body. I whip my head to Julian, pleading with him to step in. But he just backs away, hands raised in surrender, abandoning me without a word.

"Taylor—"

Her expression shifts, brows knitting with confusion.

"You shouldn't have let what go this far?" she asks.

My brain scrambles for the right words, coming up empty.

"I—it's not—"

"You didn't want me to know what?" she cuts in.

"I was going to tell you."

Wrong. That was the wrong thing to say.

"Tell me what?" Her voice cracks. "Just say it. Please."

I step closer with a hand raised, careful, like she might turn and run. Almost the way you'd approach a scared animal.

"Okay—yeah, okay. I didn't want you to know who I am. My family. But I swear, it wasn't about lying to you."

She lets out a small, disbelieving laugh.

"Alex, you literally just said you didn't want me to know who you are."

Because everything changes when people know.

I run a hand over the back of my neck, heart pounding.

"I wasn't supposed to tell anyone," I say, voice rough. "It was part of an agreement with my father. But I also didn't want this to change. Us. The way you see me."

Taylor's eyes glisten now. She shakes her head like the pieces are rearranging inside her mind in real time.

"Why are you here if none of this matters to you?"

Her usual sunny disposition has darkened, and I swallow the lump in my throat, knowing I'm the cause of it.

"You don't need the money. You don't need the networking or connections. So... what is this?"

I brace myself against the counter and drop my head.

"My last name is Harrington."

"That doesn't mean anything to me, Alex."

Of course it doesn't. That's exactly why I was sent here in the first place. To make our name mean something here in the States.

"That's fair." I take a deep breath. "My family owns one of the biggest restaurant groups in Vancouver. My father's expanding into the U.S..."

She studies me as my words trail off, searching my face. Probably looking for any sign of deception. She doesn't say anything, so I drop my eyes to the ground and continue.

"Julian and I have been working toward opening our own concept and my father threatened to pull funding if I didn't come on this stupid show. Play by his rules, win people over down here... You get the drift."

My shoulders sag in relief with the admission. I didn't realize how much keeping this from her was weighing on me. My next breath feels like the first one I've taken in weeks.

Taylor stands there with her arms crossed and her hip cocked, chewing her lower lip. She narrows her eyes as she speaks.

"And that's all fine, obviously not everyone here came with the sole intention of baking. Look at Lila."

She rolls her eyes on a scoff.

"There's plenty about my life that I haven't told you, but we've all talked about our lives back home. At some point, you aren't just concealing information." She pauses, thinking. "You're explicitly lying."

"I didn't lie," I rush. "I work in a kitchen. I do. My family just... owns the kitchen."

"Lies of omission are still lies, Alex."

"Taylor, please." My voice breaks. "I didn't know we'd become... this. By the time we did, it felt too late."

"You don't owe me anything," she says, and it hurts more than anger ever could. "But I trusted you."

Her trembling hands rise to her forehead and she begins to pace in front of me. "God, I'm going to look so stupid on TV."

I'd give anything to go back and refuse the secrecy agreement with *The Harrington Group.*

"I'd take it back if I could. All of it."

She shakes her head and steps back. The distance is small, but devastating.

"Please," I say, desperate now. "I know I should have told you. I'll tell you everything. Anything. Just—don't shut me out."

"No." Her voice is firm now. She shakes her head furiously, her hair whipping around her face with the motion.

"I need time to process this. I understand everything you're saying, but I need to work through what this all means."

She finally looks at me, and I see her trying to hold on to something. "I don't know which parts were real," she admits. "And which were just for show."

My chest caves in, and she turns to walk away.

One hand rises to her face as she goes, and I know she's wiping away the tears she so bravely fought back.

"It was all real." My voice is just above a whisper, but there's a slight pause in her retreat and I know she somehow hears me.

But she doesn't stop, disappearing through the opening of the tent.

And I stand there, completely still. Alone.

Fuck.

Chapter 21

When I park outside my apartment, Kara is already sitting on the top step, a bottle of wine dangling from one hand and a paper bag stamped with our favorite taco truck's logo resting beside her. Even from the car, I can see the grease soaking through the bottom of the bag.

I sit there for a second, engine ticking as it cools, hands still gripping the steering wheel.

I will not cry again. I've done enough of that for one day.

I slam the car door harder than necessary and square my shoulders before turning toward the building. Kara looks up at the sound. The second her eyes find mine, her expression softens.

And that's it. That's all it takes.

"Kara," I manage, my voice already breaking despite my best effort to hold it together.

She's on her feet before I reach the steps, arms open. I make it exactly one second inside them before the tears I swore were finished start all over again.

"Oh, Sunshine," she murmurs, rubbing slow circles between my shoulder blades. "Okay—yeah—that bad, huh?"

I nod against her shoulder, mortified by how quickly I folded. Three and a half hours in the car, telling myself I was fine, wasn't enough. Apparently, all it takes is one look at my best friend for me to unravel completely.

"I didn't even change," I say thickly, motioning to my flour-dusted clothes. "I walked in, grabbed my bags, and left. I didn't say goodbye to anyone. I just... left."

Kara pulls back enough to look at me, thumb swiping under one of my eyes. "Good. Dramatic exits are necessary sometimes."

A watery laugh slips out of me.

She nudges the paper bag toward me with her foot. "Come on. I brought carnitas. And that ridiculously expensive wine you pretend you can taste notes in."

"I *can* taste notes," I sniff.

"Babe, you once described a wine as 'purple' and 'grapey'."

"It *was* 'purple' and 'grapey'."

She huffs, looping her arm through mine and steering me toward the door. "Inside. Shoes off. You're telling me everything from the top. And if he's as dumb as your text made him sound, I reserve the right to hate him indefinitely."

It takes only moments for us to settle in my living room, wine glasses full and still-warm carnitas piled onto plates.

"Okay, girl," Kara says, kicking her feet up on my coffee table before taking a gulp of wine. "You have your wine. You have your food. Out with it."

The melt-in-your-mouth shreds dance a symphony of flavor over my tongue as I chew, wondering where to begin.

Because the truth is, while I'm upset that Alex didn't tell me everything sooner, I'm also just exhausted.

The competition is coming to an end. There are only a couple of bakes left. The pressure of my schedule is relentless.

I work all week, practice when I can, and bake under extreme pressure all weekend. Finding out that Alex may have been pretending for the cameras this entire time was just the final straw.

The proverbial icing on the cake.

I blow out a slow breath before turning to my best friend and recounting the entire interaction. Every word, every look, every awful, twisting second of it comes tumbling out. Kara doesn't interrupt. She just listens, humming softly when I falter, refilling my wine glass without asking.

She takes a second before speaking.

"Okay," she says carefully. "First of all? Your feelings are valid. Like, aggressively valid."

I pause mid-sip, eyeing her over the rim of my glass. She isn't as angry as she should be. She isn't gearing up to eviscerate him. That alone makes me suspicious.

"But," she continues gently, "he had an agreement in place before he ever met you, right? With his family? With the restaurant group?"

I nod in answer.

"And if he broke that, he risked his dad pulling funding."

Another nod. I don't like where this is going.

She studies me for a moment, like she's choosing her next words carefully.

"I'm not saying he handled it perfectly. He absolutely should've told you sooner. I'm not defending that part."

She squeezes my hand.

"But Tay... if someone walked up to you tomorrow and offered to bankroll your dream bakery—the storefront, the equipment, the staff, literally everything—and all you had to do was keep your last name quiet and win over an audience?"

Her brows lift when I don't answer.

"You're really going to sit there and tell me you wouldn't at least consider it?"

I narrow my eyes at her. "Whose side are you on?"

"Yours," she says immediately. "Always yours. But being on your side doesn't mean I let you rewrite the story into something it's not."

Ouch.

But she's right. I want it to be simple. I want him to be careless or shallow or manipulative. Something easy to file away under, 'lesson learned.'

But Alex isn't any of those things.

He's strategic. Intentional. Used to thinking ten steps ahead. Which means he knew exactly what he was risking by opening up to me. I can't decide whether to admire or resent him for that.

I exhale sharply. "I wouldn't turn down the chance if someone wanted to fund my dream, but that's not the same thing."

"Why not?"

"Because I'm not upset about funding or even that he didn't tell me about his family. I'm upset about... us." My voice wobbles despite my effort to keep it steady. "He let me fall for him without knowing who he really was."

Kara tilts her head. "No?"

"I knew who he presented himself as." I set my wine down harder than necessary. The deep crimson almost sloshes over the rim. "That's the problem. I don't know where the line is. I don't know what parts were him and what parts were him playing to the cameras."

Kara leans back into the couch, studying me carefully.

"Okay... Then, let me ask you something."

I brace myself, but nod for her to continue.

"You said he wasn't like that with everyone, right? Not warm. Not overly charming. Not playing golden-boy with the whole cast."

"No," I admit, thinking back on all the ways he's the exact opposite. My lips quirk as I picture his near-constant scowl. "He wasn't."

"If this was purely strategy, wouldn't he be nice to everyone? Wouldn't he spread that charm around evenly? Make sure the cameras caught it from every angle?"

I hesitate.

Because... yeah. He would.

"He didn't," she presses gently. "He was selective. And you were the only one he kept showing up for."

My heartbeat kicks up at the realization.

"That doesn't feel like someone performing for an audience," she says. "That feels like someone who forgot there was one."

Maybe Kara's right.

Maybe it doesn't have to be one or the other. Maybe he can be strategic and still be sincere. I think about the way he looks at me when he thinks I'm not paying attention, the way his hand always finds the small of my back like it belongs there, the way he stood between me and production without hesitation.

None of that felt like a performance. And yet, I don't know how to untangle my mess of feelings from logic. I don't know how to be sure I wasn't just another move on a very well-played board.

My newfound hope flickers anyway, a stubborn butterfly rising from the ashes of my anger.

I scoff, flip my phone face down, and silence it. I don't want to analyze this anymore. I don't want to reread his messages or wait for another one to come through. I just want quiet.

I just want to forget about all of it for a little while.

It's been three fucking days with no answer from Taylor.

Three days of calls going straight to voicemail. Three days of texts left on read. Three days of staring at my phone like I can will her name to light up the screen.

I've executed high-stakes dinner services with less anxiety than this. I have no leverage here. No angle whatsoever. There's nothing I can do right now that doesn't reek of desperation.

The silence is suffocating.

I'm not used to being shut out. I'm not used to not knowing how to fix something. And the longer she doesn't respond, the louder the question gets in my head: *What if she's already decided I'm not worth the explanation?*

My jaw tightens. I don't do well with helplessness. And right now, that's exactly what this feels like.

"Joe!" I bark from the doorway of my room.

I'm already moving, already halfway down the stairs before I hear his footsteps in the kitchen.

"What?" he calls back, voice thick around a mouthful of something. He rounds the corner still chewing a bagel, dragging the back of his hand across his mouth.

"Hypothetically," I start.

He takes one look at my face and groans. "No."

"You don't even know what I'm going to ask."

"I don't need to," he says, taking another bite. "The only time I've seen you this amped up was when you tore into production. Whatever you're thinking? It's not good."

I tilt my head, considering him. "How do you feel about stealing a van?"

Joe chokes on his bagel. "Excuse me?"

"Borrowing," I correct. "Temporarily reallocating resources for the sake of excellent television."

"You've lost your mind."

Yeah, maybe I have. But I have to try something. I can't keep sitting here waiting for a text that may never come.

"Hear me out," I say, stepping closer. "This could be the shot that gets you promoted next season."

He freezes. The chewing slows.

"It's been three days of radio silence with Taylor," I continue. "The audience thinks I fumbled it. They think it's over. And then—" I snap my fingers. "I show up. Almost four hours away. No warning. Flowers. An apology. Real drama to feed the audience."

Joe studies me carefully. "And you're sure she won't just slam the door in your face?"

"No." A short laugh breaks out of me. "But that outcome might actually be better for you than if she lets me in."

"For me," he repeats.

"For the show," I amend with a grin. "Whether she lets me in or not, that's the kind of footage they build promos around."

Silence stretches between us. I can see the gears turning in his head, already planning all the ways they could spin this narrative to benefit the show.

"You'd let me film it?" he asks finally. He's guarded, expression unsure and I don't blame him. I haven't been the easiest to work with.

I hold his gaze. "I'd forget you're even there."

Less than an hour later, we're piled into one of the show's passenger vans, barreling down the freeway toward Cambria.

Toward Taylor.

Toward whatever she decides to do with me.

Hours later, Joe stops at a small flower shop a few miles from Taylor's apartment. I hop out and duck inside, the bell over the door chiming too loudly.

I grab the biggest bouquet of sunflowers they have.

It isn't perfect. One of the stems leans too far out, and a couple of the petals are bent at the edges, but my girl isn't a rose kind of girl.

She's bright colors and summer sun. The kind of woman who laughs too loud and doesn't apologize for it. Someone who makes everything around her warmer just by standing there.

I run a thumb over one of the battered petals.

Yeah. These feel right.

Joe eyes the bouquet with surprise as I slide the van door closed and take my seat. The adrenaline has been simmering under my skin the entire drive, but now that we're here, it settles into a pit of nerves in my stomach.

The van turns onto her street, a narrow lane lined with low brick apartments and the faint scent of jasmine curling in the evening air. String lights hang across the balconies, casting golden pools on the sidewalks. Kids weave between parked cars on bikes, the distant hum of an ice cream truck trailing down the block. It's peaceful here, like the chaos of the last week belongs somewhere else entirely.

Joe pulls the van to a stop a few doors down from hers and cuts the engine. He nods, and I grip the bouquet tighter, feeling the rough edges of the paper against my palms.

"Alright," I murmur, mostly to myself. "This is it."

I step out, and the breeze hits my face. Every step toward her door feels heavier than the last, like the weight of three days of silence has settled squarely on my shoulders. Joe lingers behind a parked car, camera angled subtly, close enough to capture the approach but far enough to feel like I'm doing this alone.

"Go get her, bud!" he calls from behind me.

Her door comes into view, framed by a tiny wrought-iron railing and a faded welcome mat. A pot of marigolds leans against the steps. Everything about it is so effortlessly Taylor.

I take a deep breath and raise the bouquet, my hand trembling slightly. One step at a time, I move closer until I'm standing in front of her bright blue door.

My knuckles rap against it.

No answer.

I try again, a little harder this time.

Still nothing.

Just as I'm about to turn away, the door swings open and there she is. Eyes wide. Hair falling in a riot around her shoulders. Her mouth hanging open, confused.

For a second, I can't speak. I can only stand there, letting the silence stretch, letting the moment hold us in place.

"Taylor."

That's it. No grand speech—just her name tumbling out like a plea or a prayer from my lips. Her expression shifts, uncertainty flickering in her eyes, and I know this is the moment everything changes.

Chapter 22

For a second, I think I'm imagining him. That has to be it. By some combination of stress and lack of sleep, my brain conjured him because that's easier than accepting he found me.

But he doesn't fade when I close my eyes.

Alex stands there on my doorstep, holding a bouquet of sunflowers that look a tad wind-beaten, his shoulders tense like he's bracing for impact.

"Taylor."

He says my name quietly, like he isn't sure he's allowed to say it. He shifts on his feet, more unsure of himself than I've ever seen him.

My fingers tighten around the edge of the door. I instinctively move to block the view into my apartment.

"How are you here?"

His throat works before he answers. "I drove."

"That's not what I meant, and you know it." I step fully into the doorway now. "How did you find me?"

He jerks his head quickly over his shoulder, and that's when I see movement. Joe stands halfway down the sidewalk, camera trained on us.

My stomach drops. *Of course.*

I look back at Alex, rolling my eyes and crossing my arms defensively. "So this is for the cameras then?"

Alex winces at my words. A shadow of embarrassment crosses his face before he speaks. "I told him we were about to get the shot of the season," he says with a guilty smirk.

I huff out a sound—half scoff, half laugh—because he doesn't deny it.

"You used him."

"I used his ambition," he corrects, rubbing the back of his neck with his free hand. He still looks a little guilty. "There's a difference."

"That doesn't answer my question."

"I needed a ride." His jaw tightens on the confession. "I needed a way to get you since your phone has gone completely out of commission."

It's my turn to cringe. That lands somewhere I don't want it to. I have absolutely been avoiding him, hoping to put this conversation off for as long as possible. Or at least until the weekend when I'd inevitably have to face him in the house.

Joe shifts again down the sidewalk, a little closer now. I can practically feel him waiting for something dramatic.

Alex follows my gaze.

"He's not coming inside," he says immediately. "If you let me in, that is."

The choice sits there between us.

My apartment is my space. Mine. The one place in this entire experience that isn't under lights or surrounded by producers or mic packs.

He's never been here.

Whether or not he comes inside is totally up to me.

He stands there holding those battered sunflowers, not sure I'm going to accept them or him, and I feel myself start to soften.

I look down at the bouquet. They're slightly crooked. One stem leans too far to the left. A few petals are bent at the tips.

But they're perfect.

"You didn't get roses," I say before I can stop myself, a smile tugging at the corner of my lips.

His mouth lifts in response. "Didn't feel like the right choice for you. Too basic, not enough razzle dazzle."

Heat creeps up my neck. "Did you just say 'razzle dazzle'?" I tease, deflecting.

"You're rubbing off on me," he says with a casual shrug that doesn't feel as casual at all. I glance back at Joe, then at Alex again.

"If I let you in, the door closes," I say pointedly, one eyebrow cocked, daring him to push back.

"It closes." He agrees without hesitation.

"No hero speech outside, either. I have neighbors."

"Okay."

I step back and open the door, clearing the path for him to come inside.

His shoulders drop on a breath as he moves forward. Before he passes me, he lifts a hand in Joe's direction and waves.

"You got your shot. Thanks, *bud*."

Joe's face falls into something between disbelief and outrage as the door swings shut. I don't mean to laugh. It just slips out. The sound surprises both of us as I slide the lock into place.

The apartment feels smaller with him inside. He looks taller here than he does in the open-concept house and pitched baking tent back in LA. I step forward, taking the flowers from him, and leading the way further into my space.

He lingers near the entryway, unsure whether to follow me into the kitchen or move to the living room. Not that it matters, the half-wall counter is the only thing separating the rooms.

I watch him as he takes in the stack of baking books on my side table, the dish towel hanging crooked off the oven handle, the framed photo of Kara and me at the beach last summer, while I fill the only vase I own with water for the flowers.

"Do you want something to drink?"

He looks at me then, really looks at me, the full weight of his piercing blue gaze searching my expression. Being around Alex always gets my pulse racing, but the way my heart hammers as he occupies my space is on a whole other level.

I pretend to straighten that crooked dish towel, but in reality, I'm swiping my clammy palms down the fabric.

"I have almond milk," I say, peering inside the fridge, knowing it's basically empty. I grab only the essentials since I'm gone half the week between work and the show.

"And half a Gatorade."

The corner of his mouth lifts again and he laughs. Which is fair, because who offers a guest almond milk?

"I'm good."

We stand there facing each other in the quiet of my living room. Alex waits for me to drop onto the corner cushion, clutching an emotional support accent pillow to my chest. He perches on the edge of the middle cushion, bent forward with his elbows on his knees.

I can't tell if he's trying to find the right words to start the conversation or if he's waiting on me. After a minute of silence, I cave first.

"You scared me," I tell him, watching his forehead wrinkle in concern before turning to face me.

"By showing up here?"

"No. By making me think I didn't know you."

He exhales, a little exasperated. "You do know me."

"I thought I did." My voice steadies. "Then I found out you have this whole other layer you never mentioned. A father who can bankroll an empire. A deal for your future in place before you even walked into the tent."

His shoulders straighten at my accusation. I have his full attention now, and I sit up straighter in response to hold it.

"I didn't hide my family to manipulate you."

"Then why?"

"Like I said, it was part of the agreement with my father." He pauses, inhaling sharply. "But also, another part of me just didn't want to be that guy while I was here."

"What guy?" I know the answer should be obvious, but I need to hear him say it. I don't want any assumptions or miscommunication muddying the water between us any more than it already is.

"The one who's treated differently because of his family."

I let out a short laugh. "You already are that guy."

He winces, then blows out a long breath. He looks so tired, but I force myself to push forward with the conversation. No more giving passes for things that need to be addressed immediately.

"Do you know what this competition means to people?" I ask, suddenly needing to know if he understands what some of us have hanging in the balance.

"Of course I do." His eyes are sincere. I want to reach out, slip my fingers around the hand he has placed on the couch halfway between us. But I don't.

"I don't think you do." I curl one leg under myself, repositioning. "For some of us, this isn't just exposure. It isn't networking or a way to climb whatever ladder we're on. It's rent. It's a loan we can't get approved for because we don't have sufficient collateral. It's finally being able to open something of our own without begging for investors."

His gaze doesn't leave mine.

"If you lose," I continue, "you go back to a restaurant group with your last name on the building."

"I don't want that," he says quickly, afraid I'm not going to believe him. I do believe him, but what he wants is irrelevant to reality.

"You still have it, regardless."

Silence fills the space between us. His hand slides across the cushion, pinky brushing against my thigh in a featherlight touch.

"You're right."

"And then there's *us*. I don't know what parts of you were real and what parts were just an act. I don't know if I was someone you liked or someone who conveniently fit your end goal."

"You were inconvenient," he says abruptly, blue eyes flashing a range of emotions I don't have enough time to decipher.

"What?"

"You were inconvenient," he repeats. "And I still couldn't stay away from you. I came into this competition with a clear plan. Keep my head down. Win. Leave. I wasn't supposed to get distracted by someone whose laugh has taken up residence in my mind and has the nerve to challenge me in ways I haven't been challenged in years."

His admission releases tiny butterflies in my belly.

"I wasn't supposed to look for you after every bake or care if you made it or not. And I definitely wasn't supposed to let what happened between us happen. That wasn't part of the agreement."

The word agreement makes me flinch. It's so clinical.

"Chet Harrington can make me show up," he says, leaning closer to me and closing some of the distance between us. "But he has no control over what I do while I'm here."

I hold his gaze, emotion swelling behind my eyes.

"He can't make me stand between you and production when they push too hard. He can't make me stay in the practice kitchen with you, working on technique. Those things were all me."

I think back to all of our little moments in the kitchen. No one asked him to do those things, and quite honestly, it probably would have been better for him if he hadn't.

"You didn't have to do any of it," I whisper, knowingly.

"Exactly."

"Were they watching?"

He shrugs in response. "Couldn't tell you, I wasn't paying attention to them at that point."

Those dang butterflies break out into a synchronized flight pattern at the admission.

"I don't know how you did it, but you burrowed right under my skin. There's something about you that I can't quite place. I don't know how to explain it, you just... you make baking feel like it did when I was a kid." His gaze pins me in place, vulnerable and wide open and it catches me off guard.

He's letting me see into the spaces he doesn't show anyone else. Those oceans of bright blue and steely gray swallow me with their vulnerability. His words are gentle, quiet even, but my heart is racing.

He's letting me in.

"My grandparents had this tiny kitchen," he says, breaking eye contact to study his hands a little too closely. "Nothing fancy. No stainless steel or high-end gadgets. Just flour everywhere and music too loud. It was fun, you know? It wasn't about proving anything."

I smile despite my lingering hesitation. I know exactly what he means.

"My Gran taught me everything I know. She let me do all the measuring back then, and I'd end up spilling half of it across the counter most of the time."

He huffs out a laugh that almost sounds like relief. "Mine pretended not to notice when I did, too. Just quietly urged me on to the next ingredient while silently cleaning up after me."

The memories settle between us like a peace offering. Both of us lost in a different time, where everything felt simple.

"You remind me of that," he says. "Of why I started."

I look down at our hands, pinkies barely brushing. Wordlessly, I turn my hand over and slide my fingers under his palm until our hands fit together. He doesn't wait a fraction of a second before closing his fingers around mine, drawing my knuckles to his lips and kissing them gently.

The gesture warms something low in my belly, remembering all the places his lips have pressed against my skin. His eyes meet mine, and I wonder if he's thinking something similar when they crinkle at the sides, his smile growing.

"I don't care who your father is and I don't care about money." I clear my throat, needing him to hear my words for what they are. "I care that you tell me the truth. Even when it makes you look bad. Especially then."

"You have my word."

We sit in silence with our fingers twined together. The pad of his thumb traces patterns across the back of my hand. His gaze stays locked on the movement, like he's memorizing every sensation before leaning over and pressing his lips to my forehead.

"You know, you were a real jerk in the beginning," I say, pulling back to look up into his face.

"I was." He admits freely, a smirk tilting his lips.

"And pretty rude, actually."

"That sounds like me."

His eyes sparkle in the low light as I stand and pad to the kitchen, grabbing the bottle of wine I keep hidden in the pantry. If

Kara has taught me anything, it's to always have a secret stash on hand.

I glance over my shoulder, reaching into the cabinet for glasses. "If your dad was basically paying for a golden boy image in the edit, I deserve retro-pay for tolerating you when everyone else steered clear of your grumpy war path."

He barks a real laugh at that. "I'll talk to accounting."

The tension eases another notch as I set two glasses on the counter, uncorking the wine and facing him fully.

"I don't know how to do this." He pauses. "I don't know how to fix things like this. How do I prove to you that I don't give a damn about this show? That the only thing I care about is you. Say the word, and I'll drop out of the competition tomorrow if that's what it takes."

My brain stutters at his offer. "You'll what?"

"I'll throw it. I'll go home."

His eyes search mine, earnest and full of sincerity.

The thought of him leaving for Vancouver twists my chest, a tight coil of longing for someone who isn't gone yet.

"Don't you even think about it," I whisper, sliding a glass of wine across the counter toward him.

"If I want to be the best, I have to beat the best."

He nods, sipping his wine. "You're on."

Hours later, after Alex texts a disgruntled Joe that he can head back without him and we've eaten our weight in Chinese takeout, Alex stands in my kitchen with his sleeves rolled to his elbows, rinsing the dishes in my sink.

I can't help watching the way his arms flex, heat pooling between my thighs.

He catches me staring, brows lifting. He smirks my way, but there's no bite to it—just the easy confidence of a man who knows exactly how attractive he is.

I lift my wineglass for another sip.

This calm, domestic version of my grumpy storm cloud is a close second to the sight of him on his knees, blushing.

By Friday afternoon, my apartment smells like expensive espresso and the cinnamon rolls Alex insisted on baking before my shift as a peace offering for Kara, an attempt to win her over onto his side.

Little does he know, she was always on his side.

Something about Alex feels different now. The tension that used to live between his shoulders is gone, like telling the truth about who he is has allowed him to breathe again.

We leave just after my shift ends on Friday afternoon, my overnight bag tossed in the back of my car.

The highway stretches ahead of us, the city lights fading in the rearview mirror as Alex merges onto the interstate toward LA. I smile softly to myself, grateful that he insisted on driving. I get to be a passenger princess for once.

His hand finds mine on the center console.

Whatever happens in the tent this weekend, we're walking back into it together.

The semifinal is waiting.

And I've never felt more ready.

Alex

Chapter 23

Taylor's mascara runs in thin black streaks down her cheeks as she hugs her best friend in the house goodbye.

Pastry week was rough on all of us. While we've tackled pastry techniques earlier in the season, the Southern California heat made this week's challenges damn near impossible.

"Take care of our girl," RaeAnn whispers through tears when she pulls me into a hug next.

I wrap my arms around her shoulders and give her a quick squeeze. "Always."

Her laugh is wet and she swipes under her eyes before grabbing her bag. Taylor pulls RaeAnn into another hug, holding onto her for a second longer before letting go. Her shoulders slump like something inside her just gave way.

Watching RaeAnn walk out of the tent feels strange. Every week someone leaves, but this one hurts so much worse than the others. The house will feel emptier without her.

Taylor wipes at her cheeks again as she turns back toward the workstations. Her best attempt at composing herself.

Without thinking, I reach for her hand.

Her fingers slip into mine automatically, like they've been doing it for years instead of a handful of weeks. I squeeze once, grounding us both.

Swirling gold and green eyes crash into mine, and I offer a small smile, a soft place for my girl to land.

All I feel is relief.

I'm not happy RaeAnn had to go, but Taylor is still here. And that's what matters most to me right now. I don't want to imagine being here without her.

One more week and we're in the finale.

I'll spend that entire week fighting the urge to throw it and hand Taylor the win. She needs this more than anyone here. And every part of me would give it to her without hesitation.

The thought settles heavy in my chest as the crew resets the tent. Our hosts chatter quietly near the judges' table. Cameras move. Producers whisper. The familiar chaos of filming resumes as they pull Diane and Brandon for interviews.

Taylor sniffles quietly, eyes still red but she's breathing steadier now. Her thumb brushes over the back of my hand where our fingers are still laced together.

"It's just weird," she says. "Every week, the tent gets smaller. And I know I need to just be grateful that I'm still here, but I hate seeing everyone go."

I follow her gaze to the empty station RaeAnn stood behind just minutes ago. She's right. There are only four benches left now. Four bakers and one more elimination before the finale.

The semifinal is waiting for us and my only thoughts are about surviving the next two weeks without doing something reckless for the girl standing next to me.

Because if I'm not careful, I *will* break.

And the closer we get to the finale, the harder it's going to be to ignore my instincts and hand Taylor the win, even though she wants to earn it for herself.

The drive back to Cambria is quiet.

I know Taylor is still upset. She just needs time to unwind.

Somewhere near Santa Barbara, Taylor kicks off her shoes and folds one leg under herself in the passenger seat. The sun is already starting to dip, painting the sky in streaks of orange and soft pink as traffic thins the farther we get from the city.

Her hand drifts over the center console until her fingers bump mine.

They lace together without either of us looking and we drive the rest of the way like that.

The closer we get to her apartment, the more the static of the week fades. There's none of production's chaos here. Just the quiet hum of the road and the warmth of a beautiful girl's hand in mine.

By the time we pull into her parking lot, the tension that usually lives in my shoulders has disappeared entirely.

Taylor glances over at me as I cut the engine. "You realize you're stuck here for five days, right?"

"I'm aware."

"You're going to get bored. I have to work."

I huff out a quiet laugh. "I've seen how messy your kitchen is, Taylor. There's plenty there to keep me busy."

She rolls her eyes, but the corner of her mouth lifts.

Inside, her apartment welcomes us home. And it does feel like home, though I suspect that has more to do with the way we keep drifting toward each other every chance we get.

The week settles into a rhythm faster than I expect.

Mornings start with coffee strong enough to wake the dead and Taylor leaning against the counter in one of my borrowed T-shirts while she scrolls through recipe notes on her phone.

Afternoons disappear in a haze of flour and butter.

Her kitchen isn't built for two bakers, but we make it work. If I'm honest, I don't mind the tight space.

It gives me the perfect excuse to brush against her. A light graze of her hip. A gentle kiss pressed to the delicate spot where her neck meets her shoulder.

Her kitchen might actually be my favorite place to work.

Bowls crowd the counter while the mixer groans through batch after batch of practice recipes. At one point we manage to coat the floor in powdered sugar after a poorly timed bump of my elbow.

Taylor laughs so hard she has to brace herself against the fridge.

I spend the next ten minutes cleaning it up while she sits on the counter swinging her legs and offering deeply unhelpful commentary.

"You missed a spot."

"I absolutely did not."

"Right there by your foot."

I glare up at her.

She grins, eyes sparkling and I snap the towel at her legs in retaliation.

Evenings slide into something easy.

Takeout containers pile up on the coffee table while we trade bites and argue about technique. Sometimes we watch old episodes of other baking shows and critique the bakers as if we aren't going to be in that same position in a few days.

Sometimes we don't turn the TV on at all, and I spend my time pulling my name from Taylor's lips. She happily reciprocates, and I'm proud to say I haven't embarrassed myself again the way I did the first time I had my mouth between her thighs.

In the middle of the week, Kara stops by after their shift.

She doesn't announce herself so much as she appears—leaning in the doorway first, then stepping fully inside like she's taking inventory of the place.

Her gaze moves over me in careful assessment. Arms crossed, weight settled against the counter, she tilts her head slightly as if she's trying to decide if I fit into her understanding of Taylor's world.

"You're taller than I expected," she says at last.

I blink, caught off guard. "That's your first impression?"

Behind her, Taylor lets out a quiet, strangled laugh before burying her face in her hands, shoulders shaking.

Kara doesn't respond to either of us right away. She just keeps looking at me, like she's still doesn't know what to make of me.

I don't know what she sees, but I hold her gaze anyway.

By the time she leaves an hour later, the edges between us have softened. Her expression shifts from scrutiny to understanding as she steps toward the door, and I get the sense I've passed whatever test she walked in here with.

Taylor watches her go, then turns back to me, lifting a hand to pat my chest once.

"Not bad," she murmurs.

I huff a quiet laugh, but there's something satisfying in the way the room feels after. Like I've been officially accepted into Taylor's inner circle.

The rest of the week passes faster than I want it to.

That alone surprises me because I'm not just getting through it—I'm enjoying it. Way more than I ever expected to. There's an ease to being here with Taylor that has me daydreaming about the future like a damn teenager.

I can picture it, almost too clearly.

The same kitchen in the morning light. The same worn counter, the same soft routine of it all. Taylor standing barefoot by the stove, her focus split between whatever she's working on and whatever she's thinking about. Me lingering close enough to pull her attention away when I want it.

It feels so possible, and maybe that's the problem because the truth is, once the show is over, I have to go back home to Vancouver

Friday night comes sooner than it should, and just like that, we're packing our things back into her car. We don't say much as we settle in.

The drive back to Los Angeles stretches out in front of us, the road thinning as the light fades. Somewhere along the coast, the air shifts to the kind of quiet that people write songs about.

Taylor leans her head against the window, watching the world blur past in streaks of shadow and light. Her fingers find mine without looking, tracing slow, absent circles over my hand.

Ahead of us, the city waits in the dark, the tent somewhere beyond its edges. One more elimination.

And then the finale.

The four of us remaining contestants stand shoulder to shoulder at the front of the tent, hands clasped in front of our aprons, while the judges shuffle their notes. The cameras hum softly around us, red lights glowing like tiny watchful eyes.

This part never gets easier.

My shoulder brushes Taylor's. Her arm is warm against mine, but the tension in her posture is impossible to miss. I glance sideways just long enough to see her staring straight ahead at the judges' table, lips pressed together.

Across from us, Brandon stands with the same calm confidence he's carried all season. Like he already knows how this ends.

Maybe he does.

All three challenges this weekend were difficult, and the quiet in the house made it harder yet. Diane took the signature with a personal twist on a classic soufflé, while I came first in the technical thanks to some intricate sugar work.

Garrett clears his throat, drawing our attention back to the front. He stands and pulls out Magnolia's chair as she rises. Theo and Judy wait off to the side, waiting to hear the verdict.

"Bakers," Magnolia announces, folding her hands together. "This was an incredibly difficult semifinal. You were asked to create a laminated pastry showpiece featuring a baked fruit component and at least two distinct textures."

My mouth goes dry.

Breathing feels optional right now. No matter how hard I try to focus, my attention keeps drifting back to Taylor, standing just out of the corner of my eye.

"Overall," Garrett adds with a rare, genuine smile. "The standard was exceptionally high. You should be proud of yourselves."

Beside me, Taylor shifts her weight. Our pinkies brush for half a second. I don't know if she means to do it, or if her body subconsciously reaches for me like mind does to her.

I want to grab her hand, but I hold back.

"The first baker advancing to the finale is…"

The pause stretches, long enough to make my pulse pound. No one breathes.

With four of us left and three spots available, the odds feel better than they have all season. But for one of us, this is the end.

And we're so close it almost hurts.

"…Diane."

Diane gasps, both hands flying to her mouth before she breaks into applause along with the rest of us. She laughs through tears as Magnolia pulls her into a hug, Garrett shaking her hand with pride.

I clap with everyone else, smiling as she wipes at her face.

But my chest tightens anyway.

That leaves three of us.

Garrett and Magnolia exchange a long look. She gives the smallest nod, and he looks down at his card again.

"The second baker joining Diane in the finale is…"

Another dramatic pause. My heart is already hammering.

"…Alex."

For a second, I don't move. I just stare at him, like maybe I heard it wrong. Then the tent explodes into applause and relief hits all at once. I didn't feel certain today—none of us did—but hearing it out loud loosens the knot in my chest.

Diane wraps an arm around my shoulders, and Judy claps me on the back. I manage an awkward laugh as the judges step forward, shaking my hand.

But my eyes are already searching.

Taylor is beaming.

Her eyes are bright, a little glassy, but there's something genuine in her expression—like she's truly happy for me.

"Congrats," she mouths.

This isn't how I wanted this to happen because now it's down to just her and Brandon for the final spot.

My heart drops as I take in Taylor's defeated stance. It's subtle, but I know her better than anyone else. She's already preparing for the worst.

When they step forward, the space between us feels larger than it should, even though she's only a few steps away.

She glances at me and I give her what I hope is a reassuring nod. Inside, everything twists tight. Brandon is a professional. Everyone knows it. We run in the same circles. He knows my family, for God's sake.

His bakes have been flawless all season, and there's no world where that doesn't matter.

The judges turn to Taylor first.

"Taylor," Garrett begins gently. "Your showstopper today was incredibly creative."

She nods once, fidgeting with the tie on her apron.

"The flavor combination of peach and basil was unexpected, but it worked beautifully," Magnolia adds. "The filling was balanced, and the sweetness wasn't overpowering."

"However, your lamination was slightly uneven in places, which gave us a few dense layers in the center." Garrett interjects, eyeing Magnolia.

Taylor nods again.

"Overall, though," Magnolia says, raising her voice and arching an eyebrow at Garrett. "A delicious bake. Very impressive for this stage of the competition."

I let out a slow breath I didn't realize I was holding, relief loosening in my chest as I watch Taylor take in their words. Her expression gives nothing away.

That was good—not perfect, but good.

Hopefully good enough to stay one more week.

Then the judges turn to Brandon.

"Brandon," Garrett starts, lifting his pastry with obvious admiration, he takes another bite and chews slowly. "Technically speaking, this is one of the most impressive bakes we've seen all season."

My stomach drops.

Taylor's shoulders dip slightly, but she holds her head high. There's a slight quiver of her lower lip, imperceptible to anyone not watching her as closely as I am.

"The lamination is textbook," Magnolia agrees, but her voice lacks its usual warmth. "Perfect layers, crisp exterior, beautiful rise."

Brandon gives a small, confident nod.

"The flavor is excellent," Garrett adds. "Your orange crème filling is silky smooth. A real accomplishment."

Beside me, Diane mutters, "Wow."

"But Brandon…"

Garrett sets the pastry down carefully, his tone shifting—and my head snaps up.

"There's a real problem here."

Brandon frowns at the judges. "Sorry?"

Magnolia steps forward, gesturing to the pastry. "The challenge specifically required a laminated pastry that incorporated a fruit component *into the pastry structure itself*."

Brandon's brow furrows, still not understanding

"You used orange *extract* in the filling. That isn't the same as a baked fruit component."

A thick blanket of silence drops over the tent.

Brandon straightens. "But the bake itself was perfect."

"No one is disputing that. Technically, it was exceptional." Garrett says matter-of-factly.

Brandon folds his arms, waiting for the judges to go on.

"That being said, the instructions were very clear. The fruit element needed to be incorporated as an actual fruit inclusion, not just a flavor."

The way Garrett says the words and glowers over his shoulder at Magnolia, it's clear the decision wasn't unanimous.

"Wait—are you serious?"

My eyes snap to Taylor.

She's completely still. Watching. Processing.

"Because that requirement wasn't met," Magnolia's voice comes out steady, "you didn't fully complete the challenge."

Brandon stares at the table, disbelief clouding his features before he speaks, "So what does that mean?"

There's a tense moment where Garrett holds Magnolia's gaze. Finally, he exhales and delivers the final blow.

"It means that despite the quality of your bake, we can't advance you to the finale."

For a second, no one moves. Then it hits—*holy shit*.

My hands fly to my face, holding back the reaction that wants to explode out of me.

Taylor just made the finale.

"Taylor," Magnolia says, smiling. "Congratulations, you are advancing to the finale."

Her mouth falls open, gaze bouncing around to all of our faces with a manic glint flaring behind her eyes.

"What?"

It breaks out of her in a sharp, disbelieving laugh before she dissolves into tears. And something in my chest cracks wide open watching her.

I cross the distance between us before I even think about it, pulling Taylor into my arms, whispering my congratulations, and twirling her around.

The cameras are watching, but I couldn't care less.

Let them see.

Taylor making it to the finale is all that matters.

When I set her back on her feet, her glassy eyes find mine. Our chests are still heaving, but we're laughing into the space between us, breathless and a little unsteady.

I cock an eyebrow, a silent question.

She nods once.

And then I kiss her.

Watermelon lip gloss and something unmistakably Taylor flood my senses. Somewhere behind us, there's applause, laughter, and a few soft, knowing *awws*, but it all blurs into the background, reduced to the way her fingers clutch the front of my apron and the breathless laugh she lets out against my mouth.

For one perfect moment, nothing else exists.

Next week, one of us is going to win this whole damn thing. And for the first time since I walked into this tent, I'm not sure which outcome scares me more.

Taylor

Chapter 24

Walking behind Diane, hand in hand with Alex, is surreal. And not in a pretty, aesthetic kind of way. It's more of a *what is my life right now* kind of vibe. Us three being in the finale still hasn't fully settled in.

The front door swings open before I can brace myself against the deafening silence waiting to swallow us whole.

For half a second, I linger at the threshold, caught in place as the house unfolds exactly as it did that first week—loud and crowded, voices spilling through the entryway, bodies everywhere.

It doesn't make any sense.

"Surprise!"

The chorus of shouts erupts from every corner of the living room, and suddenly, people are rushing toward us. Familiar faces I haven't seen in days, some of them weeks. The energy hits me like stepping into sunlight after a long winter. Bright and overwhelming in the best way.

I barely have time to breathe before RaeAnn barrels into me. "Holy shit, you made it!"

Her arms wrap around me so tightly I nearly lose my balance. I hug her back just as fiercely, the sadness that's been coiled in my chest since her elimination finally loosens like a knot coming undone.

"I missed you," I say into her hair.

"You better have."

When she pulls back, her eyes flick past me toward Alex and then back again, a slow grin spreading across her face as she connects our very obvious dots.

"Oh my God," she whispers. "It's really happening, huh?"

"I have so much to tell you," I say quickly, keeping my voice barely above a whisper, because I absolutely cannot have this conversation with an audience. The mere thought of someone overhearing all the details has heat creeping up my neck.

RaeAnn snorts a laugh.

Before she can interrogate me further, Ace claps his hands loud enough to cut through the chatter.

"Alright, alright," he announces, stepping into the center of the room like a self-appointed master of ceremonies. "First, cheers to the final three. You all are the GOATS!"

Everyone raises their drinks toward us.

After taking a gulp from his cup, Ace gestures toward the back doors. "It's warm outside. Let's take this party to the pool and celebrate in true LA fashion!"

That's all the encouragement the group needs.

Within seconds, the energy shifts, the house erupting into movement as people head in different directions to refill drinks, change into swimwear, or snag one of the few lounge chairs beside the pool.

Jasper turns some music on, and suddenly the whole place feels like it's remembering how to be fun again. Brandon is already arguing with Chloe about who makes the best margarita, which honestly feels more on brand now than ever before.

I hang back for a moment, leaning against the archway near the foyer with a soft smile. It's strange seeing everyone again like this, outside the pressure cooker of eliminations and challenges. Like the house has reverted to some earlier version of itself, before alliances and goodbyes started carving holes into it.

After I change, I step out onto the patio just as laughter erupts near the pool. With a towel wrapped around me, I slide next to RaeAnn on the lounger she was able to claim. My body settles, but my brain is still playing catch up.

My gaze immediately searches for Alex.

He's already found a spot at the edge of the pool with Julian, feet dipped in the water. His eyes meet mine with a smirk and a wink before he turns his attention back to his cousin.

The evening air is still warm, carrying the faint scent of chlorine from the pool. String lights glow overhead, reflecting in the water in long, wavering lines.

Closing my eyes, I nestle into RaeAnn's side as she tells me all about her kids' newest shenanigans.

This is exactly what I needed. A night that is simply about being present with people I absolutely adore.

I'm halfway through that thought when Lila appears beside Alex.

I don't know where she came from. One minute she's near the patio railing talking to Ace, and the next she's there—leaning casually against his shoulder like she's done it a hundred times. Which is exactly the problem.

He shifts over, subtly creating space that she immediately takes back like it belongs to her. Her laugh carries across the pool, and my eyes narrow on instinct.

"You know," she says, tilting her head up at him, voice light and way too confident. "Now that I'm off the show, things are a lot less complicated."

She isn't... flirting with him right in front of me, right?

Alex's posture stiffens, eyes darting to mine.

She traces the rim of his drink with one finger, smiling like this is a completely normal interaction. "There's no ulterior motive this time. Seems like a waste not to finally have some fun."

Something sharp twists in my stomach.

Around them, a few people have gone suspiciously quiet. Alex and I haven't explicitly announced that we're together, but it's undeniable if you pay attention. Especially after today.

Lila's gaze flicks toward me briefly before returning to Alex, the corner of her mouth lifting. Oh, she knows exactly what she's doing. This is just another performance for the cameras.

For a second, I consider pretending I didn't hear it.

Week-One Taylor might have.

Week-One Taylor would've laughed it off, focused on her own conversation, and convinced herself Alex was a big boy that could handle himself.

But I'm not Week-One Taylor anymore. I've changed over these last few weeks, and I'm done letting people walk all over me. Just because I'm nice doesn't mean I'm weak.

Finale-Taylor isn't going to stand idly by while someone intentionally antagonizes her. If she wants to invite me into some drama, then fine. I'll accept and meet her there.

My feet move before I can second-guess what I'm doing.

"He's not interested."

The words leave my mouth calmly, almost conversationally. And I'm proud because they're in sharp contrast to the fire burning in my chest.

Lila turns to me slowly and arches one eyebrow in complete disbelief that I just interrupted her moment with Alex.

"Oh yeah? Did he tell you that?"

I hold her gaze, unflinching. "He didn't have to."

Alex stands and immediately wraps an arm around my shoulders, choosing to present a united front against Lila.

"She's right," he confirms. "And I've already told you I'm not interested. I'm not going to be as nice about it next time."

Satisfaction blooms in my chest and I give her a sweet smile as I lean into Alex's side. His body is warm against my skin.

Lila studies both of us for another moment before lifting her hands in mock surrender. "Relax, just trying to have some fun."

"Try someone else," RaeAnn quips from behind me.

A ripple of laughter breaks the tension as Lila saunters off back toward Ace, the moment dissolving as quickly as it formed.

Jasper cannonballs into the pool, sending a wave sloshing against the edge. Conversations resume. Music fills the space again. And gradually, the crowd shifts and scatters into smaller groups.

Lost in thought, by the time I realize how quiet it's gotten, the patio is completely empty. Even Alex and Julian have wandered off, probably to refill their drinks.

I'm sitting on the edge of the pool with my feet in the water, absently kicking slow circles when a familiar figure appears beside me.

Alex lowers himself onto the concrete with a soft grunt.

For a while, neither of us says anything.

The water glows faintly blue under the lights, rippling around our ankles. The party carries on, fragments of laughter carrying faintly from inside the house behind us. Here, though, it's quieter. Like the night is giving us a small, temporary reprieve.

Alex stretches his legs out, leaning back on his hands beside me. Close enough that I can feel the warmth of him even through the cooling air. "You handled that pretty well back there."

I glance over at him. "Handled what?"

He turns his head toward me, that familiar crooked smile tugging at his mouth. "Lila."

"She was being annoying." I shrug, aiming for casual, but my eyes drift back to the water like it suddenly needs my full attention.

"Mhm…" he hums, unconvinced, though his gaze stays on me. "You were jealous."

Jealous isn't the word I'd use. Not exactly.

But something tight and sharp had flickered in my chest when I saw the way Lila looked at him. It was like she was trying to climb inside a story that didn't belong to her.

I press my lips together. "I was not."

"You absolutely were." He bumps his shoulder into mine, the contact easy, familiar.

I roll my eyes, but there's no heat behind it. "You're imagining things."

"Am I?" he asks, amused, like he enjoys the question more than the answer. Probably because he already knows the answer.

I don't respond. Just bump him back.

He huffs out a quiet laugh.

"You know," he says, voice turning thoughtful, "I actually kinda like it when you get territorial like that."

Heat rushes up my neck.

"That little 'he's not interested' moment?" His smile tilts, voice dipping. "I loved every second of it."

"Oh, shut up." I laugh, shoving him.

Hard enough to knock him off balance.

Alex lets out a surprised yelp as he tips forward, splashing into the pool with a dramatic crash of water that sends ripples sloshing against the concrete. I gasp as the water soaks my legs, then immediately grin, watching as he resurfaces, pushing wet hair back from his face.

"Worth it?" I call down to him, arms crossed, thoroughly pleased with myself.

He wipes water from his eyes, then looks up at me with a slow, knowing smile. "Oh, absolutely."

Uh-oh.

He starts toward me, unhurried, water shifting around his shoulders as he closes the distance. I barely have time to move before he reaches out.

"Alex—"

His hand closes around my wrist and with one firm tug, the edge vanishes from beneath me.

Cold water rushes over me, stealing the breath from my lungs as I go under, the world turning into a blur of bubbles and blue light. When I break the surface, sputtering and laughing, he's already directly in front of me, watching as I blink the water from my eyes.

Droplets cling to his lashes, catching in the glow of the pool lights. His smile softens at the edges, less teasing now.

I don't think about it. I just move.

Or maybe he does.

Our lips meet in a kiss that starts gentle and almost questioning. Both of us holding back in case the other wants to pull away because of where we are.

Neither of us does.

His hand slides to the small of my back, anchoring me as the space between us all but disappears, and the kiss deepens—tentative at first, then with a little more certainty, like something we've been circling finally settles into place.

"Taylor..." he murmurs against my mouth, breath warm, voice rougher now. "If we keep going..."

His forehead rests against mine, his grip tightening on my hips. "...we're not stopping."

My pulse thrums in my ears.

"Good," I whisper, because there's nothing to hide anymore. Everyone already knows about us, and I'm done pretending when it comes to him.

His laugh is quiet, a little disbelieving, before his mouth finds mine again and the world beyond the pool disappears.

Warm hands glide up my back, pulling me closer until my body presses fully into his, heat meeting heat, breath catching as he lifts me with an ease that pulls a small, startled sound from my lips.

Instinct takes over and I wrap my legs around his waist.

The shift pulls me higher, closer, every point of contact suddenly more intense. My fingers find the damp hair at the nape of his neck, tugging lightly, and the deep rumble he makes in response sends a shiver racing through me.

Water trails down my skin, cool against the heat building everywhere he touches.

The rough edge of the pool drags against my shoulder blades as he moves us forward, gently pinning me between him and the tile. His hips press into mine, and the friction draws a quiet, breathless gasp from me.

I nip at his lower lip in a playful tug.

He groans into my mouth, rough and unguarded.

When we break apart, he takes a second to look at me. His eyes are darker now, heavy-lidded, like he's trying to hold onto control and failing.

"Alex…" I breathe his name the way he whispered mine moments ago. I lean in, tracing my mouth along his throat, feeling his pulse jump beneath my lips. His chest rises, brushing against mine and a shudder runs through him when my teeth graze the edge of his ear.

The way his body responds to my touch makes me braver than I've been in my entire life. My hand slips between us, searching for him, brushing with my fingertips in gentle strokes. His reaction is an immediate sound of surrender against my hair.

"Can we?" My voice comes out low, unsteady in a way that surprises me. "I'm safe. I'm—"

"I'm safe too," he says, voice rough but certain.

His gaze holds mine, as short, shallow breaths leave me and we linger there, suspended in the space between wanting and choosing.

"Are you sure?" he asks, unmoving while he waits.

There's not a single doubt in my mind.

I answer with a look, with the way my hands slide up his arms, with the way I close the distance between us again.

My fingers find the ties at my hips.

The rest happens quickly, neither of us wanting to risk the moment disappearing. Our bathing suits end up tossed in a heap at the side of the pool, then he's kissing me again.

This time it's deeper like he's grounding himself in the moment. Like he's making a decision he knows he can't take back.

When he pulls back, his forehead rests against mine. He murmurs low against my mouth, "Tell me if anything feels wrong."

"It won't." I shake my head, trembling.

A quiet, almost disbelieving sound leaves him before his mouth finds mine again.

And then there's no more thinking, only feeling. Only him.

He presses me back against the tile, the cool surface a sharp contrast to the heat that's between us. My breath catches as I feel him there, the anticipation alone enough to make my body react.

I roll my hips, chasing him, needing more.

A rough chuckle slips from his mouth as it brushes mine.

"Patience, beautiful."

"I'm done waiting," I whisper, tightening my legs around him, pulling him closer in a way that leaves no room for hesitation. That's all it takes to make him move.

The shift between us steals the air from my lungs, my head tipping back as a broken sound escapes me, my fingers tightening on his shoulders to hold myself steady.

"Fuck..." he breathes against my skin, the word ragged and wrecked as he pushes further into me.

The world narrows to sensation. To the way he moves against me with deep, intentional strokes like he's letting himself go piece by piece. Water laps around us, the rhythm of our bodies pulling me under in slow, rising waves.

My hips keep pace with his, desperate as the tension winds tighter and tighter, demanding release deep in my center.

I'm so full. So overwhelmingly full.

"Alex..." His name falls from my lips like a plea, like a warning. "Don't—don't stop."

"I'm not, baby. Not a chance." he murmurs against the sensitive skin behind my ear.

His forehead presses to mine, his breathing uneven now, like he's losing whatever control he was holding onto. Every movement sends another rush of heat through me, sharper, stronger, until I can't focus on anything else.

"I'm—" My voice breaks, and I cling to him as the tension crests, teetering on the edge.

"That's it," he whispers, the words coaxing me through it and unraveling me all at once. "I've got you, baby. Come for me."

And I do.

The last thread snaps, and everything rushes through me at once, overwhelming and all-consuming, pulling a breathless moan from my chest. I'm clutching Alex to me, fingers tangle in his hair as I pant, gasp after gasp, and ride out the wave of pleasure with nowhere else to go.

His release hits hard, grip tightening as shuddered breaths turn uneven against my skin and he follows me over the edge.

"Fuckkk…" The words break from him on a groan.

For a moment, neither of us moves, chests rising and falling together as the water laps softly around us.

"Jesus…" he murmurs, almost to himself. "That was…"

I let out a quiet, shaky laugh, resting my forehead briefly against his shoulder. "Yeah… it was."

Alex draws me in, hugging me close for a second longer than I expect, like he's not quite ready to let me go. Then he sets me back on my feet and reaches for the edge of the pool, pulling himself out with in one easy motion.

Water streams down his shoulders as he shakes his hair out, crossing to one of the lounge chairs and grabbing a towel, wrapping it loosely around his waist.

He comes back to me with another, holding it open as I climb out, shielding me from view.

"Next weekend's going to be brutal," I say with a sigh as he wraps the towel around me.

His hands linger at my arms, rubbing warmth back into my skin. I hold his gaze, letting myself stay in this moment just a little longer.

"You don't sound worried."

"Oh, I am." A crooked smirk tugs at his mouth. "I'm just pretending I'm not."

I laugh but the moment between us doesn't feel light anymore. It feels heavy with everything neither of us says out loud.

We both made it into the finale.

Only one of us can win, and I really need it to be me. Which means Alex has to lose.

Alex

Chapter 25

When I step up onto the freshly mowed grass leading to the tent, the details of production are in full swing. Patriotic bunting flutter from the fences with string lights crisscrossing overhead, and long banquet tables are lined with chairs for family and friends.

A small platform stage waits at the far end, cameras set and cables snaking across the lawn, a silent reminder of tomorrow's finale ceremony. The aroma of cut grass tangles with the smell of the tent as it's being steamed to perfection.

The air hums with the low buzz of generators and the distant voices of crew members moving props and equipment.

Garrett is already there, surveying the space with that calm, measured expression of his. Magnolia stands nearby, arms crossed, eyes scanning the horizon where the decorations catch the early light. Theo and Judy step onto the platform, arms linked, smiling wide.

"Finale day," Garrett says directly into the camera, but there's a weight to it that makes me pause.

"Three bakers left." Magnolia lets a small smile tug at her lips.

Theo waves a hand toward the lawn, voice rising so it carries across the quiet morning. "By tomorrow evening, this space will be full of friends, family, and all of our previous contestants."

"That's right, Theo." Judy beams. "And one of our final three will be dubbed *America's Next Great Baker*!"

I nod, taking it all in, committing the moment to memory as they finish their promo shot. The calm before the storm—the moment before all hell breaks loose.

Right before we enter the tent, my hand shoots out, catching Taylor by the wrist and pulling her toward me. She turns, a question forming on her lips, but before she can say anything, I brush my mouth against hers.

"Good luck," I whisper with a wink.

Her cheeks turn the most delicious shade of pink.

I saunter into the tent first, allowing the cameras to get my entrance shot and move to my station. Taylor follows immediately behind, eyes wide with nerves and excitement.

Diane is already at her station, quietly unfolding her sketchpad before tying her apron tight around her waist. She notices my gaze, squints playfully, and points two fingers from her eyes to me in the universal "I'm watching you" move. Then her eyes crinkle at the edges, and she winks.

Fucking Diane.

I shake my head, chuckling to myself.

The final challenge is here and it's go time.

Taylor gives my hand a quick squeeze as she passes, then she's gone. Off to her own station while we wait for the judges and hosts to do the official introduction to the challenge.

"For your final challenge, you'll create the ultimate showstopper cake," Garrett explains, the authority in his voice carrying above the buzz of the tent.

"A centerpiece worthy of a national celebration," Magnolia adds, hands clasped in front of her and eyes soft but serious.

Judy gestures toward the tent opening. "Tomorrow, this lawn will be filled with guests. Friends, family, viewers, and previous contestants will all be here to cheer you on!"

"But don't get too hung up on that, bakers. Because this is the finale, and the stakes have never been higher." Theo chimes in, tone dry as ever.

"You have two days to create a cake that represents everything you've learned in this competition," Garrett concludes.

Magnolia extends her hands, palms facing up, as she elaborates on Garrett's instructions. "Your cake needs to show us who you are as a baker. Let us see your creativity. Your technical mastery. Nothing less than your absolute best will do."

"Over the next two days, you can use your time however you see fit," Judy explains. "So, plan out how to best bring your ideas to life. Handle any prep, decorations, or long-setting items today, because tomorrow, you will bake in the tent for the final time."

I pull out my sketchbook, the pencil in my hand hovering over the clean page. I think of every lesson Garrett and Magnolia have given me. Of what I've learned from Taylor about tapping back into the joy of baking.

Without thinking, the design starts to flow out of me, the pencil moving in quick bursts. I make little notes in the margins: 'multiple tier heights', 'stability rods?', 'flavors that contrast but complement'.

Garrett steps toward me, crouching to get a better look at my draft. He stands there wordlessly, watching me work, as if he's weighing his words carefully.

The show's toughest critic clears his throat.

I flick my eyes up to meet his stare.

"Finales aren't about showing everything you know. We've already seen how incredibly skilled you are. There's no doubt about it. But finales are about rising to an old challenge in a new way. Show us *exactly* who you are, in here." He taps two fingers against my chest above my heart.

I nod, trying to imprint the words in my head. *Exactly who I am*. Not perfect, not flashy, *just Alex*.

Closing my eyes, I think about what makes me, well... me.

Not my last name. Not the experts I've trained beneath or the kitchens I've commanded. Not what my father demands of me.

My mind conjures up a memory, standing outside my house back in Vancouver. It's so alive and real that I can feel the crisp mountain air against my skin. Smell the pine and damp woods in the fog. Hear the faint rush of a creek behind the house. I crumple the page I started with, tossing the paper ball into the trash at the end of my station.

It was all wrong. I can do better.

That sketch is what's expected of me, not who I am.

After a moment to gather my thoughts, I start to sketch out a design that pays homage to my home. Where I don't have to perform for anybody, and am just wholly myself. Little doodles of mountains tucked behind cascading tiers, a thin layer of maple icing to represent the forest floor, flourishes that hint at the misty mornings I grew up in.

"Good man," Garrett claps a hand on my shoulder, squeezing, before he heads back to the front of the tent.

I smile to myself. This is going to be the best damn cake I've ever made.

While I'm plotting the tiered supports and sketching delicate piping, I notice Magnolia hovering beside Taylor, a quiet conversation that I can only catch in fragments.

"Bake the cake that made you fall in love with baking," Magnolia says softly. "That's what will make *us* fall in love with *you*."

Taylor's shoulders rise on a deep inhale, then she relaxes into a small smile. Magnolia's words—her encouragement and reassurance—feel tangible, and I can see Taylor's relief across the tent.

Ahead of us, Diane is methodically moving back and forth across her station, checking her sketchbook, then measuring out ingredients I can't name from here.

I can't help but notice the judges hovering a little longer around her station, leaning in to inspect sketches, discussing angles quietly among themselves.

My chest tightens with an unfamiliar twinge—*panic?*

Diane has been a quiet frontrunner this entire season; her designs are always ambitious, elegant, and somehow effortlessly perfect. And her flavors? I don't think she's ever been criticized on that front either.

I roll my shoulders, cracking my neck in the process, and focus back on my own task at hand.

By mid-afternoon, our prep work is done for the day. We've each pre-baked components, set decorations, and arranged the more delicate elements that need to cure or settle. The tent is quieter now without appliances whirring, but the aroma of caramelized sugar and buttery cake still lingers like a faint perfume.

All three of us are quietly wiping flour from our hands, re-checking our notes, or wiping down our equipment when production calls for our final pre-finale interviews.

When we exit the tent, we see three stools lined up next to one another with the festivity preparations set as the backdrop. Guests' chairs are arranged in neat rows, napkins folded in crisp triangles on the tables, bunting now fluttering gently in the evening breeze.

"Bakers, please." Hal, the executive producer who never shows his face on set, gestures with a sweep of his hand. "With this being the finale, we thought a group interview would round the moment out nicely."

Annoyance claws at the back of my throat. I still don't like the idea of giving Hal anything more than the bare minimum. God knows he doesn't deserve it, but we're so close to the end, I give in and follow Diane and Taylor to the stools, taking the one furthest to the right.

"Okay, let's make this short and sweet. This is mostly for soundbites, understand? Diane, you're up first. How does it feel to be in the final three?"

Diane takes a moment, then smiles, serene and composed, before speaking. "This is what I came here to do." Her Boston-lilted voice is steady. "I didn't make it this far to lose."

"Great!" Hal clasps his hands behind his back. "Taylor?"

Taylor straightens, her hands fidgeting as she speaks. Her hazel eyes catch the light as she stares directly into the camera. "I never imagined I'd make it this far. Winning would mean *everything*."

I linger without speaking, knowing it's my turn to answer, but I'm absorbing fragments of her words. I catch the slight tremor in her voice, the unspoken mix of nerves and excitement.

The sight of her—vulnerable and open—hits like a punch to the chest, and my heart clenches on impact. I know the stakes feel different to each of us, but her sincerity cuts straight through the noise.

Hal's exasperated sigh has my head snapping up.

"How does it feel to be in the final three?"

"Like the longest ten weeks of my life," I say, forcing a smile that lands closer to a grimace.

"And what would winning mean to you?"

I pause, weighing the answer. My eyes rove over my competition, then roll back to the camera. "It would be incredible, but I'm not the only one here who deserves it."

Hal claps once, nodding in approval, and returns to his mumbled conversation with the cameraman. When he realizes we're still sitting here waiting for direction, he waves an apathetic hand in dismissal.

Taylor reaches for my hand, tucking her body in close to mine as we walk back toward the tent's opening. Joe cuts across our path, pausing with his clipboard in hand. "Anyone planning to stay longer? Or are we calling it for today?"

"I'm ready to call it," I mutter, stretching my shoulders.

"Yeah, I'm good to head back to the house, too." Diane shrugs, nonchalant. "Whatever happens now, happens."

I can't match her ease, and judging by the way Taylor keeps shifting her weight back and forth, neither can she. I try to imagine letting the tension drain and just being good with whatever happens tomorrow, but I'm too keyed up.

I glance around one last time, at the near-complete decorations glinting in the early evening light. Crew members move to test the lights along the bunting, the banquet tables now lined with white plates, sparkling glassware catching the last of the sun. A flag flutters lazily against the backdrop of a clear sky, and the faint scent of barbecue smoke drifts from a prep station near the edge of the lawn.

Tomorrow, this lawn will be full of supportive faces as one of us wins the entire competition. Whoever it is will be standing in the center of it all with a gaudy platinum rolling pin raised overhead.

A deep breath fills my chest. The anticipation, the nervous excitement, the stakes—it all courses through me like electricity. And somehow, amid the tension, despite being forced to be here, I'm looking forward to completing the challenge. I'm about to pour everything I am into one cake.

Tomorrow, it all comes together.

Tomorrow, someone wins.

Chapter 26

Our beloved production crew must have worked all night to accomplish the mind-blowingly patriotic overhaul of the *America's Next Great Baker* lawn while we were gone.

That's literally the only explanation.

When we left last night, they had set up tables, chairs, and decorations that felt more like a barbecue than anything else.

But this is next-level.

Every table on the lawn is decorated with red, white, and blue flower centerpieces, each topped with tiny Uncle Sam hats and massive confetti balloons tethered by shiny metallic weights with tassels that shimmer in the breeze.

Jumbo chess and Jenga games have been set up for guests, along with cornhole, ladder ball, and a bubble station. Bright red and blue bounce houses—and even an obstacle course with a water slide—sit at the far end of the lawn.

"Can you believe they did all this?" I turn, breathlessly taking it all in. It immediately takes me back to time spent at Cambria's summer festival. Mom and Gran would take me and my brother every year before money got too tight and relationships too complicated.

"It's the finale," Diane answers simply. "Looks like they take the idea of 'go big or go home' seriously."

Alex leans closer to me as we walk toward the tent.

"Bet I can beat you at the obstacle course later." He pulls his bottom lip between his teeth, eyes glinting with challenge.

"Hmmm... What do I get when I win?" I hum, playfully tapping a finger against my lips in thought.

Alex dips his head, lips brushing my ear. "I have a couple of ideas."

He nuzzles briefly into my hair before we separate for our stations. When he pulls back, that lopsided smirk is waiting for me.

His expression suggests those ideas are definitely not obstacle-course related. Immediately, heat kisses my cheeks, and I press my cool hands against them as I slide into my apron.

Garrett and Magnolia step to the front of the tent while Theo and Judy fall into place beside them. All four are dressed in crisp, pristine tuxedos. Garrett dons deep blue, Magnolia elegant white, Judy sparkles in red, and Theo is impossible to miss in a sequined U.S. flag pattern. Beyond the open tent flaps, the lawn buzzes with conversation as guests settle into their seats, the soft clink of glasses and distant laughter drifting in on the breeze.

Garrett surveys the three of us, his expression measured but unmistakably proud. His intense brown eyes almost twinkle as they catch the light.

"Ten weeks ago, ten bakers walked into this tent hoping for the chance to prove themselves."

Magnolia presses a hand to her chest, her smile warm but serious. "Week after week, you've pushed your creativity, your technique, and your resilience further than we could have imagined."

Theo glances between our stations, giving a small approving nod. "Now only three remain."

Judy gestures toward the lawn outside, where family members, friends, and former contestants watch eagerly from the decorated tables.

"And tonight, one of you will be crowned the winner of Season One of *America's Next Great Baker!*"

A ripple of applause engulfs us from beyond the tent.

Garrett steps forward again, demanding to be heard.

"For your final challenge, you'll complete the ultimate showstopper cake that you started yesterday."

Magnolia nods toward the clock mounted at the front of the tent. "You have six hours."

Theo lifts his eyebrows, glancing at Judy.

She grins.

"And for the final time this season…"

They both raise their hands.

"Ready…"

A beat.

"Set…"

This pause stretches longer than the last.

Theo leans forward while the entire tent holds its breath and drops his voice to a near whisper.

"…Bake."

Instantly, the tent erupts into motion as the final bake begins, and my heart slams against my ribs.

Bowls and utensils clatter against the countertops. Mixers roar to life. Oven doors slam open and shut as the three of us launch into the final challenge all at once. My heartbeat thrums frantically in my ears.

Six hours to create the most important cake of our lives.

Might as well be six minutes when all is said and done.

My lungs constrict as I grab the first mixing bowl and start measuring ingredients, my hands just a little too shaky.

Breathe.

I've practiced this recipe dozens of times. I know every step like the back of my hand. Memorized every potential moment where something could go wrong. And because I know what *could* go wrong, I just need to make sure it *doesn't*.

Which means I need to block out the nagging thoughts at the back of my mind that keep reminding me exactly how much there is to lose.

Across the tent, Alex moves with the kind of calm precision that we've all come to expect of him. Flour dusts the front of his apron as he works quickly through his batter, barely glancing down at the recipe card beside him.

It's exactly what I expected to see from him, but jealousy still floods through me. What I wouldn't give to be that sure of myself right now.

Diane is obviously magic because she's somehow already three steps ahead of both of us. She slides a tray of cake layers into the oven with smooth efficiency before checking the notes in her sketchpad.

My oven isn't even up to temp yet.

The pressure closes in from every direction making my breathing clumsy and erratic. I really need to get a grip.

"Taylor! How's it going over there?" Theo calls from somewhere near the judges' table.

I glance up just long enough to beam a smile their way.

"Ask me again in five hours!"

They laugh in response, the sound disappearing into the noise of mixers and timers. With three ovens blasting and cameras crowding every corner of the tent, the air turns thick and sticky with heat. A bead of sweat slides down the back of my neck as I guide my first round of pans into the oven and set my timer.

I press my palms together, sending a silent prayer to the baking gods that the cake comes out perfectly golden and with an even rise. I don't have time for sunken centers today.

Working with buttercream in the middle of a heatwave is an absolute nightmare. The bowl of fluffy white clouds in front of me feels wrong.

It's too soft.

I swirl a spatula through the mixture to find it completely incapable of holding a stiff peak. Panic slams into me.

"No, no, no..." I beg, swallowing the lump in my throat.

The buttercream continues to slide down the silicone edge of the utensil, melting right before my eyes. If the frosting won't hold structure, my entire design collapses. I stare at the bowl for half a second too long, trying to decide if I even have time to fix this.

A chilled metal bowl appears beside me, half filled with water, ice cubes bobbing on the surface. I press one finger to the outside of the bowl that's coated in a layer of frost, watching the heat from my skin leave its mark.

"Ice bath," Alex says, already turning back to his station.

I blink at his back as he retreats across the aisle. Emotion prickles behind my eyes. He's showing up for me again.

"Alex—" His name is a breathless whisper.

He doesn't look back, but I hear the smile in his **voice as** he calls to me over his shoulder, "Don't make it weird."

He's been watching from across the tent, a quiet guardian while I fight with everything in me to make my dream come true.

I steal another look at him and smile to myself as I slide my mixing bowl into the ice bath. The buttercream firms up almost immediately with a few good stirs. I definitely would have figured it out on my own, but something about Alex stepping in without being asked when he thought I needed it has my insides doing somersaults.

Just because I can do it alone, doesn't mean I have to.

At the front of the tent, Diane glances over at us briefly before returning to her own cake with the same unshakable focus she's had all season. She doesn't say anything, but I know she clocked it.

The hours start dissolving faster than they should.

Layer after layer of cake stacks on the counter beside me as I work through fillings, frostings, and decorations. Vanilla and sugar billow through the tent while the steady whir of mixers blends into a kind of hypnotic rhythm.

At the halfway mark, Garrett strolls down the main aisle past our stations. He studies each of us with the same unreadable expression he's worn all season.

He pauses beside me, cocking his head as he scrutinizes my work. "What's the structure plan here?" he asks.

"It's going to be four tiers, supported by dowel rods in the middle so the layers don't collapse in on one another."

Garrett nods before speaking. "Ambitious. Best of luck."

Best of luck? Is that *good* ambitious or *terrible* ambitious? If I wasn't already terrified, his words sure would do the trick.

Before I can clarify his words or think about them too closely, he moves on to Diane's station.

I don't miss the way his eyes light up when he inspects her work. A small crowd of cameras follows him, closing in to capture his reaction. From where I'm standing, Diane's cake is starting to take shape—and it's stunning. Like, stop and take a picture, post it on Instagram, pin it to a Pinterest board level stunning.

My stomach sinks just a little as I take it in. And for a brief, envious second, all I can think is how much I wish it were mine.

"Bakers, have one hour remaining!"

One hour—holy crap, there's only one hour left. Where did all of my time go?

My hands move faster as I carefully stack the second tier, lining the cake up with the dowel rods beneath it. For one horrifying second, the entire structure wobbles, and my breath catches in my throat.

Don't fall. Don't fall. For the love of God, please don't fall.

The big man in the sky must take pity on me because the cake settles, just barely, and I'm finally able to exhale.

When Theo announces the five minute warning, the entire tent fractures into pure chaos.

I pipe the final decorations, my hands refusing to stop shaking. Blue sugar crystals scatter across the countertop as I rush to finish the last detail of my design.

Three minutes... Two... One final swirl of buttercream...

"Time!" Theo and Judy call in sync with one another.

"Bakers, step away from your cakes!"

I drop the piping bag onto the counter, hands raised in surrender, and stumble back a step, my chest heaving with adrenaline.

None of us says anything as we make exhausted eye contact and offer wobbly smile to one another.

Alex runs a hand through his hair, leaving a streak of flour through his dark waves. Diane crosses her arms, studying her own creation with quiet satisfaction.

And me? I just stare, unblinking.

Somehow, against all the odds stacked against me, I finished my bake—and it might just be the most beautiful cake I've ever made.

Three enormous showstopper cakes tower above the table in the center of the judging platform, each one elaborate and decadent in its own way. The designs sparkle under the studio lights, frosting perfectly piped, colors vibrant and bold against the patriotic backdrop of the lawn outside.

Guests return to their seats, waiting for the judges.

Garrett folds his hands behind his back and steps forward, his voice calm but carrying easily across the hushed crowd. "You've all created remarkable finale showstoppers."

Magnolia nods in agreement. "Now it's time for judging."

My stomach instantly flips. This is the moment we've all been waiting for. If I'm being honest with myself, I'm not ready for it.

Theo claps his hands together once. "Alright, folks—let's see what you've got!"

"Taylor, would you like to begin?" Judy gestures toward the center table, where our cakes now sit elevated like edible monuments.

Oh—Oh, God no. I don't want to go first.

I swallow hard and step forward, trying to summon as much confidence as I can. Up close, my cake looks even bigger than it did while I was building it.

Four tiers wrapped in soft ivory buttercream, each layer decorated with delicate piping and bursts of red and blue sugar flowers. Thin gold accents shimmer along the edges like sunlight catching on glass.

I stare at it in awe—I actually made this. My heart bursts with pride. It's everything I hoped it would be. And then some.

Garrett clears his throat, breaking through my satisfied thoughts. Pulling my attention back to where it belongs. "Tell us about your cake."

I fold my hands together, hoping they don't shake too visibly. "This is a vanilla bean sponge layered with strawberry compote and mascarpone cream," I explain, working hard to control my breathing as my chest rises and falls rapidly. "Each tier represents a different summer flavor profile. You have strawberry, blueberry, lemon, and honey."

Magnolia tilts her head as she studies the design. "And the inspiration? What does this tell us about you?"

"This is a love letter to my hometown. Summer festivals, family barbecues—the kind of celebrations where everyone brings something special from home."

As I explain, I look out across the sea of people gathered here together in support. The crowd is full of moms and dads, brothers and sisters, cousins and best friends. People I've just met but can't picture my life without.

A single tear slips down my cheek, and I swat it away with a gentle laugh. "Some people might say that it's too simple. But it's not. These kind of moments are the memories that weave us all together."

The judges and hosts listen intently, each of them responding to my words in their own way.

"So basically, it's the perfect Fourth of July cake." Theo teases, breaking the tension with his deadpan delivery and I love him for it.

"Exactly."

Garrett slices carefully into the bottom tier, revealing the clean layers inside.

The silence is deafening as he lifts the fork and takes a bite, chewing with so much restraint I want to hide my face behind my hands.

Magnolia tastes next, her expression thoughtful.

Theo and Judy follow, despite having no say in who wins the competition. Their delighted reaction makes my heart leap.

Seconds stretch into what feels like hours. And the waiting is the worst part. Nervous energy prickles over my skin until, at last, Garrett nods and points at my dish with his fork.

"The sponge is beautifully baked. It's light and moist, and has excellent structure."

Relief floods my senses so rapidly it makes me dizzy. I almost collapse under the weight of it.

Magnolia smiles warmly. "Your flavors are always so bright and balanced. This is no exception. Your mascarpone cream is velvety smooth, and it works beautifully with the fruit."

I bounce on my toes as I listen to their feedback, trying to wrap my mind around the fact that not only am I here in the finale, but that my final bake is landing so well.

"And this thing looks incredible! You nailed the celebration theme," Theo says with a grin.

Judy beams. "It's joyful in the best way."

My chest swells a little more. I brought everything that I've learned to this challenge, but I also brought the memory of Gran. This one was for her.

Garrett sets down his fork.

"The only note I'd give is that the honey tier is slightly sweeter than the others. But overall..." He points a finger at my cake. "Excellent work."

My heart somersaults behind my ribs.

Thanking the judges with a dip of my head, I step back into line with Alex and Diane.

Garrett nods once before turning. "Alex."

Alex steps forward, confident and self-assured as always. And this time, he should be. His cake is breathtaking.

Tall, architectural tiers cascade downward in shades of deep amber and forest green. Delicate sugar work shaped like maple leaves curl around the structure. The entire design feels elegant and restrained—like something out of a luxury pastry shop window. But it's also so uniquely him.

I close my eyes, picturing a little boy version of Alex running through the forest, hiding in the trees. Learning about himself and what he's capable of away from his father's overwhelming criticism.

Garrett studies it closely. "This is absolutely stunning."

"Thank you." Alex inclines his head in deference.

"Tell us about it."

"Like Taylor's, it's inspired by where I grew up." He clears his throat. "For my showstopper, you have a maple spice sponge layered with brown sugar butter cream and apple compote."

Magnolia's eyebrows lift. "That sounds lovely."

Garrett slices into the cake, revealing flawless, identical layers. "The technique here is exceptional."

"Oh yeah, that's good." Theo lets out a low whistle while Judy nods enthusiastically, waiting her turn to take a bite.

"These flavors are incredibly sophisticated." Magnolia studies the design again. "And the design is something totally unexpected from you."

Alex's shoulders relax as Garrett sets down his fork. "This is the work of a highly trained baker."

Alex gives a small nod, but Garrett continues.

"I would have liked to see just a touch more risk in the flavor profile. Don't get me wrong, it's beautifully executed. But very safe for a baker of your caliber."

Disappointment flashes but he recovers quickly, offering the judges a solemn, respectful nod. "Understood."

Magnolia turns to the final cake and Diane steps forward with a hopeful smile playing on her lips. Her cake is absolutely extraordinary.

Five tiers of delicate pastel buttercream rise in a spiral toward the sky. Intricate sugar flowers cascade down the sides like a waterfall. Tiny edible fireworks burst across the top tier in shimmering gold and silver.

Garrett circles the cake, examining every detail. "This is incredibly ambitious for a competition show like this, with the time that we gave you."

Diane smiles faintly, nodding once. "I wanted to go big."

Theo laughs. "Well, you definitely did that."

Garrett slices carefully into the lowest tier. Inside, the layers are immaculate. I was proud of how even my layers were but Diane's set the standard.

He takes a bite, then immediately reaches for another.

Magnolia's eyes widen in delight as she chews her bite of cake longer than necessary, savoring every second of it.

Judy covers her mouth with her hand mumbling between her fingers, "Oh, wow. *Diane...*"

My stomach sinks just a little at their reaction. I steal a glance at Alex, and his eyes are trained upward, slightly glazed.

Garrett finally sets down his fork. "The flavors here are extraordinary."

"Every element in your cake complements the next. I genuinely don't know how you pulled this off." Magnolia praises.

Diane shrugs lightly. "Lots of practice."

Garrett steps back, folding his hands behind his back again. "All three of you should be incredibly proud of what you've accomplished here tonight."

"Now comes the hard part." Theo nods and Judy's face falls. She looks paler than usual, like she might be sick.

"We need to deliberate." Magnolia declares.

My pulse races again as the judges step away from the table, reconvening at the far end of the tent.

Guests have been arriving throughout the day in clusters, voices rising in excited bursts. Family and friends mingle with the eliminated contestants like a reunion unfolding across the lawn. We drift out to join them, stepping into the hum of conversation and movement as we wait for the judges to deliberate.

Kara stands near the dessert table, talking animatedly with my mom, both of them holding drinks and laughing. My chest fills with something warm and a little overwhelming.

All summer, we've been baking inside that tent, sweating through challenges and whispering encouragement to one another over the whir of mixers when we could. And now everyone is here to watch how it ends.

Cameras are literally everywhere, and I'd be lying if I said this amount of attention didn't trigger my gag reflex.

Tripods line the edges of the lawn. Operators move quietly through the crowd, lenses already trained toward the platform stage. Microphones hang overhead like curious little birds.

Near the center of the platform stage sits a velvet-covered pedestal. And on top of it—*my breath catches*—the platinum rolling pin trophy gleams in the fading sunlight.

I glance toward the tent and catch sight of Alex stepping out, searching the crowd. He pauses when he sees the setup, too. His shoulders go still for a moment like the weight of it all has finally landed on him.

Our eyes lock across the crowd.

Julian calls to him from where he sits with a formidable group, fully decked out in business suits and designer sunglasses. As he approaches their table, he pauses to glance back at me over his shoulder and gifts me with a wide, dazzling smile.

Deliberation doesn't take as long as I'd hoped it would. All four of our judges and hosts take their position on the small stage. Magnolia discreetly wipes a hand under her eye, possibly wiping away a tear. I wouldn't blame her for crying.

This whole situation has been a lot.

Garrett steps forward, taking a dramatic pause and letting his signature scowl slide over the audience before he speaks.

"Thank you all for coming out to celebrate our final three bakers here in the tent," He pauses, taking a deep breath before continuing. "They have all worked extremely hard, and it's my absolute pleasure to announce our star baker."

I don't feel the wind, nor the SoCal heat pressing against my skin. I don't hear the murmur of the crowd or any of the production noise in the background.

Each second stretches into minutes, my gaze finding and holding Alex's while we stand suspended in this moment together.

Garrett looks at Diane...

Then Alex...

And finally, me.

My pulse pounds in my ears and the entire lawn has gone silent, holding its breath in wait. "The winner of Season One of *America's Next Great Baker* is..."

Alex

Chapter 27

"Diane."

Cheers explode across the crowd as confetti cannons fire from both sides of the stage, sending red, white, and blue paper spiraling through the air like fireworks. Diane's hands fly to her mouth in shock before she gasps a breathless laugh, her entire face lighting up.

A whoosh of air leaves me. I bend forward, bracing my hands against my thighs, and suck in a breath that burns on the way down.

Theo and Judy rush forward first, pulling Diane into a hug while Magnolia claps both hands together, beaming.

Garrett shakes Diane's hand firmly before moving aside, allowing a production assistant to step forward with the gleaming platinum rolling pin trophy.

Applause crashes over the lawn in waves. I clap along with everyone else, stepping to the side. Because honestly? She earned it.

I knew Diane would win before Garrett even spoke. The second the judges tasted her cake, Magnolia's eyebrows shot up and Garrett went in for a second bite. Right then, it was over for Taylor and me.

Still, a small, stubborn part of me wanted it. Ten weeks of early mornings and constant pressure to be the best does that. But the disappointment fades fast. Relief crashes into me, something tight in my chest finally giving way.

No more alarms at six a.m. No more racing the clock with cameras pressed too close. No more standing over something I made, watching it get pulled apart for ratings.

Centerstage, Diane accepts the trophy, laughing as the confetti rains down around her. She looks completely stunned. Completely happy. And all I can think is, if it couldn't be Taylor or me, I'm really glad it's her.

My attention drifts to the person standing beside me. Taylor is clapping too, her smile wide as she cheers for Diane. From a distance, anyone looking at her would think she's completely fine.

But I'm close enough to know better. It's impossible to miss the glassy tears welling in her eyes, the splotchy red blooming across her cheeks. When she lowers her hands, her fingers curl inward slightly, like she's trying to hold onto the moment before it slips through them.

Most people wouldn't notice. But I do.

I've been watching her for ten weeks now. Somewhere between week three and week six, paying attention to Taylor stopped being something I had to do and just became second nature.

Music starts blasting from every corner of the party space. Another crew member pops a confetti cannon for absolutely no reason at all, sending a fresh storm of glitter into the air.

Cameras swarm the stage, red lights blinking to life as operators jockey for the best angle. Producers shout over the noise while former contestants spill onto the platform like they've been waiting behind a gate at a horse race.

RaeAnn barrels straight toward Diane with both arms open. "You did it!" she shouts, nearly tackling her off balance.

Kara appears a second later, wrapping Taylor in a tight hug like she can hold the pieces of her best friend together by sheer force alone. Her mom joins them, squeezing both of them close.

I can't hear what they're saying from here, but Taylor's shoulders drop. She shakes as she cries.

After a minute, she untangles herself from their embrace, brushing her fingers beneath her eyes before smoothing back her hair and stepping forward to congratulate Diane.

"Congratulations," she says warmly, wrapping Diane in a quick hug.

Diane pulls back, still clutching the trophy. "Are you kidding? That cake of yours was incredible," she says, shaking her head. "Seriously, Taylor. Keep pushing. You're really something special."

Taylor sniffs, a little caught off guard by the compliment.

"Thanks," she says softly.

Then Diane turns to me, grin widening. "I knew it was gonna come down to us, kid."

"Yeah?" I let out a short laugh.

She nods, lifting the trophy. It glints in the light. I wonder where someone is supposed to keep something like that.

"First day in the house. Remember? You walked out on the patio, and I taught you how to introduce yourself. I knew then that you were gonna be my biggest competition. Could just tell."

"That's not how I remember it."

"Oh, please." She waves a hand. "You and me. I called it then—even if I didn't say it out loud."

I chuckle, shaking her hand before pulling her into a hug. "You baked the hell out of that cake. You deserve this win."

"Damn right I did."

The crowd swells around us again, voices overlapping from every direction. It's chaos.

Joe wrangles the three of us into a photo as another production assistant hands us each a glass of champagne. We smile and clink glasses on cue, flashing through a series of shots. Halfway through the mock photoshoot, my hand settles at the small of Taylor's back, keeping her pulled into my side.

When we're finally released, Julian pushes his way through the crowd. He exhales when he reaches me, giving me a firm handshake and clapping me on the back. "Sorry you didn't win. But, hey... at least it's over. We didn't need you to win—we just needed you to be likable. And I think you did that."

"We'll see. Depends on the edit." I smirk, my thoughts slipping back to my confrontation with Hal and the production team.

"Have some faith, asshole." He punches my arm. "At least we're getting the green light on the restaurant when we get back."

Those words land heavy in my chest. *When we get back.*

Tomorrow, the production vans will pull up for the last time. We'll pack our suitcases, hand in our mic packs, and scatter back across the country like this strange little summer never happened.

No more crowded kitchen counters at midnight. No more whispered strategy sessions over leftover pastries. No more Taylor humming under her breath while she measures flour. Something twists in my chest. I scan the crowd until I find her.

Beautiful hazel eyes, and those bouncing curls.

Taylor meets my gaze from across the stage. She tips her head toward the edge of the lawn, mouthing, "Escape?"

I nod.

"Julian, I gotta go. I'll catch up with you later."

Taylor and I slip away while everyone else is distracted, weaving through clusters of guests until the noise fades behind us.

My hand finds hers, our fingers lacing together in a perfect fit. Her thumb brushes easy, reverent strokes across my knuckles. I can't look away from the contact.

The bounce houses squeak in the distance. The last light of day stretches across the lawn in soft gold. We settle onto a picnic bench at the edge of the property, the world suddenly narrowing down to just us.

For a moment, neither of us speaks.

My gaze drops to her sparkly peach nails while my thumb traces gentle circles over the back of her hand.

"So... about that obstacle course." Taylor finally breaks the silence, a teasing edge in her voice.

I huff a quiet laugh. "Pretty sure that's a bet neither of us can win right now."

"If you're too scared, you should just say that." Her eyes glint, warm and playful.

She's distracting us from the truth we're both avoiding—that neither of us won, and by this time tomorrow, we'll be back in our separate lives, eighteen hours apart.

I lift her hand to my lips and press a soft kiss to her knuckles, holding her gaze the entire time. The challenge in her eyes fades as her lashes flutter and her breath catches, her attention fully locked on me.

"I was really looking forward to the prize you promised me." Her voice drops, almost a whisper.

"We can still bring those ideas to life." I wink.

The sun dips lower, painting the sky in soft peach and gold.

Taylor traces the edge of the table with her fingertips, lost in thought. A curl slips forward across her cheek, catching the warm glow of the setting sun.

I reach out, tucking it gently behind her ear, my fingers lingering as they trail down the line of her neck.

The small, pleased sound she sighs is the only invitation I need to move. I cup her jaw and pull her into a kiss.

Our lips move together in slow, deliberate passes, saying everything we don't have words for. She melts into me, her hands curling into the front of my shirt, holding me like she doesn't want to let go.

When I pull back, she doesn't open her eyes to look at me.

"How are we supposed to go back to normal after this?" she whispers, finally opening her eyes again. "Am I really going to sit in a cubicle, dealing with customer complaints and being hassled by my boss every day? Ugh."

I'd be lying if I said that hasn't been occupying my thoughts all day. While I don't love this house or LA, and I miss my own bed, I'm not ready to say goodbye to the incredible woman sitting in front of me.

There also hasn't been the right time to talk about what exactly we're doing together. I'm way too old to ask Taylor if she wants to be my long-distance girlfriend, where our dates consist of FaceTime calls and text messages.

"No," I say, bringing her knuckles to my lips again. "You're not going back to that. You've proven what you can do here. You're going to find something better."

She exhales, watching me closely. Her eyes look tired now in the fading light. "You should have won."

I glance at her. She's looking past me toward the celebration, fingers absentmindedly playing with the pendant at her collarbone.

"Nah," I say with a small shrug.

Her head snaps toward me. "Alex."

"What?"

"You know that's not true."

I lean back on the bench, tugging her closer until she has no choice but to look at me.

"Diane baked a better cake."

Her brows knit, eyes narrowing like she's planning to argue with me. "You still deserved it."

She means it. I can hear it in her voice.

"I did win," I say.

She blinks, confused. "What?"

I shift closer, bracing my hands on the table behind her, caging her in without touching her. I dip my head just enough to hold her gaze.

"Just not the show," I murmur.

Understanding flickers across her face as I close the space between us again, our noses brushing in a quiet, almost hesitant nuzzle before I kiss her—slow, deep, intentional.

For the first time all summer, the future feels uncertain in a way that has nothing to do with baking or prizes or restaurants.

The girl who showed up late and made a mess of everything somehow turned into someone I can't imagine my life without. Didn't see that one coming. Wouldn't change it either.

Now I just have to figure out how to make eighteen hours feel a whole lot smaller.

Chapter 28

Less than twelve hours ago, I was tangled up in Alex for what could be the final time. I did my best to hide the way my heart was crumpling over what happens next for us, but I'm pretty sure he saw the tears building as he opened my car door for me to slide into the driver's seat.

He brushed a thumb over my cheek and kissed me softly, murmuring against my lips, "I'll see you later."

Not goodbye, just I'll see you later, like a promise that this isn't the end for us.

God, I hope it isn't the end of whatever we are.

Never in a million years would I have thought that a carefully controlled storm cloud would fit into all the hollow places inside me. But maybe that's what people mean when they say opposites attract—all the places where you dip, they rise naturally to meet you.

Nothing explains Alex and me better than that strange, perfect balance.

A warm ocean breeze whips my hair into a frenzy as I cross the parking lot. I take a steadying breath as I step through the doors of the same mundane office building that I've spent far too much time in over the last five years.

Against every rational thought, I know what I need to do. If I don't give my resignation today while I'm still riding the buzz of the finale, I'll get trapped in the cycle of my old life before I realize it's happening.

"Morning, Sunshine!" Kara chirps, expression shifting as she takes in my squared shoulders and determined pace. "Oh shit, it's go time."

My steps don't slow as I stalk down the hall to The Trunch's office and knock on the door, sharp and loud. The timid girl who used to cower at the thought of confrontation is nowhere to be found.

I don't wait for a response. My hand immediately finds the knob, twisting and pushing the door open to find Karen staring back at me, startled.

Karen sits at her desk, a breakfast sandwich halfway to her mouth as she takes me in. Her eyes sharpen, and she smirks at me. "If it isn't Little Miss Hollywood. Oh wait... you didn't win, did you? Such a sh—"

For five years, I swallowed comments like that and told myself it was normal. No more.

"I quit."

My expression is carefully neutral as I cut her off. There's no need to play nice if I'm quitting. She's a terrible person who thrives on making others—namely me—miserable.

I don't have to stand for it.

Not anymore.

Her smirk falls, and she drops the sandwich back onto the greasy wrapper on her desk.

"What? No, you can't quit."

"Actually, I can. You've done nothing but harass me from the first day I started this job. I've done everything you and this company have ever asked, and you still crap on me every chance you get."

I stand a little taller, squaring my shoulders again.

"And I'm done. Find someone else to be your punching bag, because I quit. Effective immediately."

The words feel lighter than air leaving my mouth.

My boss's jaw hangs open, and I fight back a laugh because she looks exactly like one of those big-mouthed basses from the old fish market ads.

I spin on a heel, leaving her speechless, and snap the cheap wooden door closed behind me without another word.

I bite my lower lip to keep from smiling too hard, adrenaline tingling through my body. I shake out my hands, trying to burn off some of the pent-up energy. I feel like I could kick down a door right now.

Kara is waiting for me at the end of the hall with wide eyes. She tilts her head, raising her hands in question.

"Well...?"

"My time at *Elite Connections* is officially over."

"Hell yeah, let's go!" She pumps a fist in the air.

My best friend slings an arm over my shoulder, leading me to the main floor where our cubicles sit among the others.

"Attention, everyone! Taylor did it. She's out of here!" Kara cups her hands around her mouth, announcing my resignation to the team.

The news is met with claps, supportive smiles, and a few whistles.

"Speech, speech, speech!" Kara starts a chant that the others eventually fall in line with. One of the older guys bangs his desk with his fists, punctuating the chant.

Well, this is awkward. What can I tell these people that they don't already know?

My thoughts sift through the past ten weeks in rapid succession. My lips tip up, remembering every detail.

"I don't know what I can say to you all," I say, swallowing hard as I look at my team gathered around us.

"Ten weeks ago, I left here thinking I was just going to bake a few cakes and maybe embarrass myself on national television... turns out I only did one of those things."

A few laughs ripple through the group.

"But somewhere along the way, I realized I've been living my life on autopilot. And life's way too short to stay somewhere that makes you miserable." I shrug.

Everyone's listening now.

"Somehow, baking under a giant tent with cameras everywhere is a lot less scary than staying stuck somewhere you're unhappy."

My eyes flick to Kara's, and I give her a small smile.

"I think it's finally time I find out what else I'm capable of. And my hope is that the rest of you find a way to do that, too. If you can make it here, you can do anything."

I fold my hands in front of me, dipping my chin.

"I'm really going to miss all the free desserts!" Someone calls out from the back, drawing a shaky laugh out of me.

Each of my teammates takes turns saying goodbye and wishing me well. It's a mix of hugs, handshakes, and some tears, while I pack the knick-knacks I used to make my boring twelve square feet feel a little more alive.

A little more me.

The second I'm settled in the driver's seat of my car, I pull down the visor and fix the smudges of mascara under my eyes. I tousle my hair and reapply my lip gloss, wiping my lip line to clean up the peachy-pink that gathered along the edge.

With my phone tilted at the most flattering angle, I beam a smile directly into the camera, snap a selfie, and send it off to Alex.

ME:
the face of a girl who just quit
her awful job…

I pause for a second, thumbs hovering over the screen before immediately typing another message. We're way past a double text being a cardinal sin, right?

ME:
and if you don't look too close, you
can't tell how terrifying that was

Opening Spotify, I put on the playlist I playfully named *Bake It 'Til You Make It*. God, I love a good pun!

Lavender Haze by Taylor Swift floods the car. I put the windows down, letting the warm breeze dance alongside me while my shoulders shimmy to the beat.

GRUMP BUCKET:
That's my girl!
Scared or not, all I see is how
fucking beautiful you are.

Even though I know he can't see me, I cover my cheeks with my hands as the blush creeps in at the compliment.

I start to type, but backspace the message away only to start again. There's so much I want to say, and yet, the right words just won't come.

Get it together, it's just Alex.

I laugh, imagining him with a scowl on his face, sitting there with our message thread open, watching three little dots appear and disappear over and over again.

How embarrassing.

Before I can decide what to send, his next one comes in. He doesn't know it, but he puts me out of my misery with three simple words.

GRUMP BUCKET:
I miss you.

Pressure builds behind my eyes again, blurring the screen for a second. And I type out a quick reply. It's simple, but it says it all.

ME:
I miss you too 🖤

I spend my time baking every chance I get, texting Alex whenever we're both free, and trying to figure out what to do next.

On my way home after quitting my job, I opened Instagram for the first time in months to find my account had exploded during my social media sabbatical.

Apparently, *FluxTV* has been releasing teasers and curated scenes leading up to next week's official release on the streaming service.

They included all of our social media tags, encouraging viewers to follow along and get to know us before they start watching.

My follower count has jumped from 1,206 to nearly *twenty-four thousand.*

Absolutely insane.

I don't even *know* twenty-four thousand people.

Thanks to the follower boost, my DMs exploded—most people ask about custom cakes and catering, but there are a select few that are a bit more intrusive.

One woman sends a four-paragraph message demanding the exact recipe for the lavender-honey cake I made mid-season.

Another asks if Alex and I are secretly engaged.

Even Lila sent me a message asking if I'd consider collaborating on a series with her. She called it an olive branch to leave the past in the past.

It feels more like she's trying to capitalize on a moment, but hey, I guess I can't blame her. Maybe I'll take her up on it.

No publicity is bad publicity, right?

As luck would have it, a new bakery just opened on the far side of town. A cute little place called *Dolce*, focused on artisanal breads and pastries made with locally sourced ingredients.

The owner's daughter recognized me from the ANGB promos online. When I inquired if they were looking to hire any bakers, she enthusiastically vouched for me to her mom, saying she *just knows* that I made it to the end.

Per my NDA, I couldn't confirm or deny, but I offered a wink and told her I think she will be pleasantly surprised with how the season ends.

She clapped excitedly, and her mom hired me on the spot.

The first few shifts at the bakery are a reminder that this is what I want to do for the rest of my life.

The place smells incredible—warm yeast, caramelized sugar, and coffee strong enough to wake the dead. By the end of my first week, my hands feel permanently dusted in flour, and my forearms are dotted with tiny burns from the ovens.

And I've never been happier.

It's not glamorous work. Most mornings start before the sun even considers rising, and by the time the front doors open, the display case is already lined with rows of glossy croissants, rustic loaves, and delicate pastries that look almost too pretty to eat.

Almost.

Customers filter in throughout the day, and every once in a while, someone does a double-take when I'm cashing them out.

"You look familiar," they'll say, squinting at me across the counter.

I just smile and ring up their sourdough.

My NDA is still very much intact.

When the shop is quiet, I pull out my phone and scroll through messages.

Alex's name is always near the top.

We text whenever we can, squeezing conversations between his shifts at the restaurant and my early mornings at the bakery.

Sometimes it's a quick little update about our day.

Other times, it's photos—him sending pictures of plated dishes that look like tiny works of art, me sending back shots of whatever intricate pastry I'm currently elbow-deep in.

The time difference between our shifts doesn't help.

By the time I'm getting home and collapsing onto my couch, he's usually just starting dinner service.

Still, we do what we can to make it work.

Late one night, after I shower off the scent of the bar where I got drinks with Kara after my shift at *Dolce*, I end up curled on my couch with my laptop balanced on the coffee table in front of me.

And every single time I settle into this position, without fail, I open the bookmarked travel site and type *Vancouver* into the search bar like some strange little ritual.

The prices are... *not* encouraging.

Round-trip tickets flash across the screen with numbers that make my stomach drop. The cheaper ones feel wildly irresponsible when I've only just quit my job and started something new. Custom orders have started trickling in, but I'm still working to get caught up.

And the more expensive one? Forget about it.

I stare at the options anyway: early morning departures, red-eyes, flights with two layovers that take almost an entire day—every option the travel site is willing to show me.

I hover over the "select" button more than once, but then always close the tab. The truth is, even if I could afford to go right now, I'm not entirely sure I should.

Alex hasn't exactly invited me.

Not that he's said anything to make me think he wouldn't want me there. If anything, he's the one constantly telling me how much he misses me first, while I try to play it off like I'm way cooler than I am.

I'm honestly dying to see him, but flying to another country to see someone you technically aren't even dating feels like a bold move.

One might even call it slightly unhinged.

I rest my chin on my hand and stare at the last message he sent earlier tonight.

GRUMP BUCKET:

Just got home.

Kitchen was chaos tonight.

Tell me something good.

I send him a quick snapshot of my feet covered in fuzzy socks, propped on the table next to my open laptop. A second message follows a moment later.

GRUMP BUCKET:

Wish you were here.

My chest squeezes a little at that. I want to type something back about the flights I've been looking at. Instead, I flip my laptop closed and set it on the bottom shelf of the coffee table.

Because if I keep staring at flight prices and rereading Alex's messages, I might do something reckless.

I lean back against the couch cushions, staring up at the ceiling and holding my phone to my chest.

For the first time in years, my life feels... open.

Terrifyingly, beautifully open.

I don't have a five-year plan. But I also don't have a miserable boss breathing down my neck anymore or a job that slowly drains every ounce of joy out of my day.

Now I have the chance to do what I love every day, twenty-four thousand strangers on the internet watching my life unfold, and a complicated, wonderful man living half a country away.

It's messy and uncertain, and somehow, it feels exactly right. My phone buzzes in my hand again.

GRUMP BUCKET:
You still awake, pretty girl?

I smile before I can stop myself. I guess Vancouver can wait a little longer. For now, maybe this—whatever *this* is—can be enough.

Alex

Chapter 29

The call comes in just after noon.

I almost let it go to voicemail.

I'm standing in the middle of the space that's supposed to become Northern Flame, phone buzzing in my hand, dust floating in the air where sunlight cuts through the front windows. The place still smells like old wood and something stale I haven't been able to identify yet. It's empty except for me and our contractor, who stepped out ten minutes ago to take his own call.

My thumb hovers over the screen.

Chet Harrington.

I haven't heard from my father since the finale aired.

That's not unusual. Silence and avoidance have always been his default setting unless he needs me to do something for him. Praise, when it comes, is doled out in rations.

The phone buzzes again, and this time I answer.

"Chet," I drawl sarcastically, balancing the phone on my shoulder. "To what do I owe this immense pleasure?"

There's a pause on the other end, just long enough that I wonder if the connection dropped.

"Alexander."

Same dry greeting as always. If my tone gets under his skin at all, he isn't letting it show. He almost sounds bored, like we'll just be discussing a casual business arrangement instead of the last ten weeks of my life and what it means for my future.

"Hey," I shift my weight and run a finger through the dust collecting on a nearby windowsill just to give me something to do with my hands. "What's up?"

"I watched the season. Finale included."

Finally, it's been out for a couple of weeks at this point.

I let out a breath through my nose. "Yeah?"

"You handled yourself well."

I nod to myself, knowing he can't see it. "Thanks."

Another pause. Papers shuffle faintly on his end. I picture him at his desk at Harrington Group HQ, perfectly organized, pen lined up parallel to the edge, everything in its place.

"You did exactly what I needed you to do."

I push my free hand through my hair, staring at my reflection in the hazy window. This is about as close to approval as it gets with my father. While we don't exactly have a close relationship, hearing that I did well hits me square in the chest.

"Even though I didn't win?"

"Yes." He says without hesitation. "You won them over just like we needed you to. Viewers, judges, sponsors. The exposure alone—"

"I know," I cut in sharply, before I can stop myself.

Silence meets me from the other end of the line.

I close my eyes briefly, pressing my thumb against the bridge of my nose. "Sorry. I just... yeah. I get it."

There's a shift in his tone when he speaks again. Not warmer necessarily, because Chet Harrington doesn't do *warm*, but it's far less clipped now than it usually is.

"The opportunity you've been looking for is there now," he says. "If you're going to move forward with your concept, this is the time."

My gaze lifts, scanning the space again. The bare walls desperately in need of new paint. The outlines done in painter's tape on the floor where equipment will go. The skeleton of something that can be really special if I can pull it together.

"I've already started," I admit. "The lease is signed. Plans are in motion."

"I assumed as much."

"I'll need to review your projections. Costs, timelines, staffing, menu concepts—everything."

It's more demand than question, but all I can focus on is the fact that this feels a lot like permission. A lot like he's agreeing to the Harrington Group investing in Julian and my concept.

"Yeah," I breathe out quickly. "I can send that over."

Another pause. Shorter this time, but still poignant.

"You have my approval to proceed."

Finally.

Starting my own restaurant, away from my family's legacy, has always felt just out of reach. Like there will always be one more step, one more hoop to jump through.

"If you execute this properly, it will position you well for expansion within the next three to five years."

I huff out a small breath that might pass for a laugh if you're not paying close attention. "Already planning the second location, eh?"

"You should always be planning ahead."

"Right." I clear my throat.

We fall into a brief silence that stretches longer than it should. This is always the awkward part with him. Even when we aren't at odds, we don't have much to say.

"You did well," he says again, like he's checking a box. Without a doubt, Mom is standing near the desk, coaching him into being more encouraging.

I hum in acknowledgment.

"That will be all."

The line clicks dead, and I lower the phone slowly, staring at the screen for a second before it goes dark.

That's it?

No questions about how I'm doing. Nothing beyond the show or the business. Just confirmation that I met expectations. I shake my head. I hadn't expected anything more, yet a small part of me had hoped for it anyway.

I slip my phone into my pocket and look around the space again, trying to imagine the concept coming together.

You did exactly what I needed you to do.

The words echo, but they don't sit the same way they used to. A few months ago, that and the official approval of Northern Flame would have been enough. More than enough. Now...

I drag a hand over my jaw and exhale.

"Yeah," I mutter to the empty room. "Guess I did."

The rest of the afternoon is a mind-numbing montage of back-and-forth moments with the contractor.

We walk through the layout again, nailing down all the details: equipment placement, ventilation, how the line will flow during service, and what needs to be in place to make that happen.

I nod, ask questions, jot down notes, and make decisions faster than I used to.

It should feel *good*.

This is what I've been working toward. My own place. My own concept. No one looking over my shoulder, no one telling me how to plate a dish or when to adjust a menu. Except for Julian, but we almost always see eye to eye.

Freedom.

Instead, I keep catching myself reaching for my phone.

It happens without thinking. A break in the conversation, a pause while the contractor double-checks a measurement, a second of silence that my brain fills automatically.

My hand goes to my pocket every single time. And every single time, there's nothing new.

Or there is, and its hours old.

A message I didn't see because I was busy. A photo I didn't respond to right away.

Even though nothing's coming, I check again anyway.

"Alex?"

I look up.

The contractor is watching me, clipboard in hand. "You with me?"

"Yeah," I say, straightening. "Sorry. Go ahead."

He points to the back corner. "If we shift the prep station here, you'll have better flow into the line."

I follow his line of sight, forcing my attention back to the room. "That works."

We talk through it for another twenty minutes before he wraps up for the day, promising to send over updated plans by morning.

When he leaves, the space goes quiet again.

I stand there for a minute, listening to the faint hum of traffic outside, the distant sound of a door closing somewhere down the block. I drop my head between my shoulders, leaning against the counter.

Then, out of habit, I pull my phone out and a message from Taylor is waiting for me.

My chest tightens as a photo appears on the screen.

Her hand is dusted with flour, clutching a tray of pastries I can't make out at first. The light is warm—or maybe that's just how she makes me feel. A smear on her wrist catches my eye. I wonder what it is. Knowing her, it could be anything.

PRETTY GIRL:
burnt my arm twice today
but look how pretty these turned out

Another image comes through, a close-up of one of her pastries cut in half.

I zoom in, taking my time to study it.

Croissants. Perfect layers. Deep golden color. Slight sheen on the surface.

"Jesus," I mutter under my breath.

I type back before I can overthink it.

ME:

Those look better than anything

I've seen all week. Fucking epic!

Three dots appear almost immediately, then disappear and reappear a few times.

I wait for her response.

And wait.

And wait a little bit longer.

Nothing.

"She's working," I tell myself out loud before locking my screen and shoving the phone back into my pocket.

It's hard to believe the competition ended almost two months ago.

The first month of planning passes in a series of long days and short nights.

Julian and I meet with suppliers and go over budgets. I argue with a designer about materials that don't make sense for the kind of kitchen I'm building. Julian spends long hours interviewing chefs to build our line for success.

It's everything I expected. Everything I've ever wanted.

And still, there's this low-level distraction running in the background—*I miss her*.

Taylor's messages come in throughout the day.

It's an eclectic mix of photos and random thoughts that don't need a response but make me want to give one anyway.

I do my best to answer when I can. Sometimes it's immediate. Sometimes it's hours later. But I always do answer, eventually.

By the end of the second month, the shift between us is almost too much to bear.

Where we used to fall into long conversations, back-and-forth without thinking, now it's broken up. Stretched out over time.

We're both busy with new routines. New jobs and projects. I tell myself it's temporary. That it makes sense given all the changes we are both handling right now, and that it will get better once everything is settled.

It has to.

Now halfway into the third month post-competition, I'm starting to split my time between Prism back in Vancouver and Northern Flame's home in San Francisco.

Tonight, I'm standing outside the restaurant after a fourteen-hour training day, phone in my hand, trying to decide if it's too late to call her.

Better to ask for forgiveness than permission.

After ringing a good number of times, it clicks over to voicemail, and I hang up before leaving a message. Blankly, I stare at the screen, willing it to change.

Not even a full minute later, it buzzes, and I answer the call immediately.

"Sorry, was just in the shower." Taylor's melodic voice carries over the line. "What's up?"

My lips tip up, both at the thought of her in the shower and at how quickly she called me back.

'Nothing..." I trail off, hand pushing my hair back away from my forehead. "Just wanted to hear your voice. It's been a day."

"I'm really glad you called. I miss you," Taylor sighs.

I lean back against the brick wall behind me, closing my eyes for a second. I can practically see the small, content smile I hear in her voice.

"Miss you, too, pretty girl. Hey, look... so I'm in San Francisco for a couple of weeks, and I'd love to see you."

"Wait, what?" There's a scuffle of noise, like she's repositioning against one of her ridiculously ruffled pillows.

"Yeah, San Francisco..."

"That's a lot closer than Vancouver..."

I bite my lip, dancing around what I actually mean to say. I haven't seen Taylor in over two months, and it's killing me.

"Come visit."

It comes out more demanding than I mean it to, but I'm desperate to close this distance that is growing between us.

She sighs. "I don't know, Alex. I don't have back-to-back days off ever, and it's a four-hour drive one way..."

I'm silent for a beat, trying to figure out if she's hung up on the logistics or if she just doesn't want to come.

"I'm obviously going to book you a flight," I say, cautiously. "If you're willing to come, that is... Please come, Taylor."

She hums noncommittally, thinking over my offer, while I stand, holding my breath and waiting for her answer.

"Yeah, okay." Her voice is small. "Let's find a day that works for both of us."

We pick a day that fits both our schedules.

Not ideal for either of us, but the only one we could make work. Nothing about this relationship has been ideal since we left LA, anyway.

She flies in early. I meet her between prep and service training at the restaurant, time carved out where it doesn't really exist.

I see her before she sees me.

She's standing near the entrance when I pull up to the pick-up area in a sleek black car, looking around like she's not sure where she's supposed to be. She's wearing a white sundress that ties behind her neck, and strappy sandals that twist around her ankles. Her hair is pulled back, and she has vintage-style sunglasses perched on top of her head.

She's so damn beautiful, it hurts.

For a second, I just watch her.

Then, unable to wait any longer, I get out and circle around the front of the car to where she's waiting.

When she finally turns, our eyes collide.

And everything else drops out.

I cross the distance without thinking.

She barely has time to smile before I'm pulling her into me, arms tight around her, face pressed into her hair.

She smells like citrus and something sweet I never want to go another day without.

"Hey," she says, voice soft against my chest.

"Hey."

I don't let go right away.

Neither does she.

When we finally pull back, there's this moment where we just look at each other, taking it all in.

"You're here," I say, because I don't know what else to say.

She huffs out a small laugh. "I'm here."

I brush my thumbs over her cheeks, committing every curve of her face to memory.

"You look tired," she adds, studying my face.

"So do you."

"Rude." She playfully swats my chest.

I grin. "*Accurate.*"

She rolls her eyes, but she's smiling.

It feels the same and different at the same time, and I can't quite place why.

I press a soft kiss to her lips, that same watermelon lip gloss meeting me on contact. She pulls back first this time, smudging away the glisten from my lower lip as she does.

In all of the times we've been together, I don't think I've ever noticed her pull away from me first. Usually, it's a mutual drift before diving back in for more.

Maybe we just need some time to get used to each other again. A dull ache forms in my chest at the realization, but what else can I do except give her the time she needs?

"Come on," I say, quirking an eyebrow and nodding toward the car. "We've only got a couple hours."

"Then let's not waste a second of them," she beams, that quintessential Taylor-ness shining through.

Without much time, I zip us over to Burlingame to spend the afternoon together.

We walk along The Ave with no real destination in mind. Just moving together, talking about nothing in particular.

She tells me all about her time at *Dolce* and how her custom dessert business is starting to take off through social media.

I share the progress Julian and I have been making with Northern Flame, including a tentative grand opening set for this March.

But there's an awkward discomfort underneath it all now. A slight delay in responses, like we both are choosing our words carefully. A brief moment where we check ourselves before speaking.

At one point, she reaches for my hand.

I take it without hesitation.

Our fingers fit together like they always have.

At least that part hasn't changed.

We stop at a small place on the corner for coffee and a quick bite. I let her order for both of us, which she gets a kick out of as she orders the quirkiest sandwich on the menu.

I watch her while she talks, catching up on stories I've only gotten in fragments over text. Her eyes dance, jaw working against the food in her mouth, while she tells me all the details that were too much to type out.

The burns on her arms.

The customers who recognize her.

The way she lights up when she talks about the bakery, gesturing animatedly with her hands and shimmying around her chair, is infectious.

"You're happy," I murmur against my coffee mug, sipping the hot liquid carefully but never taking my eyes off her.

She pauses, then nods. "Yeah. I am."

"Good."

And I genuinely mean it.

There's just a small part of me that wishes I were there to see it and be a part of it. That we weren't hours away working toward separate dreams when our time in the tent made it so clear how well we work together.

She studies me for a second.

"You are too," she says, a flicker of something crossing her gaze before she casts her eyes away.

It's not a question.

I hesitate before answering, "Yeah."

It's true, I am happy. It just doesn't feel complete. I'm getting everything I thought I wanted, and it's pulling me away from the one thing I didn't expect to matter this much.

We fall into a quieter moment after that.

"I wish we had more time," she says eventually, picking at the crust of her sandwich, leaving a flurry of tiny crumbs across her plate.

"I know."

"I get it," she adds quickly. "I do. It's just—"

"I know," I repeat, softer this time.

She nods, looking down at her cup.

We sit there for a minute without speaking. Then she looks up, forcing a smile. "Show me your restaurant?"

Something in my chest loosens.

"Yeah," I say. "Okay."

It's not finished, but I pull out my phone and start flipping through the progress photos I've taken of the renovations. I ramble on and on about the layout, the vision, where everything will go, and she listens like it's the only thing that matters.

She doesn't roll her eyes or drift off into her own thoughts like everyone aside from Julian does. She keeps her big, hazel eyes locked on me, smiling and nodding in encouragement.

"That's going to be incredible," she says when I'm done.

"Yeah?"

"Yeah."

I nod, looking down at the layout on my phone again. For a second, I picture her there. Flour on her hands, moving through my kitchen like she owns the place.

I don't say it out loud because I don't know how that would work, but I tuck the thought away in the back of my mind to ponder later.

My phone buzzes, and I glance down—*time's up.*

"Shit," I mutter, feeling my stomach flip.

Taylor's eyes go wide. "We have to go?"

"Yeah, I have to get you back to the airport so I can make it to the restaurant on time for service training." I sigh, pressing my palms to my eyes so hard I see stars.

"It's okay," she says, reaching across the table to brush her fingers over my forearm. "My flight isn't for a while, I think I'll hang out here for a bit and just Uber back later."

Unease pools in my gut. I wanted to be the one to drop her off—to steal just a little more time in the car before she's gone again.

"It's okay," she repeats, smiling, excusing herself to the bathroom. All I can do is watch her go, white skirt swishing around her perfectly tanned legs.

While she's gone, I pay our tab and wait for her at the entrance. I slide my hand across her lower back, leading her out to the main street.

We stand there for a second, neither of us moving.

Then she steps closer, tracing one hand up my chest. A small groan escapes, and I dip, bringing my mouth to hers.

The kiss is slow, intimate, tongues moving together like old friends. I bring both hands up, cupping the back of her head, angling her to deepen it.

She moans into my mouth, tangling her fingers in my hair and pressing her body against mine.

Mindlessly, I undo the clip holding her wild curls in place and attach it to the strap of her bag without breaking the kiss. She smiles against my mouth as my fingers circle her scalp.

When we pull back, my chest is rising a little too fast.

She's doing her best to hold back tears.

"I'll text you, I promise."

"Okay," she says quietly. I reluctantly start back toward the car, still hating the idea of leaving her to explore without me. She smiles, raising a small hand in a wave. A single tear breaks free, trailing a hot streak down her cheek.

I hold a hand to my chest and turn for the car door.

I don't look back.

If I do, I'm not sure I can walk away.

Chapter 30

Six Months Later

There's a rhythm to my life now.

It's not the kind I used to force before the show—rigid schedules, back-to-back calls, counting down the hours until I could go home and feel like myself again. This one is different. This one is mine.

It shifts when it needs to, stretching and folding around the things I didn't know I'd been longing for: quiet mornings filled with the aroma of coffee and dough, room for my creativity to wander, and the freedom to make each day matter.

Most mornings start before the sun, and I don't mind.

While it took a couple months to prove how reliable I am, Theresa—the owner of *Dolce*—happily let me take over the opening shift.

The bakery lights flicker on while the world outside is still dark, and for a few seconds, it feels like I'm the only person awake. There's something peaceful about it. The quiet hum of the ovens warming, the low whir of the mixers, the smell of yeast and sugar coming to life.

By the time the first batch of croissants goes in, caffeine is zipping through my bloodstream.

By the time the doors open, I'm fully in the groove.

This morning is busy in a way that makes me feel alive. The steady rhythm of shaping dough, glazing pastries, plating things people will actually stop to admire before they eat them feels good. Customers filter in every few minutes, keeping me on my toes and smiling.

I've even started recognizing regulars.

There's an older man who comes in every Tuesday and Friday like clockwork, always ordering the same sourdough loaf and black coffee. A mom with two kids who press their little faces to the display case while they try to choose just one thing. A college girl who pretends to browse but always ends up ordering the lavender-honey pastry and smiling like it's the highlight of her week.

Sometimes they recognize me, too.

Today, my lavender-honey connoisseur tilts her head like she's trying to place me.

"You look familiar."

I just smile. "Must have one of those faces."

It's easier this way.

My NDA is technically up now that the season has aired, but I really enjoy not having the spotlight on me when I'm here. The show still plays in the background of people's lives, and every now and then I'll catch someone watching it on their phone while they wait in line.

It's surreal.

But it's not my whole life anymore.

By the end of my shift, my arms ache and my hair is half falling out of whatever attempt I made to tame it when I first arrived. Before I head out, I slip into the bathroom to freshen up. There's almost always a smear of something on my cheek, and a lingering scent of toasty bread and espresso that follows me everywhere.

I've never felt more like myself.

And I sing alongside Sabrina Carpenter the whole way home, dancing in my seat like nobody can see through my un-tinted car windows.

Heating up a plate of leftovers from Mrs. Delgado, I drop into a chair at my tiny kitchen table. Chewing thoughtfully, my fingers open my laptop and navigate to the Google form I set up for all the custom order requests flooding in.

I initially tried to manage it all by hand, keeping a log of all inquiries from DMs across every social media account in a composition notebook but it quickly became too overwhelming for that.

Custom cake orders with specific theme or flavor requests are the most common, but there are some event inquiries and open-ended requests asking about pricing, timelines, and availability.

I've gotten good at saying no when I need to, and even better at knowing my limits.

Some nights, I sit cross-legged on my kitchen floor, sketching out designs with an extra pencil tucked behind my ear. Other nights, I'm elbow-deep in buttercream, music playing in the background while I lose track of time completely.

It's not glamorous, or easy, but it's mine.

"Okay, but hear me out," Kara says, kicking off her shoes the second she steps into my apartment without knocking like she owns the place. "What if we start a tradition where we only go out for drinks if we have a reason to celebrate something."

I glance up from the cake I'm smoothing frosting onto, one eyebrow lifting. "That feels like a slippery slope into finding reasons to celebrate everything."

"Exactly," she says, grinning. "You get it."

I huff out a quiet laugh, shaking my head. "We don't need a reason, Kara."

"Wrong," she counters, hopping up onto my counter and swinging her legs. "We always need a reason. Today's reason is that you turned down three orders because you're fully booked for the next two weeks."

I pause for a second.

"Okay," I admit, setting the spatula down. "That might be worth celebrating."

"Thank you," she says, like I've just proven her point.

"God, I love being right."

We end up at the same bar we always go to, tucked into a corner booth with drinks we didn't really need but ordered anyway.

We talk about everything and nothing.

All the new drama with The Trunch at *Elite Connections* and the weird guy who tried to flirt with her at the gym by asking if she believed in fate. Still laughing, I regale her with a retelling of the customer who asked me if I could make a cake shaped like their dog and then sent me seventeen reference photos.

As the night winds down and the drinks settle me into a warm, sleepy stupor, she nudges my foot under the table.

"You're smiling at your phone."

I blink, glancing down to see Alex's nickname at the top of the screen. Somehow, I hadn't realized I was looking at the message he sent me earlier.

"I'm not," I say, a little too quickly. But it's too late, the blush is already creeping in. The telltale warmth covering my cheeks.

Kara's expression doesn't change. "You are."

"It's nothing." I exhale, setting my phone face down on the table and idly tracing a finger over the textured edge of the sunflower case Alex sent me a couple months ago.

"I don't believe that for a second."

"It's just... he texted earlier. About some dish he's working on for the new restaurant."

"And?"

"And nothing," I shrug. "We just... still talk sometimes."

And that's the truth of it. We do still talk; except it's not like we used to. Not constant. Not effortless in that same way where hours would pass without either of us realizing it.

Now it's a message here, a reply there.

Sometimes it's a full conversation, but more often than not it's just a quick exchange that fades when one of us gets pulled into something else.

It makes sense.

We have lives that don't overlap the way they did before, back in LA. Nothing dramatic happened, we're just both busy.

Still, I don't mute his notifications. I don't archive the thread, and I don't stop my heart from doing that small, frantic flutter when his name lights up my screen.

Kara watches me for a second, then sighs. "You miss him."

I pick at the chipped label on my glass. "Of course I do."

She waits patiently for me, knowing there has to be more.

"But I'm okay," I add, glancing up at her. "I really am."

There's a difference between missing someone and needing them. I don't feel like something is missing from my life without him.

I feel like something meaningful happened, and now it's over. And maybe that's enough. We both just go our separate ways, remembering our time together for what it was.

Kara studies me like she's trying to decide if she believes me. Then she nods once, like she's come to a conclusion she's not going to argue out loud.

"Okay," she says simply.

She takes a long sip of her drink and we move on.

That's the thing about Kara. She'll push when she needs to, but she also knows when to let something sit. And this is something I definitely don't plan on digging into right now, especially not in the middle of a dive bar surrounded by desperate men waiting for the first sign of vulnerability to move in on.

Later that night, after I've washed off the day and changed into one of my oversized sweatshirts, I curl up on my couch with my laptop balanced on my knees.

My phone buzzes softly beside me—*Grump Bucket.*

A picture loads.

A plate, intricate and precise, with components arranged in a way that looks almost too perfect to touch. I don't even know what half of it is, but I know it took time. Skill, intention, and finesse that Alex has in spades.

I smile before I can stop myself.

ME:

Garrett would weep with

pride 😄

Three dots appear almost instantly.

GRUMP BUCKET:

Tastes better than it looks

I huff out a quiet laugh. Knowing Alex, it's probably the most delicious food imaginable. But, for whatever reason, I don't type that out as a response. Instead, I keep it short.

ME:

that seems unlikely

There's a pause this time. My head lulls back against the couch cushion with my phone in hand, waiting to see if he says anything back. This is already the longest conversation we've had all week.

GRUMP BUCKET:

Long day?

I glance around my apartment. At the half-finished sketch on the table, a dirty apron dangling off the counter in the spot I tossed it when I came home earlier.

Me:

good day

Another pause that stretches far too long and feels deafening.

GRUMP BUCKET:
Good.

And then nothing.

I stare at the screen for a second longer than I need to before setting my phone down, because what am I supposed to say in response to *good*?

That's how it is now.

We keep it to simple check-ins, always light and efficient.

Not heavy or dripping with everything we can't say.

I press back into the couch cushions, letting the pillows absorb as much of my body as they can and stare up at the ceiling.

Maybe not everything that feels big is meant to last.

The thought comes easily now. It isn't sharp or painful like it might have been months ago. It's just... true.

Maybe some people show up for a short period of time, just change you, and that's it.

I sigh, folding my hands over my stomach.

Still, for reasons I don't fully understand, I never quite treat it like it's over. If I did, this would all be so much easier.

A few days later, I find a crisp, black envelope at my door.

It's tucked just above the handle, half-hidden inside the frame like it was slipped there in secret.

There's no postage or return address, just my name written across the front in clean, deliberate handwriting.

This was hand-delivered.

My stomach drops at the sight.

I already know who this is from. After seeing Alex's notebook every week for months, I'd recognize those strokes anywhere.

I stand there for a second, staring at it like it might disappear if I look away. Like opening it will shift something I'm not ready to disturb.

"Okay," I mutter to myself, reaching forward to grab it, dislodging it from its resting place.

It's heavier than I expect. Thick, expensive paper if I had to guess.

I run my thumb along the edge before finally sliding it open to find a single card with elegant, foil lettering across the top.

Northern Flame

Grand Opening Invitation

March 27th

5:00 PM

The address scrolls across the bottom in small, clean font that's easy to read.

My eyes scan the words once, then a second time, slower.

I flip the card over like there might be more. Like there should be more, but there isn't.

I sink down onto the top step without meaning to, the envelope creasing in my grip.

It's been six months.

Six months of building something new. Of settling into a life that feels steady and good and mine. It's the closest I've ever been to having everything I've ever wanted.

And now *this*.

The questions start coming uninvited, sharp and sudden.

I press my lips together, closing my eyes.

Was our connection real? Of course it was. I know it was. There would be no way to fake it all that well.

Hadn't Alex moved on? If he had, then why would he bother inviting me?

I stare at the card again, tracing the embossed lettering with my finger.

Does this mean something, or is it just polite?

A courtesy extended to everyone from the show?

A strategic move to create more buzz for the opening?

I groan a sigh—Do I even *want* to go?

The last one lingers longer than I expect it to, because the truth is—I don't know if I want to go.

Going means stepping back into something I've spent months learning how to carry differently. It means seeing him again. Standing in his space, his world, and pretending like it doesn't matter more to me than it should.

Will it just stir up all the feelings I've finally figured out how to hold at a distance?

I let my head fall back against the door behind me, thoughts more confused than ever.

"I don't have to go," I say out loud.

Just because he invited me doesn't mean my attendance is required. Nobody is forcing me to go.

My life is good.

I'm happy.

I don't need to reopen something just because it's there.

I push myself up off the ground and finally enter my apartment, setting the invitation on my kitchen table like it's just another piece of mail.

Like it's not quietly unraveling every carefully folded thought I've had about him for the past six months just by existing.

Before taking the hottest shower my chilled skin can tolerate, I send a quick SOS text to Kara and by the time I'm out, she's already perched at my kitchen table with two bowls of ice cream.

"You always know exactly what I need."

She smiles, kicking out a chair for me with her foot. With a single finger, I slide the invitation across the table for her to read on her own and scoop a heaping spoonful of Ben & Jerry's into my mouth.

As she looks it over, I launch into my thoughts.

Kara doesn't let me finish explaining before she interrupts. "He built a restaurant and invited you."

I blink at her from across the table. "I—yeah, but…"

"You're going."

It's not a suggestion or question, but a declaration.

I open my mouth to argue, then close it again racking my brain for the right words to convey, well… everything.

"It's not that simple," I try instead.

"It *is* that simple," she counters immediately, tone sharper than I expect. "You just don't want it to be."

I cross my arms, leaning back in my chair and eyeing my best friend suspiciously. "You don't think it's weird? Not even a little bit?"

"No." She rolls her eyes at me.

"You don't think it might just be a general invite?"

Kara gives me a look that I know all too well. It's the *don't-be-an-idiot* look she uses at work all the time.

"A general invite that was hand-delivered to your front door?" She deadpans.

"Well—"

"Taylor."

I drag a hand down my face. "I just don't want to accidentally read into something that isn't there." I drop both hands to the table on a heavy sigh.

"And I don't want you to pretend something isn't there when it clearly is." She arches an eyebrow, punctuating her point with a swivel of her neck.

We stare at each other for a second.

She softens, but not much.

"If you don't go, you're going to think about it forever. If there's even the slightest chance that you'll regret not going, to you owe it to yourself to go."

I look down at my hands, picking at the edge of my sleeve. She's right. If I don't show up, I'll always wonder what it would have been like to see him again.

To stand in the space he's been working toward for so long, and find out if what we had was really just something temporary or something that just needed better timing.

I faceplant on the table with a groan.

My life feels steady and good and full.

But this? This feels like a turning point. Like something I can either step toward or away from. And either way, it's going to matter because it's going to change everything.

I glance up at Kara.

She doesn't say anything this time, just spoons ice cream into her mouth while she watches me. She knows she doesn't have to push any further. I already know the answer.

"Fine," I say quietly. "I'll go."

Her grin is immediate. "Hell, yeah!"

I shake my head, but I can't quite stop the small smile pulling at my lips. Part of me is more nervous than I want to admit. Another part of me feels something else entirely.

Something I haven't felt since leaving the *America's Next Great Baker* tent—anticipation.

Alex

Chapter 31

The restaurant looks nothing like it did the first time I stood in the empty space, dust in the air and a lease agreement burning a hole in my pocket.

Now it's finished. Alive in a way that doesn't feel real.

Soft lighting glows against dark wood and brushed metal, catching on the edges of glassware and the clean lines of the tables spaced carefully across the dining room. Every detail, down to the specific shade of cream for the cloth napkins, has been argued over and agreed upon. Every decision intentional.

It's exactly what Julian and I pictured.

And somehow, not what I'm focused on at all.

My phone sits heavy in my hand, screen dark, thumb brushing over it every few seconds like that might magically make a message appear.

But no amount of manifestation seems to be working.

"It's barely five o'clock." Julian's voice cuts through the quiet as he steps up beside me, adjusting the cuff of his jacket like this is just another night of service instead of the biggest opening of our careers.

"And you know that girl has the propensity for being late."

I glance at him, then back at the door.

"She didn't say she was coming."

He huffs out a quiet breath, not quite a laugh. "And in your hand-delivered invitation, did you ask her to RSVP?"

A crease furrows my brow, but I don't answer his question, because no, I didn't ask her to RSVP. That's a little desperate, isn't it?

"Thought so. You can't send an open invitation like that with no context and expect a response."

"I expected one," I grumble.

The early invitation had felt like the right move at the time. Taylor's invite was custom and should have her arriving a full hour before anyone else. It ensures there will be enough time for a conversation we've been dancing around for months.

Enough time to say what I haven't said.

Assuming, that is, she actually shows up.

I drag a hand over my jaw, exhaling a slow, measured breath as I glance at the clock on the wall behind the bar.

Ten minutes.

She's ten minutes late.

Or she's not coming—a possibility I hadn't given much thought to until now. I've been nervous about seeing her after all this time, not concerned she wouldn't show up.

For a second, I consider what that would mean. What it would feel like to walk through this entire night, shaking hands and smiling for investors and critics and guests, knowing the person I want here the most couldn't bring herself to attend.

My grip tightens around my phone.

"That's not happening," I say under my breath, like I can demand it to be true.

Julian watches me for a second, then claps a hand against my shoulder. "Relax. Worst case, you open a wildly successful restaurant without her being here tonight. You'll survive."

I shoot him a look.

He shrugs. "Best case... she walks through that door, and you stop looking like you're about to jump out of your skin."

My gaze drifts back to the entrance.

The glass windows reflect the interior of the restaurant back at me. All I can focus on is how empty the space is.

I check my phone again.

Still nothing.

"Jesus," I mutter, shoving it into my pocket.

Fine, she isn't coming. I should be focused on tonight's opening anyway. On the fact that everything I've worked for is finally here, tangible and within reach.

Instead, every thought loops back to one thing.

Is she coming?

The handle on the door shifts; my head snaps up so fast my neck cracks with the motion. Adrenaline spikes in my system as I will time to speed up, to show me who is behind the door.

She's here.

Taylor stands just inside the doorway, one hand still resting lightly against the door as it swings closed behind her. The city lights catch on the smooth fabric of her dress—black, simple, elegant in a way that startles me.

Her hair is pulled up, soft and neat, exposing the line of her neck. A few loose strands frame her face, but it's controlled. All her reckless curls smoothed straight into a smooth chignon.

No one looking at her would guess the kind of chaos she carries just under the surface.

The kind I know by heart.

My chest tightens.

"She came," Julian murmurs beside me, like I hadn't already noticed. He gives me a reassuring smile before slipping through the swinging doors to the back of the house.

I don't answer or watch him go, because I'm already moving.

The distance between us closes faster than I expect, my steps steady, though my chest is hammering out its own erratic beat.

She watches me carefully as I approach, and for a second, there's something unguarded in her expression before it immediately smooths over.

"Hey," she says softly.

Her smoky, charcoal-lined eyes survey the room, taking in every detail. She's looking everywhere but my face. If I didn't already know her better, I'd wonder if she was just shy.

"Hey."

I stop just short of reaching her.

And then there's that moment.

The one where neither of us is quite sure what to do.

Six months ago, this wouldn't have been a question. I'd wrap her in a tight embrace and kiss those glossy lips until they're swollen and bright pink.

Now, I step forward first, pulling her into a hug before I can overthink it. One of us has to break the tension. I don't mind being the one to cross the line.

She folds into me easily, arms wrapping around my back, but there's a hesitation in it. A slight delay that wasn't there before.

I notice everything as she's pressed against me.

The smooth fabric of her dress under my hands.

The familiar scent of her—something citrusy, something sweet that hits me all at once like muscle memory. I breathe her in before I can stop myself.

"Hi," she murmurs against my chest.

"You came."

We don't let go right away, and I wonder if she's being sucked back through time and space to every shared moment back in LA like I am.

I step back just enough to look at her, taking her in properly this time.

"You look…" I trail off, shaking my head like I can physically disrupt the million different thoughts running through my head. "Different."

"Good different or bad different?" Her lips curve into a small smile.

"Good," I say immediately, eyes wide, afraid I might have offended her. "Just… different."

She huffs out a quiet laugh. "I'll take it."

A beat passes between us, both of us just taking the other in. I want to kiss her so bad it hurts. To take her in my arms and erase all the distance that's grown between us.

The thought hits hard and fast, instinctive in a way that makes my fingers twitch at my sides. But I don't move toward her, because I don't know if I can. I don't know where we stand. I don't know if she *wants* me to.

"Shall we?"

Her brows lift, glancing around the otherwise empty room. "Where's everyone else?"

I clear my throat, not wanting to explain the invitation I slid into her door had an earlier time printed on it than everyone else. "I wanted to show you around before everyone gets here."

"Okay." She falls into step beside me, and for a second, it feels almost normal. *Almost.*

We start in the dining room.

It's the easiest place to begin. Neutral ground in a way we desperately need right now. Something I can talk about without overthinking every word because it's just furniture and aesthetics.

"This is the main dining floor," I say, gesturing around us. "Seating's a mix of tables and booths. We kept it open so it doesn't feel cramped, even when it's full. We also have a private dining space upstairs we'll eventually use for hosting small events, but right now it's being used as a makeshift training room."

She turns slowly, taking everything in.

"It's beautiful," she admits, and there's no hesitation in it.

"Yeah?"

"Yeah."

Something in my chest loosens at her tone. It's soft and dreamy in a way that I've come to associate only with Taylor.

I nod once, then lead her toward the back. "Kitchen's this way."

We move through the space together, close but not touching. There are moments where our arms brush, small accidental contact that lingers just a second too long before we both shift away.

The silence between us sits just shy of uncomfortable.

There's too much simmering underneath it.

I push through the swinging doors into the main kitchen, already alive with last minute prep before the first official dinner service of *Northern Flame*.

"This is where the magic happens," I say lightly.

Her eyes light up immediately, scanning the room with interest. The chefs and line cooks don't acknowledge us, completely absorbed in their task at hand.

Exactly as they should be.

Distractions equal mistakes and mistakes have consequences, especially for new concepts.

"Okay, this is incredible," she says eyes sparking to life, stepping further in. "Look at this setup."

I watch her instead of the kitchen.

How she moves through the space, carefully staying out of the way, curiosity pulling her forward. My attention hyper-focuses on the trail of her fingers over the counter as she looks around.

Having her in the space I built is almost as surreal as owning my own restaurant. And, while this is the first time, if I have it my way, it won't be the last.

I look away before I get too caught up in the thought.

"There's more," I say, nodding toward the back hallway. She follows without question. We walk in silence for a few seconds before I stop in front of a closed door at the back of the kitchen.

"This is the last part."

My heart starts beating wildly in my chest, hands going clammy with nerves. This is the moment I've been working toward these past few months.

"Oooh, mysterious!" She tilts her head, teasing.

"Something like that."

I push the door open, stepping inside and flipping the light on.

"This space is separate for a reason," I start, leaning casually against the counter as she steps in behind me. "Savory kitchens are brutal on pastry. Too many smells, too much heat. It messes with everything."

She considers that as she analyzes the pristine prep room with state-of-the-art appliances and flawless chrome countertops.

"That's why this is back here, isolated in a controlled environment. No interference."

Her gaze moves across the room, lingering on the equipment, the layout, the way everything is set up with intention for optimum flow.

"It's perfect," she murmurs.

I swallow. "It needed to be."

She glances at me, curiosity flickering in her expression.

I push off the counter, moving toward the second door at the far end of the room. My lips tip up on one side.

"There's one more thing."

I don't look at her as I reach for the handle.

I just open it.

The space beyond is quiet as natural light filters in through a large front-facing window, catching on glass display cases and clean white counters. The entrance to the street sits just on the other side, opposite from the main restaurant, exactly as planned.

I step back, letting her take it in.

She doesn't move at first. Then slowly, she steps past me.

Her heels click softly against the floor as she walks further inside, her gaze sweeping across every detail: black and white checkered floor, chrome bar and stools, pink accent wall with TT in bright white script.

I watch her carefully; every reaction etched into memory. Her fingers brush along the edge of one of the display cases.

Her breath catches as she peeks out the front window, seeing the neon pink awnings hovering above the sidewalk outside.

She turns in a slow circle, taking in the space from every angle not saying a word.

"This…" she starts, then trails off. Both hands cover her mouth, eyes glittering in the light.

I stay quiet, arms casually crossed while I let her get there on her own. She stops near the center of the room, turning back toward me.

"What is this?"

I hold her gaze, unblinking.

"You know what this is" My answer hangs between us.

She shakes her head, blinking in confusion. Disbelief.

"I built this side of the business with someone very specific in mind." My voice stays steady, though my pulse is hammering. "She just didn't know about it until now and hasn't decided if she wants it yet."

She stares at me like she's trying to piece it all together, like she's not sure she heard me right.

"You built this... for me?" she asks, voice quieter now.

"Yeah."

"That's..." She exhales sharply. "Alex, that's a lot."

"I know."

"And what if I say no?"

It's my turn to suck in a sharp breath, but I nod once before speaking. "Then you'd say no."

Her brows pull together as she processes my words. "Right but then what? You'd just keep it?"

"I'd figure something else out," I say honestly.

She folds her arms waiting for me to go on.

"I have a stack of resumes in my office from different pastry chefs who submitted inquiries, and I'd have to step in in the interim period if you don't want it, but I wasn't going to not build it just because I didn't know what you'd say."

Taylor paces across the tile, hands resting on her hips but her eyes never stray from my face. She narrows her gaze, searching. "Why?"

God, how do I even answer that question?

Because I miss you.

Because nothing has felt right since we left LA.

Because I've been building this place and thinking about where you would stand, what you would do, how you would fit into this place like you were always supposed to be here.

A lump forms in my throat, and I swallow hard against it as my thoughts try and fail, to transform into coherent words.

Instead, I take a step closer.

"Because you're too special not to have something of your own," I say quietly. "And I knew if I waited, you'd go find that space somewhere else, without me. And I don't want a version of this that doesn't have you in it."

Her breath hitches, tilting up to hold my gaze.

"I'm not asking you to give anything up. I won't do that because I know you've created something you love back in Cambria—" I stop myself and steal a breath. "I'm offering you a place here. If you want it."

She looks around the space again, and I can see it happening. The realization that this is what she told me she'd do if she won the competition.

"You built my dream," she says softly, bringing a gentle hand to my chest. I look down at her chipped yellow nail polish and smile—there's a little bit of that quirky chaos I love.

"Yeah."

Her eyes find mine again briefly before she closes the distance between us. And thank God she does because I don't know how much longer I could hold back.

Her hands find my shirt, gripping lightly as she pulls me down toward her.

And then she kisses me.

It's everything we didn't let ourselves do the second she walked through the door.

I kiss her back immediately, one hand coming up to cup the back of her head, the other wrapping around her waist and pulling her flush against me.

She tastes like that watermelon lip gloss I can't get enough of and hope and happiness and everything that's good in this world.

She makes a soft sound against my mouth, and I lose whatever restraint I had left.

I dip her without thinking, one arm supporting her back as the other tangles in her hair, loosening the careful style she showed up in.

She laughs into the kiss, breathless and bright, and when I pull back just enough to meet her eyes, I can't help but smile.

"There's one condition," I murmur, lips brushing hers.

Her eyes flicker with amusement. "Oh yeah?"

"You can never smooth your hair out like this again," I say, tugging lightly on one of the loosened strands. "I love your curls, they are part of what make you... you."

She laughs, full and unguarded in a way I haven't heard in months.

"Deal," she says, breathless.

I kiss her again before she can say anything else.

Because I've waited long enough.

And this time—I'm not letting her go.

Taylor

Epilogue

One Year Later

The sky is barely light when I unlock the front door, the bell chiming softly overhead as I step inside. The bakery smells faintly of yesterday's citrus tarts—another take on my favorite lemon-blueberry pairing.

I flip the lights on one by one.

Warmth fills the space slowly—glowing against glass display cases, polished counters, the black-and-white tile I once stood on in disbelief, trying to convince myself it was real.

Even a year later, it still feels a little unreal.

Just surreal and dreamy in the best way.

"Morning, boss."

I glance over my shoulder to find Kara slipping in behind me, already halfway through tying up her freshly dyed, bubble-gum pink hair, a coffee balanced in one hand and her phone in the other.

Now that she's no longer under The Trunch's dictatorship, she shows up with a different hair color every other month.

"You're late," I say, not even trying to hide my smile.

She scoffs. "I'm three minutes behind schedule. That's not late, that's fashionably *delayed*. Besides, I came in right behind you."

"And I'm also late. Plus, you literally made the schedule."

"Exactly," she says, pointing at me like I've proven her point. "Which means I get to interpret it however I see fit."

I shake my head on a laugh, turning back to the counter as I reach for my apron.

Kara moves through the shop with practiced confidence, like she belongs here now—because she does. Six months ago, she signed the lease on the apartment next door to the one Alex and I share, and somehow, between that and taking over the logistics side of the business, she's become just as essential to this place as the ovens themselves.

She handles orders, inventory, staffing, customer inquiries; everything I used to try to juggle on my own until I was one minor inconvenience away from a full breakdown.

Which means now, I just get to do what I do best.

Bake.

Well... mostly, anyway.

The day side of *Taylor's Treats* runs like a proper storefront with customers in and out, display cases filled, a steady hum of business that still makes something in my chest swell every time I step back and take it in.

And at night, the other half of the dream kicks in.

Northern Flame's dessert menu is all mine with my vision feeding into Alex's. Our individual businesses are still very much their own things, but connected and deeply intertwined.

Just like we are.

"Okay," Kara says, snapping her fingers as she examines our detailed agenda on her phone. "We've got three custom pickups before noon, a last-minute cupcake order for some kind of corporate thing, and..." She pauses, squinting at the screen, "Gladys asked if we could recreate her dog in cake form again."

I freeze mid-reach for a mixing bowl. "No."

"That's what I'm saying," she replies immediately with a laugh. "I'll just tell her we respect animals too much for that, and that one time was more than enough."

I snort. "Thank you."

"You're welcome."

She sets her coffee down and hops up onto the counter like she used to in my old apartment, completely ignoring the very professional, very real business we're standing in.

Some things never change.

I work steadily through the familiar motions of preparing the shop for customers. The peaceful stillness before opening is still my favorite part of the day.

It feels like endless possibility.

Like anything in the world could happen.

The bell over the door chimes again.

Neither of us looks up right away.

"Signs not flipped," Kara calls out automatically. "We're not open for another—"

"Relax," a deep, familiar voice cuts in.

My whole body stills, half inside one of the display cases, while rotating the macarons for maximum freshness.

Kara's head snaps toward the front with a smirk. "Oh, look. The other half of your personality just walked in."

I roll my eyes, but I can't stop the smile that pulls at my mouth as I turn.

Alex stands just inside the door, unfastening the buttons on his sleeves and carefully rolling them up to his elbows in neat creases. I try not to stare as his forearms flex with the movement.

His gaze finds mine immediately and everything else fades a little at the edges. It's not the dramatic, overwhelming, knock-the-breath-out-of-you kind of moment like it used to be, but it's full and familiar, and that just might be even better.

"Hey, pretty girl" he says as he crosses the space between us without a single ounce of hesitation. One hand comes to rest lightly at my waist as he leans in, pressing a quick, easy kiss to my lips.

The butterflies in my stomach kick up like they always do, still, after all this time, because this incredible man is somehow mine.

"Morning," he murmurs against me.

"Morning."

And just like that, he pulls back, already reaching for a clean apron like he didn't just rewire my entire brain with that kiss.

Kara makes a dramatic gagging sound behind us. "Wow. Disgusting. You guys are really leaning hard into the whole domestic bliss thing, huh?"

"You moved in next door by choice." Alex calls over his shoulder, not breaking his stride toward our shared prep kitchen. I fall into step behind him, looping an arm through Kara's and dragging her along with us.

"I make sacrifices for this business," she says solemnly.

"For the record," I add, grabbing a whisk from the utensil rack as we pass, "you also make yourself at home in my fridge, and I feel like that's repayment on its own."

"That's called *community*, Taylor!" She shoots back.

Alex huffs out a quiet laugh, stepping up beside me at the counter while I'm silently reading the prep list.

"Where do you want me?" he asks in a low voice.

The timbre sends a shiver down my spine, because that tone is laced with alternative meaning and innuendo. But we have too much to do and too little time, so I don't take the bait.

Instead, I glance at him, pulling a face before I answer.

"Ganache needs to be redone. It broke yesterday."

He grimaces at my words. "Who made it?"

I give him a look.

Because *he* prepped the ganache yesterday morning.

He pauses. "...I'm going to fix it."

"Good call."

He takes over the stove, melting chocolate with the kind of intensity that used to intimidate me. Now, it just makes me shake my head. A year and a half ago, I'd never criticize Alex's technique, but I'm much more confident now than I was back then.

"You're overheating it," I say, watching over his shoulder.

"I'm not."

"You are."

"I'm literally not."

"You literally are, though," I repeat, reaching over to adjust the heat slightly. "You're treating it like a reduction. It's chocolate, not a sauce."

He glances at me, unimpressed. "I know what it is."

"Do you?"

Without a word, he dips a spoon into the mixture and holds it out toward me. "Try it."

"If this is bad, I'm firing you." I narrow my eyes at him.

"You don't have that authority."

"Julian and I can vote you out at any time, buddy."

His eyes glint with amusement as I take the spoon.

The second the chocolate hits my tongue, my eyes flutter closed and I moan softly at the smooth, rich flavor. Alex's heated gaze snaps to mine.

"Okay," I admit reluctantly. "That's actually really good."

"I know." He winks, patting my hip to scoot me away from the stove so he can continue without interruption.

I bump my shoulder lightly into his. "Don't get cocky, this isn't the same quality you produced yesterday. Very inconsistent, Alexander Harrington. You're better than that."

Kara makes another noise from behind us. "This is unbearable. Truly. I'm surrounded by insufferable talent and sexual tension that somehow still exists even after a year. Gross."

"There's no tension," I say automatically, tucking a stray curl behind my ear. Alex raises a brow, glancing at me and heat immediately creeps up my neck.

"...okay, maybe a little," I amend.

"Unreal," Kara mutters, hopping down from the counter with another one of her famous eyerolls. "I'm gonna go do actual work while you two flirt over chocolate."

"You love it," I call after her. Alex just laughs.

"I tolerate it," she corrects, disappearing into the front.

After the morning rush of customers, things slow down before lunch. While we focus on delicious desserts, we also offer a coffee bar and simple café items, like mini quiches and artisanal sandwiches.

Kara is at the register, counting back the drawer as a reset before the second half of the shift. It was busier this morning than usual, which is a good problem to have but she had to jump in and help with last minute touches on our last custom cake.

Her pastel bun is tousled with long, wavy strands falling over her glistening forehead. I suggested she take a break before handling the register but she refused. I think doing something familiar gives her brain a chance to relax, so I don't push it.

The bell above the door chimes as Julian breezes in.

His warm brown eyes narrow on Kara who is completely oblivious to him. Alex gives a quick nod, and I smile in greeting.

"Kara," he drawls, sliding onto the stool nearest to her.

Her eyes flick up, leveling him with a flat stare while he props his chin on one hand, looking her up and down with genuine appreciation.

"Looking gorgeous, as always."

If looks could kill, Julian would be six feet under from the daggers Kara is shooting his way. I cover my mouth with a hand to hide my smile.

"Don't start with me, Julian. I'm not in the mood for your shit. We just got our asses handed to us in here while you were sleeping in." She folds her arms, glaring.

"What can I say?" His smirk is downright mischievous. "I needed my beauty sleep. I wanted to look my best for you."

Kara grips the edge of the counter so tightly, her knuckles turn white. Alex lets out a low whistle, watching her square her shoulders like she's preparing for war.

And knowing her, she probably is.

While my best friend goes toe-to-toe with Alex's cousin, and the love of my life seeks refuge in the prep kitchen, I pause to take this moment in.

People always talk about the good ol' days, wishing they knew that they were living the best moments of their lives while they're happening.

I take a second to commit this mental snapshot to memory, because these are absolutely the best days of my life so far, and I don't want to look back for a minute, wishing I'd have paid more attention.

I'm living the life I always dreamed of.

And I didn't have to give up anything to have it.

I didn't have to shrink myself to fit into Alex's vision or sacrifice my own dreams to make our relationship work. My best friend escaped her dead-end fate by following me to a new, exciting city to start over.

If anything, my reality is leagues beyond what I ever could have hoped for. The dream expanded, changing when it needed to, and found its place amongst those I love most.

Maybe not everything that feels big is meant to last.

I used to believe that.

Used to think some things or people were just meant to pass through your life—important, meaningful, but temporary.

And maybe that's true for some things.

But not this.

Alex appears next to me, sliding a hand into my back pocket. His thumb brushes against my hip so instinctively, I doubt he even realizes he's doing it.

I rest against him, inhaling the scent of his skin, the warmth of his body, the quiet, confident rhythm that is all him. It drifts through me, fills me, threads through my lungs until it feels like I am breathing him into my very soul.

No, things don't last because they're easy.

They last because, somehow—despite timing, distance, and everything standing in your path—you find your way back to them anyway.

Taylor's Bake It 'Til You Make It Playlist

Breakaway - Kelly Clarkson

Golden - Harry Styles

Electric Love - Børns

I Like Me Better - Lauv

Mystical Magical - Benson Boone

Sweetness - Elliot James Reay

Lavender Haze - Taylor Swift

Slowly - Ed Sheeran

Please Please Please - Sabrina Carpenter

Do I Wanna Know? - Arctic Monkeys

Sunflower - Post Malone, Swae Lee

Steal The Show - Lauv

Dress - Taylor Swift

Sapphire - Ed Sheeran

Listen on Spotify!

Letter from the Author

Hi friends,

This book started as a 3 p.m. daydream in the school pickup line—one of those *stare off into the distance while inching your car forward* kind of moments. I found myself wondering what would happen if a show like *The Great British Baking Show* had a baby with *The Real World* (you know… that old MTV show where people stop being polite and start getting real). And from that slightly chaotic "what if," this story was born.

It was so important to me that Taylor, our sunshine optimist, still felt like a real person—not just a trope or a schtick. I wanted her joy to feel earned, her struggles to feel honest, and her heart to be something you could recognize pieces of yourself in.

And Alex… I really wanted to challenge the typical grumpy, alphahole stereotype. He's controlled, he's a little jaded, but he isn't cruel. He feels deeply, even if he doesn't always know what to do with it, and loving Taylor was never about changing her. It was about learning how to meet her where she is.

While you'll find all the markers of a dreamy love story here, the things that mattered most to me were a little quieter: enthusiastic consent, not abandoning your dreams for someone else, and loving someone in a way that doesn't try to reshape them into a life they were never meant to live.

I hope all of that landed. And more than anything, I hope you had fun with *Bake It 'Til You Make It*.

As always, thank you really just isn't enough.

Love,

Kassie

Acknowledgments

Cover design by Marge at *Caravelle Creates*—thank you for your kindness and collaboration. You took my jumbled pile of screenshots, color suggestions, and vibes and ran with it. Everything about this screams sunshine romcom, and I couldn't be happier.

Thank you to my friends and family for all of your support on this book. I was so overwhelmed by the outpouring of love for *Messy & Bright*, but your constant excitement and belief in me are the biggest reasons I didn't quit when my mental health took a nosedive in the middle of writing it.

To the babes in the Bookish Collective, ♥ Ruined Book Besties ♥, Book Besties Supporting ♥ and Book Besties ♥ over on TikTok—I freaking love you guys. Thank you for showing up every day and for welcoming me into your circle. Long live Corny and Bookmark.

And last, but absolutely not least, to my readers—*holy crap*, I have readers!—thank you for taking the time to read my words. I'm not anybody special, I just like to yap and make up stories. I love reading so much and thought, *"Hm... I can do that."* And then I did. If there's anything in your life that makes you feel that way, you owe it to yourself to give it a chance.

About the Author

Kassie Jones is a lifelong storyteller from the Detroit suburbs, finally sharing her words with the world. Her writing style has been described (mostly by herself) as a tornado with the best of intentions.

When she's not writing, you can usually find her baking, lost in a book, dancing at concerts, or diving headfirst into whatever ADHD hyper-fixation has her attention that week. She lives with her husband, two daughters, and a mischievous puppy, who keep life full of love, laughter, and just the right amount of chaos.

Kassie hopes her stories leave readers feeling seen, loved, understood, and maybe even a little inspired.

Connect with Me

I love connecting with readers! Follow along for updates on new books, behind-the-scenes looks, and a little extra holiday chaos.

Website & Newsletter:
www.kassiejones.com
Sign up for my newsletter to get book updates and bonus content!

Social Media:
Instagram: authorkassiejones
TikTok: @authorkassiejones
Facebook: facebook.com/authorkassiejones

I love seeing your photos, reactions, and reading moments—let's stay in touch!